I0823214

Love is patient.

—1 Corinthians 13:4 (NIV)

MYSTERIES *of* BLACKBERRY VALLEY

Where There's Smoke
The Key Question
Seeds of Suspicion
A Likely Story
Out of the Depths
Run for the Roses
Crooks and Christmas Cookies
Smoke and Mirrors
No Love Lost

MYSTERIES *of* BLACKBERRY VALLEY

No Love Lost

BECKY MELBY

Guideposts

Published by Guideposts
100 Reserve Road, Suite E200
Danbury, CT 06810
Guideposts.org

Cover and interior design by Müllerhaus
Cover illustration by Bob Kayganich at Illustration Online LLC.
Typeset by Aptara, Inc.

ISBN 978-1-965859-17-9 (hardcover)
ISBN 978-1-965859-18-6 (softcover)
ISBN 978-1-965859-19-3 (epub)

Printed and bound in the United States of America

No Love
Lost

Chapter One

Pond Creek Coal Mine
Pike County, Kentucky
March 9, 1921

Talbert Haley braced both hands against the cold, damp tunnel floor as if he could stop the earth from shaking, its rumbles still echoing. The draft that usually flowed past his face no longer blew. Instead, thick ashy air filled his lungs.

Next to him, Oren Benton coughed. "You hurt, Tal?"

"Not bad." Talbert eased to a sitting position. His head throbbed. He gently touched his right temple, confirming the source of the pain. His pulse hammered over the ringing in his ears.

"What happened?" Oren asked.

"Cave-in," Talbert rasped. He'd been on his feet, pickax in hand, chiding Oren and Linus Moss about working too slowly, and then the earth had flung him about like a rag doll.

Linus. He reached out with both hands. Hands he couldn't see in the thick blackness. A jolt of fear shot through him. Was he blind? "Linus?" He raised his voice. "Linus!"

"He's down." Oren coughed again. "He has a pulse, though. Linus! Linus, wake up!"

A groan answered him. "Can't feel...my legs."

Talbert forced away the panic that tried to close his throat. How many times had he had this exact nightmare, awakening with his heart pounding, his nightshirt clinging to his back with cold sweat? And then Viviene's arm would slide across his chest as she whispered, "It's only a dream, Tal. Everything's fine."

But this time it wasn't a dream, and nothing was fine, as evidenced by Linus's ragged breathing.

A clang ricocheted off the walls as his foot made contact with something metal. He leaned down, running his hand across the uneven rock floor. His headlamp. "Either of you got matches?"

"Shirt pocket." Linus's voice was barely above a whisper.

"Got 'em. There are four." Oren's outstretched hand collided with Talbert's elbow. "Don't drop any."

Talbert gripped the four small sticks as if his life depended on them. Maybe it did. Maybe Linus's life hung in the balance, and they could do something for him if they could get some light.

Holding the small brass lamp between his knees, he tucked three of the matches in his shirt pocket and stuck the end of the fourth between his teeth.

Securing the lamp with one hand, he turned the lever that would let water from the upper chamber drip into the calcium carbide in the base. In seconds he smelled the acetylene gas the combination produced. He struck the match on the floor and was rewarded with a hiss and a flash. He wasn't blind. Thank the Almighty for that anyway. He held the lit match to the burner tip and murmured a prayer of gratitude as the flame, magnified by the reflector, filled the space with light.

The collapse had created a room no more than eight feet square. How long could three men...

He halted the thought before it could paralyze him. Lifting the lamp, he adjusted the reflector, directing it at Linus. His gut clenched. A beam, six inches square, pinned Linus's legs. One end of the beam was buried under the still-settling mound of rock and debris that blocked the entrance.

Talbert locked eyes with Oren. Tears made streaks down his friend's blackened face as he slowly shook his head.

There was nothing they could do for Linus.

Chapter Two

Hannah Prentiss inhaled the heavenly scent of chocolate wafting from the Hot Spot kitchen and tried to concentrate on untangling a string of red heart-shaped fairy lights. Distracted by the endless to-do list in her brain, the sniffles coming from the corner booth, and the wafting chocolate, she was making a mess of things. In frustration, she switched to addressing envelopes for the Valentine's Day birthday lunch she was planning for the young woman quietly crying in the corner.

When she'd sealed the last envelope, she stood and stretched. As she walked out of her office, she glanced up at the double-sided clock that had hung between the arched doorways since the old firehouse was built in 1898. As she surveyed the exposed brick walls covered with memorabilia from the early days of the fire station, she felt the same sense of awe she'd experienced after signing the papers that made the building hers.

Several of her friends in California had thought she was crazy for deciding to leave a successful career at a high-end restaurant to return home to Blackberry Valley, Kentucky, and turn the historic firehouse into a farm-to-table restaurant. In truth, there had been days—in the midst of remodeling, developing a firehouse-themed menu, sourcing local ingredients, interviewing staff, marketing, and transforming the upstairs apartment into a comfortable living space—when she had wondered if they were right. But now, she wouldn't trade this life for anything.

The old clock told her it was almost lunchtime. A 1942 wall calendar with dates that matched the current year told her it was Tuesday, February 3. She had about a week and a half to get ready for Valentine's Day.

She padded past Raquel Holden, the usually upbeat waitress who'd shown up six hours before her shift started because "work gets my mind off things." Hannah had spent close to an hour listening to Raquel's relationship dilemma as they wrapped silverware in napkins. She'd listened and nodded, prayed and offered tissues.

Hannah pushed through the swinging double doors to the kitchen—then stopped in her tracks. "Oh my goodness." It was all that came to mind as she stared at the thing of beauty in the center of the spotless stainless-steel table.

"Triple Dark Chocolate Raspberry Truffle Supreme Valentine Cheesecake." Head chef Jacob Forrest wiped his palms on his chocolate-streaked apron and beamed at her. "Chocolate cookie crust, smooth dark chocolate cheesecake with raspberries folded in, a thick layer of satiny ganache, fresh raspberries, and handmade raspberry truffles on top." He swept the toque from his disheveled dark brown hair and bowed at the waist.

Hannah clapped. "We can't serve this. It belongs in an art gallery."

"Thank you, ma'am." Jacob stroked his closely trimmed beard. "Think a slice of this will help Raquel?"

"I'm sure it will go a long way toward cheering her up at least. But let's get some protein in her first. What do we have for that?"

"I thought you'd never ask. I may have whipped up a too-large batch of the soup I'm testing for our spectacular Valentine's Day culinary extravaganza."

Hannah grinned. Part of her job as Jacob's boss was keeping his enthusiasm within manageable bounds, but she never wanted to squash it. She'd been promoting their reservation-only Valentine's Day dinner with words like *intimate*, *romantic*, and *elegant*. Left to Jacob, who favored words like *extravaganza*, it might come off sounding like a super sale at the car dealership down the street.

"What kind of soup?"

"Tomato basil with cheese tortellini. Tomatoes grown and canned right here in Blackberry Valley, tortellini made with eggs from chickens we know by name and locally sourced cheese, and basil from the window herb garden." He gestured toward the greenery soaking up the pale February sun in a window.

"Sounds like a winner. I'll have Raquel pop back here to sample it."

A ding from her phone grabbed her attention. She slid it from her pocket and smiled at the name on the screen. Liam "Completely Smitten" Berthold. It was the current nickname he'd given himself in her contacts list. The text read, I'M HERE.

"Tell your boyfriend to come join us for lunch." Jacob grinned.

"How did you know?"

"Your smile. Dead giveaway. He's out front, right?" When she nodded, he shooed her out of the kitchen.

Hannah laughed as she went. She was thirty-six. Liam Berthold, Blackberry Valley's fire chief and the man she'd been officially dating for three months, was thirty-eight. And yet the giddiness she felt at the thought of seeing him rivaled that of any young girl with her first crush.

Raquel must have let him in, because Liam met Hannah in the center of the dining room with a warm embrace. After a quick kiss, Liam gave her a lopsided smile and an almost imperceptible nod toward his fellow firefighter and best friend, Archer Lestrade, who had come in with him. Usually brimming with *joie de vivre*, Archer seemed strangely subdued.

Hannah motioned to a four-top. "Do you have time for lunch?"

Liam nodded. Archer shrugged.

"Jacob's warming up some tomato soup." She tipped her head toward the corner booth. "I was about to ask Raquel if she wanted some."

Both heads swiveled to the shadowy corner where Raquel wiped menus with a vacant stare. She appeared to have stopped crying, but her uncustomary silence seemed to draw Liam's attention. "Hey there, Raquel. Come join us."

Raquel ambled across the room and joined them. "Hi, Liam. Archer." She did a double take after her lackluster greeting to Archer. "You okay? You look different."

Archer rubbed the stubble on his chin. "I'm growing a beard. Bryn's always said she wanted to see me with one. Though now... Anyway, I should ask you the same. What's going on?"

Raquel pulled out a chair and plopped onto it. "Marshall got a job offer in Chicago."

"Wow. That stinks." Archer, usually the one to give a quick joke to try to snap someone out of a bad mood, had nothing but empathy in his tone. "I feel your pain."

"I knew it wasn't just the five o'clock shadow. What's going on with you and Bryn?"

"You don't know? You guys are so close. I thought she would have told you."

Raquel shook her head. "I know she's up in Wisconsin where she can work on her dissertation without interruption. Is that it?" She gave a small laugh. "You're sad because she chose a place with no phone service or internet, and you have to endure a few days without talking?"

"If only." Archer rested his elbow on the table and his chin on his hand. "We had a fight."

"Seriously? I talked to her while she was loading her car on Friday. She didn't mention anything about a fight."

"It was after that, so I'm not surprised."

Before he could explain further, Jacob emerged from the kitchen carrying a tray with four steaming crocks of soup. He gave a slight bow to Liam. "I took the liberty of bringing a portion of my humble soup for you, great fire chief, tamer of flames." Turning to Archer, he asked, "Will you also be lunching at our fine establishment, sir?"

His horrible British accent earned him an eye roll from Liam. "Since when do chefs in fine establishments eat with the clientele?"

"Since I make the food, so I make the rules," Jacob shot back. "I mean, *she* makes the rules." He gestured to Hannah. "But she has graciously allowed the lowly kitchen help to break bread—or in this case, tortellini—with her."

Hannah waved him off with a laugh. "Go get another bowl, please."

Liam nudged Archer's elbow. "While we're waiting, show the ladies your mysterious photos."

"Mysterious?" Hannah leaned in.

Archer reached into his jacket and pulled two manila envelopes from an inside pocket. His name was written in black ink in a medieval-style calligraphy on the front of each. He opened one and slid out a black-and-white photograph, then did the same with the other envelope. One showed a tree stump. At its base, grass poked up through a thin layer of snow.

The other photo was harder to decipher at first. Hannah studied it, turned it vertical, then horizontal. It appeared to be the top half of an arched window or doorway. "Looks a little like one of our doors here, but the bricks are different. Where was this taken, and why is it mysterious?"

"I don't know where it was taken. The envelope with the photo of the doorway was leaning against the door of my apartment on Sunday morning. The other one came to the firehouse yesterday."

"I found it behind the No Parking sign out front," Liam added.

Hannah rubbed her hands together. "They're obviously clues. You just have to find out where they were taken. I bet they'll lead you to more clues."

"A treasure hunt." The first smile Hannah had seen on Raquel all day lit her eyes with a tiny glimmer of her normal optimism.

Whatever this was, it might become a much-needed distraction. "Maybe it's a contest of some sort. Or maybe Bryn left them for you. Something fun to keep you busy while she's gone."

Archer's mouth scrunched to one side. "I'm not so sure Bryn is interested in my having fun right now. You know all the stereotypes of clueless men who say clueless things?"

"Uh-oh." Hannah patted his hand. "What did you say?"

"She called when she stopped for groceries at some tiny town in Wisconsin on her way to Pittsville. She said it was probably the last time she would be able to talk to me. She'd been driving for almost twelve hours, and she sounded exhausted, so I said, 'Are you sure this is worth it?' She hung up on me, and I can't say I blame her. It must have sounded like I was questioning her whole career."

Liam clapped him on the back. "That's nothing, man. A simple, 'I'm sorry I'm a clueless insensitive dude' should clear that up."

"Maybe some flowers along with it," Raquel added. "And groveling."

"And chocolate." Hannah pressed her lips together. Archer's distress was real, but she was sure Liam was right. This probably wasn't nearly as serious as Archer seemed to think.

Jacob set another bowl of soup on the table then pulled out a chair. "Sorry it took me a minute. Carrie from Sweet Caroline's delivered our bakery order."

If Hannah hadn't been looking at Archer, waiting for his reaction to her suggestion, she would have missed the grimace that flashed over his face when Jacob mentioned the bakery. Had he had a bad experience at Sweet Caroline's?

"No clue what you guys were talking about," Jacob went on, "but I second what Hannah said. Chocolate makes everything better, and I'll prove it to you after the soup."

Hannah picked up her spoon. "Bryn Reynolds is not the kind of woman to carry a grudge over a careless comment like that."

Archer stared at the contents of his bowl. "True. She's usually pretty quick to forgive. But that wasn't my first offense this week."

Hannah winced. "Dare I ask?"

"Her original plan was to hole up less than an hour away in a hotel in Bowling Green to finish her dissertation. She had all of her research compiled, and she just needed a week in a quiet place to put it all together. I was totally supportive. But then I made the mistake of telling Colt that this would be the first time we would be apart for more than a couple of days."

Liam groaned. "Not Colt." Colt Walker, one of the youngest firefighters, was known for his practical jokes.

"What did he do?" Hannah asked.

"He suggested that I write down a list of things I could do when Bryn was gone that I couldn't do when she was here. I thought he was trying to be helpful, because focusing on that kind of thing rather than missing the person can ease the difficulty of the separation. But I also know what a jokester he is, so I wrote things I would never, ever actually do." Archer slid his hand down his face. "It was all in fun, but then he went and gave it to her."

"Uh-oh." This time the two dire syllables were proclaimed by a quartet of voices.

"Yeah. The next day she announced she was going to her grandparents' cabin in Wisconsin. For *two* weeks. She said she wanted time to decompress after she finished working. Walk in the woods and commune with nature in a place that holds memories for her." His cheeks puffed out on a ragged exhale. "But I think when she said it was the last time she would be able to talk to me, she meant *ever*."

The empathetic silence that followed was broken by Archer's phone vibrating against the wood tabletop. The lit screen said *Mom*. After pressing a button, he lifted the phone to his ear. "Hi, Mom. Yeah, go ahead and open it. Can we switch to a video call?" He tapped the screen then set it in the middle of the table. "She found an envelope with my name on it under her welcome mat," he told the group.

Mindy Lestrade's face showed on the screen briefly. "It's a photograph." The picture flipped, and the next thing they saw was another black-and-white photo. It appeared to be part of a decorative wrought iron fence. The metalwork was intricate, with two swags of ivy leaves pinched in the middle by a bow. One side of the fence was attached to a charred wooden post or board.

"Does this mean anything to you?" Hannah glanced at Archer and saw the color drain from his face.

Archer made eye contact with Liam, whose eyes widened slightly as he nodded.

"This is the balcony on one of the apartments above the jewelry store," Archer said quietly.

"Where the fire was last month?" Jacob asked.

Archer nodded. "It was a Sunday night. I was across the street, out for a run. I heard yelling, and at first I thought it was just a couple of people arguing. Then the front door of the store flew open. Two people came running out, and I saw flames behind them. They said no one else was in the building. I called it in and told them I was with the department."

"We had the fire out in under half an hour," Liam chimed in. "But the next day, the owner came in to the station and blasted Archer, saying he shouldn't have waited for the team. He should have gone in and tried to save his inventory."

"So what do you think this means?" Raquel asked.

Archer was quiet for a long time. "I think someone's trying to tell me something. And I don't think it's something good."

Chapter Three

I think you're right. It sounds like Archer is seeing it as a bad thing because of the mood he's in. I bet it's a treasure hunt." Lacy Minyard, Hannah's best friend since grade school, sat across from her at Jump Start Coffee on Wednesday morning, hugging a mug of hot chocolate.

"I'm hoping it is. Archer's picking up extra shifts while Bryn is gone. He says it's because he has extra time, but I'm starting to suspect that he's saving up for a ring. Anyway, he doesn't have time to try to figure out who sent the pictures. So, being the good friend I am, I offered to help."

"The good friend who occasionally happens to be too curious for her own good." Lacy sipped her cocoa. "I hope he'll split the treasure with you when you find it."

"I hadn't thought of that. Maybe I need to draw up a contract for him to sign."

Lacy gave her a thumbs-up. "Now you're talking. Show me the pictures."

"I will. But first, how are you feeling and how are the kids?"

"I'm tired but happy. All the kids are fine." She patted her still-flat tummy and grinned.

Hannah had been asking about the goats that were born the previous year, but realized the term now included the little human

Lacy expected in six months. "I suppose it's cliché to say you're glowing, but you are."

"Is glowing another name for tired?" She yawned. "I just hope I can keep up with all the work on the farm this spring. But let's get back to Archer. He has no idea who these photos are from?"

"Not a clue." Hannah swiped her phone and turned it so Lacy could see the screen. "This is the one he got first." She pointed to the picture of the arched doorway. "I have no idea where this is."

"I do," Lacy said at once. "It's an oval window on the alley side of the Stanton Building."

"Where is that?"

"It's that big, stately building with the cement pillars. It was originally a bank. I think it was an antique store when we were in high school. It's been vacant for a couple of years, at least on the main floor. There might be apartments upstairs. It was sold maybe six months ago to a couple from Nashville, who plan to turn it into an event venue."

Hannah bit her bottom lip. Why would someone send Archer a picture of a window on an old building that wasn't currently being used for anything? "Look at these two. I'm trying to find some connecting thread between them." She showed Lacy the photo of the balcony railing. "We figured out that this was part of the balcony above the jewelry store."

"Where the fire was?"

"Yes." She told her about the owner's accusations against Archer.

"You need to ask Archer and Liam if there's ever been a fire in the Stanton Building. Maybe whoever sent these is upset with how the fire department is handling things."

"Sounds plausible, but what does the tree stump have to do with anything?"

"Good question. But the more important question is why are we still sitting here? We need to be out there, canvassing the town and talking to people." Lacy stood and picked up her hot chocolate. "I'll get this in a to-go cup."

Hannah took a few steps into the alley and held her phone up next to the oval window. She pointed to a crack in a brick. "The photo is definitely the bottom half of the window. Why would someone take a picture of only part of it?"

Lacy shrugged. "Add that to the growing list of questions."

Hannah followed Lacy to the front of the Stanton Building. She stopped and took in the grand entrance, featuring massive double doors with vines and flowers carved around the frosted windows. "Do you know the people who are doing the remodeling?"

"I met them last fall at the farmers market, not long after they moved here. They were just making plans at the time. They said they'd be doing as much of the work as possible themselves and hoped to open this spring. They were asking about caterers, and I told them you don't cater, but you own a farm-to-table restaurant. I remember telling them the two businesses would complement each other nicely."

"Way to network. Someday I'll have to put you on the payroll."

"A girl can dream." Lacy pulled out her phone. "I've been racking my brain to remember their names. I wonder if they have a website."

She tapped and swiped for a minute. "Okay. It's Stan and Stephanie Carlson. Ooh. I love what they're calling it—the BV Forum."

"That's perfect. BV for Blackberry Valley, and 'forum' fits with the Greek-style columns. Can't wait to see how they're decorating."

Lacy reached for the brass handle on the old front door.

"Wait a sec. What are we going to say?"

"How about if I reintroduce myself and then introduce the illustrious restaurant owner I told them about. I'm sure you'll have tons of remodeling stuff to talk about."

"Sounds like a plan." Hannah felt a rush of anticipation as Lacy opened the door. This was where the first photo had been taken. Did that mean the Carlsons were sending them? If so, why?

The interior of the building was every bit as beautiful as the exterior. Octagonal tiles covered the small foyer. Drop cloths draped half of a marble-topped counter. The pressed tin ceiling was painted gold, and teardrop crystals hung from gold filigree chandeliers.

"Hi!" A voice came from the top of a ladder, where a woman was pressing a strip of gold-and-navy striped wallpaper around a window. Her hair was kept under control by a bandanna. "As you can see, we're not open for business yet. Can I answer any questions?"

"I'm Lacy Minyard. My husband and I own Bluegrass Hollow Farm. We met—"

"At the farmers market!" the woman finished for her. "One sec. There." She finished with the wallpaper and scrambled down the ladder with the agility of someone who'd spent a lot of time doing just that. "I'd shake your hands, but I'm a sticky mess. Nice to see you again, Lacy." She turned to Hannah. "I'm Stephanie Carlson."

"Hannah Prentiss. I own the—"

"Hot Spot! Sorry, I keep interrupting." Stephanie's laugh was easy. "I'm excited to see both of you. My husband and I have wanted to get over to your restaurant, but we're swamped."

"Been there, done that. I opened the Hot Spot last spring. It takes a ton of work, but it's worth it."

"That's encouraging. Some days I wonder. We're hoping to open the first of May. We already have a retirement party, two weddings, and a fundraiser booked."

"You're off to a good start."

"This has been my husband's dream since he was a kid. Stan grew up here and always loved this building. It used to be the town mercantile. His great-grandfather added the stone façade when he owned it as the bank."

"Oh!" Hannah felt her eyebrows rise. "Is Stan short for Stanton?"

"Yes."

"I don't remember the name. When did he live here?"

"Until he graduated from high school in 2011, and then for a while a few years ago. After we met, I lured him to Nashville where I was working, but we're both ready for the slower pace of a small town."

Hannah did a quick calculation. Stan would have been a freshman when she and Lacy were seniors. That would explain why his name wasn't familiar. But she knew someone who would have known him. "We have a friend who graduated the same year as your husband. Did Stan ever mention Archer Lestrade?"

"Now there's a name I haven't heard in years." A muscular, dark-haired man dressed in dusty overalls walked into the room. He extended his hand to Hannah. "Stan Carlson."

"Hannah Prentiss. And this is—"

"The chicken lady." Stan held out his hand to Lacy. "Sorry. That didn't come out right. But I can't remember your name."

"Lacy Minyard." Lacy grinned. "But I do also answer to 'the chicken lady.'"

"Nice to see you again, Lacy. We really enjoyed the produce and eggs we bought from you." He focused his attention on Hannah, then back on Lacy. "Which one of you knows Archer?"

"We both do," Hannah answered. "Were you and Archer friends in high school?"

Stan's smile quirked up on one side. "Well, I guess you'd call us mostly friendly rivals. We wrestled in the same weight class. I left town for college, but we picked up our rivalry a few years ago when I moved back to help my dad after he had surgery. Archer and I would meet up for racquetball."

"And tried dating the same woman," Stephanie added with a snicker. When Hannah and Lacy gaped at her, she held up her hands. "No. Not me."

Stan's gaze swept the ceiling. "Never should have let her in on my old secrets. And that's not exactly accurate." He raised his arm and tapped his watch. "Sorry to cut this short, but we have a meeting with a supplier in a couple of minutes."

Stephanie nodded. "We'll have to meet up sometime and talk more."

Hannah fished in her purse and pulled out a flyer. "We're hosting a special Valentine dinner. We still have some openings."

Stan took the paper. "Sounds fun." He tapped his chin with a paint-spotted hand. "Will my archrival be there?"

"I think he will be."

"All the more fun then."

Hannah zipped her jacket higher as the wind picked up. They'd walked the block from Jump Start Coffee to the Stanton Building, but the temperature had dropped in the past few minutes.

"Will I sound like a bored small-town housewife if I admit I'm curious about who the woman is that Archer and Stan both 'tried' dating, whatever that means?" Lacy asked.

"It might if you actually had time in your life to be bored, which you don't. Nothing wrong with a little curiosity. Besides, if we're going to investigate the source of Archer's pictures, we can leave no stone unturned. Anyone in his past or his present could be sending them."

"Good point. And a romantic triangle could be motive for someone to do something, whether good or bad."

"Do you know anything about Archer's romantic history before Bryn?" Hannah asked. Her friend had kept her finger on the town's pulse while Hannah had lived in California for several years.

"I knew who Archer was, but didn't really get to know him until you started hanging out with firefighters." Lacy winked as they reached her black pickup and climbed inside. "Jewelry store next? Or do you want to drive around and hunt for a tree stump?"

"Let's drive past the jewelry store. I don't want to talk to anyone though. It's pretty clear what that place has to do with Archer."

As Lacy started the car, Hannah had a sudden image of her a few months from now, when it wouldn't be quite as easy for her to slide behind the steering wheel. "Tell me you're still going to be my spontaneous friend after the baby comes." She tried to make the comment sound lighthearted, but it really was something she worried about. People always said that a baby changed everything. Would it change their friendship?

Lacy paused before shifting into drive and twisted in her seat to face Hannah. "Of course I will. Babies are portable. I already have a sling, a front pack, and a backpack. I've started reading all about sleep and feeding schedules versus on-demand, and Neil and I have already decided we're 'on demand' people. We may feed our four-legged kids at the same time every day, but we want our family to be flexible. So, Auntie Hannah, I'm going to keep my diaper bag packed at all times, so the baby and I are ready to join you on whatever adventures come our way."

Chapter Four

The three firefighters at table three on Wednesday night looked like they'd put in a long day.

After hostess Elaine Wilby seated them and Raquel brought them water, Hannah approached the table. "Rough shift?" she asked, letting her gaze fall first on Colt, then Archer, then linger on Liam, who offered her a tired smile.

"You could say that." Archer rubbed a hand over his face.

"We did drills most of the day," Liam explained. "They're not too happy with me at the moment."

"He nearly killed us," Colt added, putting on a woebegone expression.

Hannah gave a slight bow. "On behalf of the residents of Blackberry Valley, thank you for working so hard to protect us."

Colt rolled his eyes. "You pay her to say that stuff, Chief?"

"Yep." Liam winked at her. "We'll settle up later, Miss Prentiss."

Raquel rushed past, saying she'd be with them as soon as she brought out another order. The Hot Spot was packed, and Raquel seemed unusually frazzled.

At the next table, waiter Dylan Bowman balanced a drink tray in one hand while handing a packet of crackers to the mom of a fussy toddler. He'd been a clumsy disaster when Hannah had first hired him, but he seemed to have found his stride. He shot his coworkers a concerned glance, but Hannah waved him away.

"Raquel," Hannah called, holding out her hand as Raquel whirled around. "I'll take this table."

With a grateful look, Raquel handed over a spare order pad and pen.

"What'll it be, gents?" Hannah asked.

Colt ordered the Five Alarm Burger and Archer and Liam both asked for the Rookie Meltdown, Archer's with onion rings and Liam's with fries. They all requested black coffee to drink. Not for the first time, she wondered how these guys could sleep after strong caffeine with their supper.

After putting in their order, she brought them a complimentary basket of Mini Turnout Tacos. "I met someone you know today, Archer. Stan Carlson."

Archer's lips tilted into a smirk. "Heard he was back. He and his wife are fixing up the Stanton Building, right?"

"Yes. Did you know Stan's great-grandfather owned the Stanton bank?"

"Nope. Can't say as that ever came up while I was pinning him to the wrestling mat or whipping him at racquetball."

"According to his wife, you competed at something other than sports too."

Archer wrinkled his nose. "If you mean Carrie Moore, that was a sad comedy of errors I'd like to leave in the past. Where'd you run into Stan?"

"Wait. Carrie Moore of Sweet Caroline's?"

"Yes." Archer closed his eyes for a moment. "Back to Stan."

Hannah let it go—for now. "We met him and his wife at his building. We went there because Lacy figured out your first mystery photo was a window in the Stanton Building."

Archer stopped, his hand poised in midair as he reached for a taco. "Why would someone send me a picture of some random window?" He flopped against the back of the seat, then pulled out his phone. "I got another one today."

It was almost eleven when Hannah walked out of her office and into the empty dining room. She let out a weary but contented breath. It had been a good night.

"Tired?"

The welcome voice caught her midyawn. She grinned at Liam, who sat with his feet propped on a chair and arms crossed over his chest. "I should ask you the same thing. Knowing you, I don't imagine you were just standing around all day putting your men through their paces."

"Gotta set an example." He lowered his feet to the ground and sat up. "The wind's died down, and the moon is nearly full. Do you have enough energy for a walk?"

With you? Of course. "Sure. I'll go change my shoes and be ready in a second."

"That's one of the things I like about you, you know."

"That I wear sensible shoes?"

His rich laugh filled the air. "That you're spontaneous."

Was she? It wasn't something she'd really thought about until this morning when she'd worried that, in a few months, Lacy wouldn't be as available for spur-of-the-moment adventures as she was now. "I like that about you too. With our schedules, it's vital."

Hannah and Liam had recently shared several long talks about whether their relationship was important enough to both of them to carve out time together around two busy and often unpredictable schedules. Thankfully, they'd both agreed it was. On paper, Liam was scheduled for four twelve-hour shifts each week but, as the town fire chief, he was always on call. And when his shifts ended, she still had five hours to go at the restaurant. They were committed to making time to be together, but the struggle was ongoing. She'd been reminded of that more than once as she'd prepped for the Hot Spot's upcoming event. On her first Valentine's Day with Liam, all her time would be focused on making it special for other couples.

At least they had already planned for that. Going out for Sunday brunch the day after Valentine's Day wouldn't be quite the same as a romantic evening in a swanky restaurant with white tablecloths and candlelight sparkling on crystal, but the important thing was being together.

She poked her head into the kitchen, where her chef was untying his apron. "Thanks for everything tonight, Jacob."

"Sure thing, Hannah." He nodded pointedly to the right.

Raquel sat on a stool at the end of the worktable, chin resting on both palms, a tissue sticking out of one hand.

Hannah glanced from her to Jacob. "Could you tell Liam I'll be out in a few minutes, please?" After Jacob stepped out, Hannah pulled up a stool next to Raquel and put an arm across her shoulders. "Something new?"

Raquel shook her head. "No. Just me being the same sad mess." She sniffled and gave Hannah a weak smile. "I made it through a whole twenty-four hours without tears, but then Marshall called and said he'd decided not to take the job in Chicago. But I know he really wants it. He's only saying that for my sake, and I don't want to be the one who stands in the way of him realizing his dreams. I mean, *Chicago Magazine* has over a million subscribers! So I told him he should take it, but I didn't mean it. I keep praying, you know? Giving it to God and then..."

"Taking it back?"

"Yeah." Raquel blew her nose. "I read somewhere that the definition of love is wanting God's best for someone else, no matter what it costs you. I want to be able to want that, but I really just want Marshall to stay." The tears started again.

"When does he have to give them his decision?"

"Not until the end of next week."

"He must be so torn. It's obvious how much he cares for you, but that job is an amazing opportunity."

"It is. It's also way too early in our relationship for me to uproot my entire life and follow him to Chicago."

"Not that I'm any kind of expert on these things, but I think you have to be careful you don't swing too far on either side. He needs to know you'll support him in whatever he decides, but you need to be honest about your feelings. He also needs to hear how much you're going to miss him."

Raquel dabbed at her eyes. "I don't know if I can tell him this is killing me without laying a guilt trip on him. I want him to stay, but not because I've made him feel bad."

"How about we pray together?" When Raquel nodded, Hannah closed her eyes. Before she began, part of a verse she'd read that morning came to mind. *Love is patient, love is kind.* She prayed aloud for wisdom, comfort, kindness, patience, and peace of mind for both Raquel and the man who clearly adored her.

After a deep, shuddering breath, Raquel said, "Thank you. Now I've taken up enough of your time. Liam is waiting for you." She smiled and waved.

Hannah turned to see Liam poking his head through the door. "I didn't mean to interrupt. I just wanted to tell you we can walk another time."

"No!" The emphatic reply came from Raquel. "You two don't have enough time together as it is. And take it from someone who knows—time together is a precious thing." She hugged Hannah, grabbed her purse and coat, and slipped out the back door.

Liam stepped into the room. "And that's something else I like about you, Hannah Prentiss. You always take time for your friends."

It was a perfect night. Still and bright, with moon shadows stretching across the ground. The air was crisp, but Hannah was barely aware of the temperature as Liam took her hand and thanked her for taking an interest in Archer's mystery.

"I still think it's some kind of prank," he said, "but he's starting to get worried about it, and he doesn't have the time or the headspace to focus on it this week."

"So you don't think it could be some kind of warning or intimidation tactic?"

"If it was an actual threat, why not be more obvious about it? Why play games?"

Hannah had been wondering the same thing. "I only caught a glimpse of the photo he received today, but it looked like bricks on the corner of a building. Did he figure out where it was taken?"

"Not yet. He was pretty wiped out after work."

"If you think about it, can you ask him to send me a picture of it? And I didn't think to ask how he got this one."

"It was stuck under the windshield wipers on his truck when we came out of the station."

They moved on from speculation about Archer's photos to talking about plans for the rest of the week. "You're off Saturday?" she asked.

"I am. But I promised Archer we'd take the kayaks up to Cave City."

"In February?"

"It'll be in the mid-sixties by noon." When she didn't comment, he said, "I hate feeling torn between wanting to spend time with you and wanting to keep him occupied."

"You're a good friend." Despite a twinge of disappointment, she meant it. "What time does the health fair end on Sunday?"

"Four o'clock. Think you could carve out a little time for some pad thai afterward?"

"I suppose I can be patient until Sunday night."

Their footsteps echoed on the wood planks of the bridge at the park. They stopped in the middle, gazing down at the moonlight reflected on the creek. The water was low this time of year, trickling softly around smoothed rocks. The sound lent the perfect backdrop to the moment Liam put his arm around her. "Speaking of patience, I need to ask for a bit more."

Hannah's jaw tensed. Where was this change of topic leading? "Oh?" Her response hung in the cold air along with her breath.

"I got a message from the organizers of the KFA conference. They asked if I could fill in for one of the instructors."

Hannah let out a silent sigh of relief. The Kentucky Firefighter's Association conference in Owensboro didn't start until the sixteenth. She already knew he'd be leaving that Monday and would be gone for a few days. But why was he bringing it up again? "And?"

"And they want me to come early and help set up."

There it was. "Early, as in Sunday?"

Now it was Liam's turn to sigh, only his sounded more like pent-up frustration being released. "As in I need to be there by six o'clock Sunday morning, which means I'll probably have to leave the day before. They have to have the expo set up by ten on Sunday because there's a wedding starting at eleven, and the hotel doesn't want vendors hauling things in and making noise during the ceremony or reception."

Hannah swallowed a lump of disappointment. There would be no day-after-Valentine's-Day date to look forward to. Her advice to Raquel replayed in her head. *You need to be honest about your feelings.* How could she strike a balance between supporting him and letting him know she'd miss him?

"I'm sorry, Hannah."

So much for hiding her disappointment. "It's not your fault. I mean, who gets married on a Sunday, anyway?" She smiled up at him, trying to inject a bit of levity into the moment.

"I'll make it up to you. How about a Valentine's Day rain check?"

"Absolutely. Besides, Valentine's Day is just a commercial holiday anyway. It's a day for businesses like mine to make money." She smiled at him, doing her best to make it appear light and breezy. She tugged at his hand, and they walked down the slight slope on the other side of the bridge. "We're together now, so let's just enjoy it."

Liam stopped suddenly, bringing her to a halt as well. "That tree stump." He pointed to a spot along the creek about ten yards away. "Is it the one from the photo?"

Hannah stared at the curved stump, about three feet high and a foot and a half in diameter. The pale outer rings of the cut surface surrounded a hollowed-out center, forming a perfect circle. She reached into her purse for her phone then swiped through her pictures until she got to the one she'd taken of the second photograph Archer had received. "That's it. But what would that have to do with Archer?"

"A lot." Liam rubbed the back of his neck. "He's the one who cut it down."

Chapter Five

Pond Creek Coal Mine
Pike County, Kentucky
March 9, 1921

"Do you hear that? Shovels." Talbert pulled his handkerchief from his pocket and used it to mop Linus's brow. The usually cold air felt thick and hot. His lungs were starting to burn. "They're coming for us, Linus. It won't be long now."

The lamp sputtered. It wouldn't last until the shovels reached them. Was it running out of fuel? Or out of oxygen?

Linus raised his hand and patted his chest. "Josephine," he gasped. "Give this to her."

"Whatever it is, you can give it to her yourself," Oren said.

"No. Won't have the chance. She can have the land. And the ring. Here." He slowly raised a shaking hand and tapped the top pocket of his jacket. "No one else to give it to. She didn't want me, but I never stopped loving her." His eyes closed. His breathing stopped.

Talbert pressed his thumb and forefinger into the hollows on either side of his nose, but it didn't stop the tears.

Linus was a good man. The kind people called the salt of the earth. He'd left his farm somewhere in the middle of the state to spend a year in a coal mine in Pike County to "earn enough to build a nice little house for my Josephine and ask her pa's permission for her hand." He'd shown everyone the photograph tucked into the cover of his pocket watch. Josephine had been his world.

And then, just days ago, he'd gotten a letter. Josephine had met someone else. The man whose body had been broken by the explosion had already been crushed in spirit.

Oren gently moved Linus's still hand and pulled a paper from his coat pocket. "It's a letter, two pages. All smudged and wrinkly. Looks like he's been carrying it since he started. The first page is what they call a plat map." He shifted so more light fell on the page then tapped a blue dot next to *L. Moss*. "That be Linus's land." He flipped the paper over. "This says Josephine can have it. The other page is a hand-drawn picture. A tree with a circle at the bottom of the trunk. No. Not a circle. It's a ring. Maybe his grandma's wedding ring that he always said he was going to give Josephine before she dumped him."

"Does the letter say anything about the ring?"

Oren held the paper closer to his face as the light dimmed. "On the drawing. There's an arrow, and it says, 'Dig here.'"

Talbert laughed. It sounded strange in the echoey cave. Out of place, and yet not. "Remember him talking about playing pirates with his friend when they were boys?"

"Yeah. Sounds like he never outgrew it."

"What I can't figure is why he didn't just sell the ring and get her a cheaper one instead of coming here. He said he had a jeweler look at it and offer him more than a thousand dollars for it." Talbert let out a low whistle. "Think what that could buy. Who'd give up farming in the fresh air for killing yourself underground when you have something like that?"

"The ring was sentimental, he said. Been in his family for generations. Guess I can understand that."

"Maybe so, but I'm sure Viviene would rather have me safe than have some expensive doodad on her hand." Talbert was quiet for a moment. They shouldn't be talking. They should be conserving air. "When we get out of here, we'll find her. We'll find his Josephine."

"Not sure she deserves his land after what she did to him."

"But it's what he wanted. Got to honor that." Talbert closed his eyes and sank back against the wall. Cold and hard. Like much of his life.

Unlike Linus, he hadn't chosen this life. It had chosen him. He'd grown up in a coal camp. Third generation. He'd met Viviene when he was sixteen and she was fourteen. Two years later they were married. Ten months after that they had a daughter.

Evangeline was twelve now. Such a tender child, with a heart for anything in need. How many baby birds and stray cats had she brought home and nurtured? His Evangeline was strong. If he didn't make it out of here, she'd take care of Viviene and the younger ones.

Just as the light sputtered for the last time, he glanced at Oren, his best friend from the cradle. Words weren't needed. They'd grown up next door to each other in identical tar paper-covered shacks, married the same year, and had kids three months apart. Oren's oldest, Micah, was sweet on Evangeline. Not that she knew it. To her, Micah was like a brother.

Talbert wondered if that would change someday. "Lord, watch over them." He closed his eyes, wondering if, like Linus, he'd never open them again.

Chapter Six

Even though she could have slept in on Thursday morning, Hannah woke before dawn and stared at the ceiling for several minutes before sitting up and propping a couple of pillows behind her.

She'd slept like a baby after Liam's final text last night. How about an early Valentine date? Rearranged the schedule so I'll be off on Monday. I don't have a plan, but if you're free, let's spend the day together.

She'd answered with, Sounds perfect. And I have an idea.

To which he replied, I look forward to it.

She flipped on her bedside lamp and reached for her phone. Five days ago she'd started reading a two-week devotional based on the "love chapter" in 1 Corinthians. It was written to be read in the fourteen days leading up to Valentine's Day. Before finding today's message, she reread yesterday's verse out loud.

"Love is patient, love is kind. It does not envy, it does not boast, it is not proud."

"I'm listening, Lord," she whispered. "I'm going to need some help in the patience department." If she could just, as the cliché went, "Let go and let God," things would fall into place. Like Liam arranging to be off on her day off.

She ticked through the other words, and *envy* popped out at her. When she'd first moved back, she'd experienced twinges of envy while watching Lacy and Neil together. But then God had brought Liam into her life. "Thank you," she whispered, "for working everything out in Your time."

She flipped the page and read the day's verse. "It does not dishonor others, it is not self-seeking, it is not easily angered, it keeps no record of wrongs."

"Ouch." She closed her eyes and spent a few minutes confessing her recent self-seeking moments, then moved on to praying for her father, brother, and uncle, Liam, the fire department, Raquel and Marshall, Archer and Bryn, and several other names the Lord brought to mind.

When she finally swung her legs over the edge of the bed and headed to the shower, she felt ready to face a rare not-too-busy day that included lunch with her dad and a list of errands.

As she drove up the gravel drive to the house she'd grown up in, Hannah remembered the things her mother had done every February to ward off cabin fever. Hannah had probably been ten or eleven before she realized it wasn't an actual disease.

Her dad sat in his rocking chair on the porch, Zeus the border terrier by his side, when she parked in front of the house. He wore a stocking cap and a down jacket, but the plaid throw blanket she'd bought him for Christmas was draped over the empty chair next to him instead of on his lap.

Zeus jumped up and dashed down the steps when she opened the car door. After giving him some undivided attention, she walked up the steps and hugged her dad.

"Have a seat." He gestured to the other chair. "I have butternut squash soup warming on the stove, and I just took a loaf of sourdough out of the oven."

"Where's Uncle Gordon?"

"Helping Pastor Bob install a new kitchen sink at church. He said to say hi."

The two brothers had been living together after both losing their wives. With their respective former trades as electrician and plumber, volunteering their skills kept them both busy.

"Think you've mastered sourdough this time?"

"This one's a beauty. Pretty enough to make my restaurateur daughter proud."

Hannah laughed. "It doesn't take bread to make me proud of you, but if you feel the need to keep impressing me with your new baking skills, who am I to try and stop you?" She sat back, letting the familiarity of the chair and the view bring their usual sense of peace. "Mom would love that you're baking bread. I was reminiscing about the things she did to keep us from being bored in the winter. Remember the year she insisted on keeping the artificial tree up after Christmas and decorated it with heart lights for February?"

"I remember. That thing started shedding like a real tree after two months."

"But it was fun. I remember the red glow in the room on our popcorn-and-movie nights."

"Good times. I was thinking about her while I made the soup. She was the queen of comfort food." Dad smiled. "You know, I think your love of cooking probably started exactly twenty-six years ago this month."

Hannah squinted at him as she tried to recall what he was referring to.

"Your mom was down with the flu, and so were several other people from church. When she said she wished she was feeling well enough to make meals for the Wilbys and Stantons, you said you'd do it for her."

"The Stantons? As in the people who used to own the Stanton Building?"

"Yep. Why?"

"I'll tell you all about it over lunch. There's been some interesting stuff happening."

"Sounds intriguing." Dad stood and led her inside. "I heard one of the Stanton boys was back in town to renovate that building. Heard they uncovered some old papers from when it was the Haley Mercantile. Is that part of the interesting stuff?"

Hannah walked to the cupboard and took out two stoneware bowls, then stopped to admire the round, crusty loaf of bread sitting on a cutting board. "No. Though that sounds interesting too. It all started on Sunday, when Archer Lestrade found an envelope outside his door."

As her father ladled soup into the bowls, she told him about Archer's mystery. After he'd prayed over their lunch, she showed him the photos on her phone. "Archer sent me this one on my way here. I haven't had time to examine it yet." She swiped to the message from Archer and showed her father the picture of bricks on the corner of a building. The grooves between the bricks were filled with snow.

Her father laughed. "I'd recognize those bricks anywhere. I had a close encounter with them back when I was a paper boy." He pointed to a miniscule scar on his nose.

She'd never thought to ask how he'd gotten the scar. "What happened?"

"I was probably twelve at the time. I thought I was so cool on my neon-yellow stingray frame bike with the banana seat and tall handles. I turned to say hi to a girl crossing the street, hit a crack in the sidewalk, and face-planted into the corner of the bakery."

Hannah laughed. "I bet you didn't tell Drew that story when he ran into the mailbox on his bike."

"I did not. That was a completely different story. Your brother was playing on his portable video game console while riding down the driveway. That was careless and irresponsible." His eyes twinkled.

Smiling, Hannah took a sip of her soup. "Mom would definitely be proud." She buttered a piece of bread and closed her eyes as she chewed. "You know, Jacob could use an extra hand in the kitchen."

He laughed. "I've known too many guys who tried turning a hobby into a business with disastrous results. I'll stick to woodworking and baking just for fun."

After a few more bites, Hannah studied the picture still open on her phone. Light-colored bricks that appeared to be cut from stone dovetailed with darker, smoother ones. "The bakery, huh? Do you know if there was ever a fire there?" Even as she asked it, she had a feeling the bakery's connection to Archer had nothing to do with fire.

"Not that I can recall. Seems to me you've got a direct line to someone who can answer that question for you."

"Yes, I do." And she didn't intend to stop at one question.

After putting gas in her Subaru Outback, buying a birthday card for Raquel, and dropping off more flyers about the Valentine's Day dinner at Blackberry Market, Hannah stopped at the library. She'd reserved a new rom-com novel, and it had just become available.

Librarian Evangeline Cooke greeted her with a smile and a wave as Hannah gravitated toward a display on the history of valentines. Elaborate, lacy, nineteenth-century cards with verses as flowery as the roses and daisies depicted on them alternated with what a caption called *Vinegar Valentines.* The first one made her cover her mouth to keep from laughing out loud.

You asked to see me home, kind sir.
I thank you, but decline.
One beau is quite enough for me.
I'm satisfied with mine.
You need not set upon the fence
To see me going by.
I cannot give you such a chance.
There now! Dear me, don't cry.

"The genteel Victorians were not always very gentle, were they?"

Hannah glanced over her shoulder, then nodded as she took in Evangeline's bright red blouse, three rings on one hand, and heart-shaped earrings with a necklace to match. "You're very valentine-y today."

"I've always thought we should have a season to celebrate love, not just a day."

"I agree." And the thought made celebrating on the Monday before Valentine's Day much more appealing. Hannah tapped the glass. "This was the 1800s version of speaking your mind on social media." She took a step to the right and leaned in to read one from the early 1900s. "'Valentine Greetings, the time I hope for lip to lip to plight my love.'" She wrinkled her nose.

"I believe kids today would call that 'cringe.'"

"I'd have to agree with them." Hannah studied a card featuring a chubby cupid with curly hair surrounded by hearts and doves. The words below his bare toes said simply, *To My Sweetheart.* "That's more my style. Simple and to the point."

"What are you and Liam doing for Valentine's Day? I know you're going to be working Saturday night. Ted and I are looking forward to your dinner."

"We've synced our schedules for a whole day, so we're celebrating five days early."

"I know what that's like. When we were dating, we were both working second shift and taking classes during the day."

"But you made it work. That's encouraging."

"My stepmother found me crying on the back step one day because it had been a week since I'd seen Ted. In a rare sympathetic moment, she told me, 'Anything worth keeping is worth fighting for.'" Evangeline's eyes lit. "Years later, when it was careers and kids keeping us too busy for quality time together, I had that printed on a pillow. We still have it because we still need that wisdom."

"I think I need to keep that in mind myself." Hannah turned back to the display. A pencil sketch caught her eye and stole her breath for a moment. It was clearly old, the paper smudged and yellowed and curling at the corners. Bold, back-slanted letters above the drawing said, *Evangeline, my Valentine, will*—Beneath that was a drawing of a window. The bottom half of an oval window she'd stood in front of less than twenty-four hours before. Beneath the drawing was the rest of the question: *meet me here at closing time?*

When she recovered from the shock of realizing the sketch matched the first photo Archer had received, she read the words out loud. "'Evangeline, my Valentine, will meet me here at closing time?'"

"Will *you* meet me here," Evangeline corrected her.

Hannah stared at the drawing for a moment before she saw it. "I get it. The window is shaped like a letter U, so it forms the 'you' in the question. That's so clever. Did Ted draw this for you?"

"Oh no. That was for some other Evangeline, long before I was born. Kind of fun, though, as it's not a particularly common name. There's a date on the back. February 14, 1932."

"Where did you get it?"

"The historical society set up this whole display. It's all from their collections." She nodded toward the back of the library where a placard next to a door read *Blackberry Valley Historical Society.*

Hannah glanced at her watch. She had almost an hour free before her meeting with the string trio that would perform for the Valentine's Day dinner. "Anyone in there?"

"Not until three today, but I think they're in all day tomorrow."

"Okay. I'll come back in the morning then." Next stop, the fire station. She took out her phone and snapped a picture, then rested her fingertips on Evangeline's arm. "I promise I'll explain everything tomorrow and get the book I came in for, but right now I need to run."

"Are you okay?"

"Yes. Fine." Hannah dug her keys out of her purse. "Really confused, but totally fine." With any luck, her next stop would provide some more pieces to the puzzle.

Chapter Seven

Before leaving the library parking lot, Hannah pulled out her phone and texted Liam. DO YOU AND ARCHER HAVE A FEW MINUTES TO SPARE FOR AN AMATEUR SLEUTH?

In seconds, she got her answer. IF SAID SLEUTH IS BLOND AND PRETTY AND HAS LEARNED SOMETHING THAT WILL CHEER UP A HEARTSICK FIREFIGHTER, YES.

With a smile, she typed BE THERE IN A FEW. She wasn't sure that what she'd learned would cheer him up, but hopefully it would get Archer's mind off his troubles with Bryn, at least temporarily.

She drove to the station and found Liam waiting for her just inside the door with a hug and a quick peck on the cheek. "Our depressed friend is in my office."

"Poor guy. Has he heard anything from Bryn?"

"Not a word. He called her mom and found out that Bryn made it to the cabin safely."

"That should be a relief."

"It should be, but he's still moping. I'm tempted to drive him up there on Monday so they can work this out and he can get his head back in the game."

But Monday was when Hannah and Liam were supposed to celebrate Valentine's Day together. She'd heard people joke that it was dangerous to pray for patience because God might provide an opportunity to work on it. Would Liam really—

"Kidding." He nudged her with his elbow as they walked toward his office. "I just wanted to see your reaction."

She nudged him back. "That's cruel."

"I'm sorry. I should know better. I've been attempting humor with Archer all morning, but apparently it's not in my skill set." He opened the office door.

Archer sat in front of Liam's desk, bent over his phone. He nodded an unenthusiastic greeting.

Hannah took the chair next to Archer and glanced down at his phone screen. "Ooh. Shuffle. That'll strain your brain." She played the online word game with her brother, but he was far more competitive than she was.

"Bryn used to send me her results every morning." Archer blew out a slow breath. Anyone who didn't know the reality of it would think Bryn was a long-lost love he hadn't seen in years. Finally, he made eye contact with her. "It doesn't strain my brain as much as whatever game somebody's playing with me."

"Did you get another photo today?"

He shook his head. "But you look like you know something."

"Before I tell you my new theory, Liam told you we found the tree stump, right?"

"Yeah."

"He wanted me to hear the tree-cutting story from you," she said.

"It's not much of a story. During that freak ice storm in December, the tree came partway down and fell on power lines. The trunk was just hanging there, suspended. If it had fallen all the way, it would have brought down the power lines and smashed a shed on the neighboring property. The power company was overwhelmed, so they cut the power and asked us to help with the tree."

"Doesn't sound like something that would make anyone mad."

"It shouldn't have, but I trimmed off a big branch, and it didn't fall where I thought it would. It crushed a dirt bike that was leaning against the shed. This kid, probably fifteen or so, came running out and started screaming at me. Fortunately, Liam stepped in."

"I told the kid his parents' insurance would most likely cover the bike, but he was still irate," Liam explained. "He'd built the bike himself and said he could never get another one like it."

"You'd think I'd killed a beloved pet or something," Archer groused. "Anyway, Liam said you figured out that yesterday's picture was taken at the bakery."

"My dad figured it out." She told him the story of her father crashing into the bricks as a young man.

Archer actually laughed at the tale, then sobered again. "We racked our brains, but neither of us remember a fire or any other emergency there. Not since I've been here, anyway."

"Then there must be some other connection." She raised an eyebrow, hoping he might mention Carrie Moore, but all she got in return was a deadpan stare. "I found out something at the library this morning that might break this case wide open." She used her best detective voice, but Archer's answering smile didn't reach his eyes. "Do you have the photos?"

Archer reached for an envelope waiting next to him in the chair.

"Lay them out in the order you got them." Hannah stood and moved a stapler and a cup of pens to make room on Liam's desk.

Liam reached forward to help her make room, and Archer laid out the photos.

When they were done, Hannah said, "Now, forget about where they were taken. That might have been the wrong approach." She waited a moment for effect. "What if they're letters?"

Archer gaped at her in confusion, then back at the pictures. "What…? Oh. Wow. Why didn't I see that sooner?" He traced the shape of the window. "That's a *U*, and the tree stump is an *O*. The balcony, *M*, and the bakery..." He scratched his head. "The lighter-colored bricks form an *E*. *U-O-M-E*."

"Huh." Liam winked at Hannah. "You're not just a pretty blond sleuth. You're brilliant too. But what does UOME mean?"

"I have no idea, but—"

Archer's eyes widened. "You. Owe. Me."

"Who would send you that, and why?" Liam asked.

Archer stretched his neck to one side and then the other. "I want to say I don't have a clue. Unfortunately, I think I might. I've heard those words before."

"From whom?" Hannah asked.

Archer leaned back in the chair. "Right before I met Bryn, Winter Bronson tried setting me up on a date with someone who'd apparently been interested in me for a long time. Winter gave me her name. I scoped her out on social media and decided we had nothing in common, so I told Winter I wasn't interested. Shortly after that conversation, I met Bryn but hadn't told anyone about her except for Liam here. The next time I saw Winter, I happened to mention to her that I was picking up Goldilocks for the Chamber of Commerce gala the next week."

"Goldilocks?"

Liam sighed. "She was a sweetheart."

"Who is she? Or, rather, who was she?"

The men exchanged amused glances. Liam's smile turned down. He gave a loud sniff. "Goldilocks is no more."

"Who *was* she?"

"She was the prettiest 1974 Camaro Z28 LT you ever laid eyes on. Got her from my uncle for only five hundred bucks. Metal flake gold, not a speck of rust, only thirty-seven thousand miles and—"

"A *car*?" Hannah interrupted. "I thought we were talking about a woman."

Archer grinned. "Therein lies the confusion. Winter had the same thought. How was I to know the woman she was trying to set me up with was called Goldilocks by all her friends?"

A tiny groan escaped Hannah. "This story is not going to end well, is it?"

Archer grimaced. "*My* Goldilocks was in the shop. I figured everyone knew that was what I called my car. But Winter was evidently the one person in town who didn't, so she called her friend and told her she must have missed a text or voicemail from me saying that I'd changed my mind and wanted to ask her out. The two of them took off to shop for what was apparently a very expensive outfit."

Hannah matched Archer's grimace. "What happened?"

"I picked up Goldilocks the next day, then picked up Bryn for our second date at the gala. About an hour later, Winter shows up with this blond woman who was all decked out in this sparkly dress with matching shoes and purse. The woman stomped up to me and hissed, 'You owe me for this.'" Archer threw up his hands.

"I had no idea who she was or what she was talking about. I found out much later that Stan Carlson had invited her to go with him, and she'd turned him down because she thought I was taking her. Anyway, as you guessed, the story didn't end well, but that's not the worst of it. On our way home from the gala, Goldilocks's engine blew up."

Hannah shook her head, hoping that the poor woman had developed the ability to see the humor in the comedy of errors. "So let me guess. The woman you apparently owe for her sparkly attire is the new bakery employee, Carrie Moore."

Archer nodded miserably. "You got it."

Hannah walked through the Hot Spot dining room with her mind whirling.

Archer had received a photo of the bakery. Carrie Moore, the woman who felt he'd humiliated her, worked at the bakery. Was there a connection? They had to look at all the possibilities. Who else might think Archer owed them something? But maybe what they'd thought were a *U* and an *O* didn't actually stand for "you owe." Maybe she'd been wrong, and they weren't letters at all.

After leaving her jacket and purse in her office, she joined Jacob in the kitchen. He was listening to his favorite radio station while shaping burger patties. She'd told him more than once that she was fine with using premade patties, but he was adamant that frozen burgers were too dense and "not made with love." He greeted her with a greasy hand wave and a head tilt toward his phone. "You can turn that down if you want. I was going to ask you about the menu for Raquel's birthday bash."

She laughed. "Birthday plans are exactly what I need right now." Better than the questions on repeat in her brain. She reached across the table and tapped the pause button on Jacob's phone. "Tell me your thoughts. Turning twenty-five is a big deal, and I know she's often felt that her birthday gets overshadowed by Valentine's Day. Let's make sure that we do something fun and light and very non-valentine-y, especially since Marshall might not be here."

"I couldn't agree more. I tried getting her mind off Marshall yesterday by talking about favorite foods. You saw how successful that was, but I did learn a few things. She loves Italian, so I was thinking we could do a traditional Italian buffet of lasagna, garlic bread, and Ceasar salad with tiramisu cake for dessert."

"Tiramisu *cake*?"

"Yep. Three layers of coffee-soaked vanilla sponge cake, frosted with a fluffy mascarpone cream and dusted with cocoa powder."

"Sounds heavenly. I'm sure she'd love it, but is that putting too much on you?"

"Not at all." Jacob flattened a burger patty and pointed to a roll of parchment paper. "Would you mind?"

Hannah grabbed the box and pulled out a stretch of brown paper that matched the length of the tray Jacob was filling. She tore it off and covered the two dozen identical burger patties.

"Thanks." Jacob pulled a portion of ground beef from a massive bowl. "I'll make the lasagna ahead of time and freeze it. The rest is easy."

"I'll help wherever I can."

"Any idea how many people I should prep for?"

"I've invited thirty. So far I've gotten ten yeses and two nos. I'll follow up early next week." Another thing to add to her pre-Valentine's Day to-do list.

"As if you have nothing else to do next week."

"My list is a bit daunting. Which reminds me. Do you know of any good restaurants in Hopkinsville? I want to take Liam to the firefighter museum there on Monday and then out for lunch."

Jacob raised his eyebrows. "What a great idea of a date for him. Liam seems like the kind of guy who values good food over fancy ambiance, so I'd recommend the Wood Shed. Best pulled pork I've ever eaten."

Hannah typed it into her phone. "Thanks."

"Any updates on Archer's mystery?"

"What's the last you heard?"

"Just what he showed us on Tuesday. Did he figure out who sent the pictures?"

"Not yet. Sorry. I should have kept you in the loop, since you were there for the start of it." Hannah filled him in on the additional photos and their theories so far, leaving out the identity of the woman nicknamed Goldilocks.

"Wait. Some woman he never intentionally led on is now trying to get him to pay for the dress she bought for a gala because she thought he was taking her, even though he'd never said a word about it to her?" Jacob's eyes were wide with incredulity.

Pressing her lips tight to suppress a laugh, Hannah nodded. "That kind of sums it up. Of course, it's only a theory."

"Sounds a bit far-fetched."

"It does, but Archer's grasping at straws. I don't blame him. He doesn't have much else to go on, and at this point we have to consider everything."

Jacob turned a patty in his hands, pressing out the cracked edges. "I suppose you're right."

"It's only a theory." She tapped her hand against the worktable. "Guess I'd better get something done. I don't have a ton of paperwork today, so let me know if you need me in here."

"Will do."

Hannah turned, then stopped. She intentionally hadn't told Jacob the real name of the woman whose friends called her Goldilocks. She didn't want to be accused of gossip or slander if she was way off base. But Jacob knew her, which meant she couldn't afford to pass up the chance that he'd be able to fill in any blanks. "Before I go," she said in her most nonchalant voice, "how well do you know Carrie Moore?"

"Not well. Other than the fact that she's an early riser. Before it got really cold, I saw her out walking a couple of times before five in the morning."

"She sounds very disciplined."

"I don't think she's walking for exercise. She's always carrying a big purse."

Chapter Eight

Hannah was at the library two minutes after Evangeline unlocked the doors on Friday morning. She walked up to the circulation desk and checked out the book she'd reserved, but the whole time she chatted with Evangeline, her eyes were on the door at the back, waiting for it to open.

"They'll be here any minute now," Evangeline said with a knowing smile.

"Sorry to be so distracted. I'm just really curious about the 'Evangeline my Valentine' drawing." She told the librarian about the first photograph Archer received.

"It was exactly the same as the sketch? Only the bottom half of the window?"

"Yes. I'm guessing the person who took the picture got the idea from your display."

"When did you say Archer got the photo?"

"On Sunday."

Evangeline shook her head. "The display didn't go up until Tuesday night after we closed."

Hannah felt her pulse quicken. "Well, that might help us narrow it down. Now we just need to find out who donated the drawing."

"Could have been someone volunteering at the historical society."

Hannah nodded. The sound of a door clicking open echoed off the high ceiling and hardwood floor. A young woman stood in the doorway of the room at the back. "That's my cue."

"I'll pop in when I can. I'm curious about the other Evangeline."

"Maybe she's a long-lost relative, and you were named for her."

"That would be fun. My mother passed away when I was seven. My father wanted nothing to do with her family, especially after he remarried, so I know almost nothing about them, but my father's mother was named Hortence. Glad I wasn't named after her."

Hannah laughed. "Evangeline is much nicer." As she walked toward the back, she watched a silver-haired woman select a thick novel and settle into an overstuffed chair in the corner. She had a wistful moment, wondering if things at the Hot Spot would ever get to the point that everything ran like clockwork and she'd have time to sit for hours and read. That had been one of the factors that influenced her decision to only open for dinner. So far, the times she allowed herself a day just to relax were rare. Even rarer were those downtimes that coincided with Liam's.

But Monday was only three days away.

She was smiling as she walked into the room lined with bookshelves and maps and old black-and-white historical photographs.

"Hi! Can I help you?" Up close, the young woman appeared much younger, maybe still in her teens. What were the chances she'd be able to help?

"Hi, I'm Hannah Prentiss. Is Phyllis going to be in soon?"

"Yeah. She had to take one of her grandkids to school. She figured I couldn't mess things up too bad before she got here."

"I come here often, but I don't think we've met."

"Probably not. I'm new. Doing community service." She grinned. She must have noticed the doubt on Hannah's face because she quickly added, "Because I'm a senior, not because it's court-ordered or anything like that. I'm in a work program at school that allows me to be here, especially since I've already met my graduation requirements."

Hannah chuckled. "That does ease my mind."

"I'm Amethyst." Emerald-green eyes, likely enhanced by contact lenses, sparkled as she smiled.

"Nice to meet you, Amethyst. Hannah Prentiss."

"You own the Hot Spot. That place is great. How can I help you?"

Hannah smiled. "I'm curious about one of the items in the Valentine's Day display up front."

"Aren't those hysterical? Some of them are so mushy, while others are plain rude. Like, who would send someone a valentine that basically says, 'No way, man, I'm so not into you.' Right?"

Hannah couldn't help but laugh. "Right. Anyway, the one I'm interested in is the one with the pencil drawing that says 'Evangeline, my Valentine' at the top. I was wondering if I could find out who donated it, or if anyone here knows who wrote it or who Evangeline was."

Amethyst pursed her lips. "I don't know any of that, but there's a box marked 'Vintage Valentines and Love Letters,' and another one with old letters that all that stuff came out of. I helped a little with the display, and it was awesome reading some of the old-time love letters."

"I believe that."

"People talked so differently a hundred years ago. Last night my boyfriend sent me a text that just said L-U-B for 'Love you, babe,' but back in those days a guy would get out a pen and paper to write something like 'My darling, I am so besotted with your beauty that I cannot eat or sleep or think of anything other than how much I will love you for all eternity and beyond." She ended with one hand pressed against her heart and the other stretched up in a beseeching gesture.

Hannah burst out laughing. "Please tell me you're taking drama in school. And I'm impressed you know the word 'besotted.'"

Amethyst giggled. "My lit teacher last year was really into Tennyson. He loved saying people were besotted. And I am in drama. We're doing 'You Can't Take It With You' in May. I'm playing Penelope. I was typecast because I love to write like Penelope in the play. Anyway, the boxes are back here." She waved her hand for Hannah to follow.

"You're sure it's okay if I look through them?"

"Yeah. Phyllis told me just to make sure people handle things carefully and no one absconds with anything."

Absconds? Hannah smiled at Amethyst's back. She'd been so wrong about this girl.

Amethyst set two bankers boxes on a table. "Have fun. You can take pictures if you want."

"Thank you."

Amethyst walked back to the front desk, and Hannah lifted the cover off the box labeled VINTAGE VALENTINES AND LOVE LETTERS–PROPERTY OF BLACKBERRY VALLEY HISTORICAL SOCIETY. A little surge of adrenaline coursed through her as she thumbed through the titles on the folders. The first half were filed by date, the rest by name. The oldest were from the 1800s. Driven by curiosity rather than the mission that had brought her here, she quietly read out loud as she thumbed through the alphabetical names, looking for anything familiar, and stopping to read a few old letters along the way.

She stopped when she spotted an envelope with a heart penciled on the front and pulled out a stack of yellowed envelopes held together with a rubber band. The top one was postmarked March 19, 1921, in Russell, Kentucky, and addressed to Mrs. Roman George in Blackberry Valley. She slid her finger carefully under the rubber band, but the aged rubber snapped and fell away. The top envelope was the only one with a drawing. She opened the back flap and slid out a single piece of tissue-paper-thin stationery and began to read.

> *My darling Mary,*
>
> *How I wish we were together on this beautiful spring night. I look up at the stars and thank every one of them that you are living under this same sky. As much as I miss you, I know I did right to send you to your family. The sickness in the camp is spreading, and I would be sick at heart if you or our darling Minnie succumbed to it. Please give her a kiss on her little nose from her pa, and tell her we will be together soon as the weather warms a bit more. Yes, I heard the news about the Pond Creek collapse. We had a time of prayer here for those who were lost. Don't you worry your pretty little head. Nothing like that is going to happen here.*
>
> *Your loving husband,*
>
> *Roman*

Hannah blinked back to the present. She could spend hours reading through these. For now, she continued to peek into each folder for anything resembling either the pencil sketch of the Stanton Building window or the heavy, bold print with a backhand slant. She stopped occasionally to pick up an old greeting card—some elaborate, others clearly homemade.

Nothing in the first box jumped out at her. The next box was labeled LETTERS – 1920 THROUGH 1940. ON LOAN. She opened it. Also alphabetized. Again, she started with the beginning of the alphabet. As she flipped through, one name struck her as familiar. *Haley*. Where had she just heard that name? She closed her eyes and took a deep breath, trying a trick she'd learned as a little kid. *Walk backward through your mind.* She was pretty sure it had been in the midst of a long conversation, so that ruled out stopping at tables to greet guests at the Hot Spot.

She'd spoken to Liam, Archer, Jacob, Raquel, Lacy, Dad…*Dad.* The Stanton Building. Dad had mentioned that it had previously been the Haley Mercantile. He'd also mentioned that Stan and Stephanie Carlson had found something in an old milk box while they were renovating. It was a long shot that what she'd find in the folder marked *Haley* was in any way connected to Stan Carlson, the other corner of the unintentional love triangle, but she wasn't about to ignore the possibility.

When she opened the cover of the file, she immediately gasped. Sitting on top was a page with several small sketches, one of the Stanton Building window. The next looked like the wrought iron end of the bench in front of the Hot Spot—scrolled iron she'd never before realized resembled an *R*. The third was of the Eiffel Tower. Next to it was a drawing of a peach. If she was right that the first few images stood for letters, the message was, "You are a peach."

Below that was written, *Meet me at our favorite place. We will dream of summer, and I'll tell you of Paris as we plan.*

"Plan what?" Hannah asked out loud.

"What?" Amethyst walked toward her. "Find something?"

"Maybe." She held up the page. "This was likely drawn by the same person who made the one out in the display."

Amethyst nodded. "Sure looks like it. My grandma has pictures hanging in her dining room that are words spelled out with architectural elements. One says 'Love,' and one 'Family,' and the other says 'Pray.' Who knew that was a thing back before cameras?"

Hannah didn't bother to tell her that cameras had been around since before the Civil War. "Maybe this person invented it." She set the paper face down on the table. "I'm looking for anything with the name 'Evangeline' on it."

"I asked Mrs. Cooke about that other one, and she said it wasn't made for her."

"I asked her too. That drawing was made for an Evangeline that lived before Mrs. Cooke was born." Hannah picked up the folder and slid the box aside. "I'm going to go through all of these."

"Can I help? I love historical stories, and this is kind of a mystery, isn't it?"

"It definitely is." Hannah handed the top half of the stack to Amethyst, who took a chair across from her.

The top page on her own sheaf contained another drawing, this one of a young girl and her puppy. The next depicted an old rickety barn and a windmill. Both of them held similarities to the window and the Eiffel Tower, but she'd guess they were done by a younger person, or the same artist at a younger age.

"Hey! Look at this." Amethyst laid a crumpled, black-smudged piece of paper in front of Hannah. "At first I thought it was just a picture of a tree, but there's something written on it." She smoothed it out and jabbed a purple fingernail in the center. "See that?"

Amethyst's fingernail tapped on an arrow pointing to the base of the tree where a circle was drawn. On the other side of the arrow were two words: *Dig here.*

Chapter Nine

Near Blackberry Valley, Kentucky
March 21, 1921

Evangeline Haley hugged her knees, forming a cradle on her lap for Tucker as the truck bounced over deep ruts in the dirt road. Pa figured the pup was about three months old. "Barely old enough to be away from his ma," Pa had said when she'd found him wandering outside the camp six weeks ago.

As they jostled along, mile after mile, the sun had slowly arced overhead and now sat low on the horizon in front of them. "Heading west," Ma had said, "just like pioneers."

Sadness mingled with excitement with each bump in the road. She'd been born in the mining camp and figured it was where she'd someday raise a family, just like Ma had. But the explosion had changed everything. She and Micah had crouched on the Bentons' porch under the window, listening in while Pa and Mr. Benton talked about Mr. Moss. They'd sent a telegram to his girl, but she'd replied that she was marrying a rich banker and didn't want Mr. Moss's land. She'd told them he had no next of kin and to keep it and his "paste and tin" ring. So they were moving, and her pa and Micah's were going treasure hunting soon as they got there.

Isaiah, her ten-year-old brother, lifted his head from the stack of pillows he slept on, then lay back and closed his eyes again. Esther, who'd just turned six, was sitting up front between Ma and Pa, and baby Ruth was on Ma's lap.

Everything they owned was piled around Evangline and Isaiah in crates and baskets. It wasn't much. Their beds and kitchen table had belonged to the camp. The only piece of furniture going with them was Ma's rocking chair, the one Pa had made when Evangeline was born. They had some dishes and some blankets. Pa said they'd buy more, lots more, when they dug up the ring. He said Miss Josephine, Mr. Moss's intended, was wrong. The ring buried on the Moss land was real—and mighty expensive.

Her sadness lifted like morning fog when Micah stood up in the bed of the Bentons' truck that was right behind them and waved at her. She returned the wave, grinning at him. Micah wasn't sad. He'd said since they were little that he couldn't wait to get out of the camp. He wasn't going to be a miner, no matter what. The last few days he'd bragged to all their friends that he was going to be a farmer.

They were all going to be farmers now, in Blackberry Valley. With a name like that, it had to be a pretty place. She imagined lush green hills covered in blackberry bushes. She'd pick pails full, eat as much as she wanted, and still have enough for pies and jam.

There were cows on the farm, Pa said. Mr. Moss had paid another farmer to care for them. Were there other animals? She'd seen pictures of a farm in a book. She imagined a big white house with a porch that wrapped all the way around it. And a bright red barn. And sunflowers and corn taller than she was.

Was there a school nearby, and a church? Micah had always been her best friend, but she already missed Suzy and Betsy. She used to tell Micah everything, but now that she was almost thirteen, there were things she couldn't tell him. Like how much she liked it when he carried her books home from school, or how mad she got when he talked to Colleen McFadden.

The sun was setting, blazing the sky orange and pink as the truck lurched to a stop. "This is it!" Pa called out the window.

Evangeline scrambled out of the truck ahead of Isaiah. She'd braided a collar for Tucker, and now she tied a rope to it. She laughed as he ran in circles around her, sniffing the ground.

As she gazed around, searching for the big red barn and the white farmhouse, Ma gasped. Not the happy kind of gasp. Evangeline walked around to the front of the truck to see what had caused it. Two buildings sat in front of them. An unpainted barn leaned to the left. Swallows flew in and out of a gaping hole in the roof. A tiny shack, no bigger than the one they'd just moved out of, was surrounded by weeds as tall as she was.

The six Bentons joined them, and Mrs. Benton started to cry.

"Everything's going to be all right," Pa said. "Don't look like much now, but we got forty acres and a buried treasure. We'll take the barn for the night. Meet you at first light, Oren?"

Mr. Benton nodded. "Sounds like a plan. By breakfast time tomorrow, all our troubles will be over."

Chapter Ten

"A treasure map?" Phyllis Taft stared at the smudged paper. At seventy-eight, and a fourth-generation Blackberry Valley resident, she not only knew everyone in town, but could also rattle off fascinating tidbits about many families' ancestors.

"Not like an 'X marks the spot' map," Amethyst said. "But maybe a circle marks the spot." She pointed to the circle at the base of a tree with leaves that were detailed enough to tell it was a red oak. Two gnarled limbs spread over what appeared to be a narrow stream like a giant's outstretched arms. "Look at the detail on the tree. I think it would actually be possible to find it. And why would it say 'Dig here,' if there wasn't something buried there?"

"The problem is, it could be anywhere in the world," Hannah said glumly.

She stood across the table from Amethyst, looking at the picture upside down. Amethyst had grabbed two magnifying glasses from the front desk. She and Phyllis were bent over the paper, making it hard for Hannah to get a good look at it. While she waited her turn, she glanced over at the stack of papers she'd given Amethyst. The next thing on the stack was a map.

Yellowed, crumbling around the edges, the paper appeared to have been ripped out of a book. Spidery lines wove across the page. Roads, streams, and what appeared to be a railroad line. The map was crowded with words. Only a few, in bold caps, were easy to read. *SLICK ROCK. CAVE CITY. GLASGOW.* Was this a map of Barren County? She held out her hand. "Can I have a magnifying glass, please?"

Phyllis offered hers. "What did you find?"

"I think it's a county map." She picked up the page. With the magnification, faint grid lines appeared. The words were actually names. *J. Bales, M. Huggins, R. Parrish.* None that she recognized. "It's a plat map."

Phyllis came around to her side of the table. "It is." She pointed to miniscule letters that formed a familiar name—King Farm.

"That's Elaine Wilby's farm." Any frustration she'd felt a minute ago was now replaced by excitement. "I wonder how old this is."

"Easy way to find out." Phyllis stepped to a small table pushed against the wall and opened a laptop. "We have plat maps all the way back to the mid-1800s." Her fingers tapped so quickly it sounded like popping corn. After a moment, she picked up the laptop and brought it to Hannah. "This might be it—1919."

Hannah glanced between the enlarged map on the screen and the image under the magnifying glass. "Yep. That's it. Other than King, I still don't recognize any names. Do you?"

Phyllis expanded the map. "Sure do. Not many properties still owned by the same families, but I see quite a few that are in our archives. Darter, Mayfield, Moss."

Phyllis bent closer to Hannah, peering through the magnifying glass. "Think that blue dot next to 'L. Moss' is intentional?"

The dot was tiny, but perfectly positioned next to the *L*. "Looks like it, doesn't it?"

"Let's see if I can find any records on an L. Moss. It's not familiar, but that doesn't mean anything."

Hannah set the magnifying glass on the table and stretched her neck from side to side. When she glanced at her watch, she was surprised to see she'd been there for over an hour. She had other things to do, but she knew where she'd be at nine the next morning. As she lowered the map to put it back in the folder, she noticed a spot near the top where ink seemed to have bled through from the other side. She turned it over.

"There's something written on the other side. A letter. No, it's more like a document of some kind." The handwritten words were smeared in spots and the penmanship, spelling, and grammar made it look like it could have been done by a child, all making it hard to decipher.

> *In the event I don't make it outa this job alive, I hereby do bequeath my property to Miss Josephine Hamilton of Blackberry Valley, Kentucky, my one true love for eternity. Everthing on and under my land shall be hers for good and legal in perpertuity after I meet my maker.*
>
> *Signed,*
> *Linus K. Moss*
> *Stone, Kentucky*
> *April 5, 1920*

When Hannah lifted her gaze from the paper, the two other women in the room voiced the words ricocheting around in her head. "On and *under*?"

Tapping the delete key seven times, again, Hannah chided herself for too many simple mistakes. Formatting the Valentine's Day menu wasn't a task that required extreme focus. But it did require some. She glanced down at Jacob's handwritten list and tried again.

Soup:

Tomato Basil with Cheese Tortellini

Salad:

Iceberg Lettuce Wedge, Praline Walnuts, Blue Cheese Crumbles, Applewood Smoked Bacon, Blistered Tomatoes, House Ranch Dressing

Entrée:

Seared Filet Mignon with Béarnaise Sauce

Charred Scallion Whipped Potatoes

Prosciutto Wrapped Asparagus

Yeast Rolls with Herb Butter

Dessert:

Triple Chocolate Raspberry Truffle Cheesecake

The second time she misspelled *potatoes*, she gave in to her impulses. She opened an internet browser and researched Linus Moss and Josephine Hamilton. She quickly hit a dead end with them, so she moved on to the town where Linus Moss had penned what could have served as his last will and testament. She'd discovered that Stone was a coal-mining community named for Galen Stone, head of the Pond Creek Coal Company.

It took her a minute to remember where she'd recently read the name Pond Creek. The letter written to Mary George had mentioned the Pond Creek collapse.

The black smudges on the paper and the reference to the possibility of not surviving the job told her Linus Moss had probably been a miner. Was he working when the mine collapsed?

That question led her down a rabbit hole into Kentucky mining in the 1920s. She read about the dangerous working conditions. Miners often worked in the dark, in low-ceilinged areas lit only by their acetylene headlamps. As they mined by hand with shovels and pickaxes, they were constantly at risk of explosions and collapses, as well as diseases like black lung. Pay was minimal, and rent, coal for heating, and medical expenses were often deducted from their paychecks. Their families lived in small, dilapidated shacks. Black-and-white photographs depicted men with deeply creased coal-blackened faces, row upon row of cookie-cutter shanties lining treeless streets, barefoot children playing with sticks and rocks, and too-thin women in flour sack dresses.

When she finally clicked out of five open tabs on coal mining, a sense of sadness pervaded her mood. Such hard lives. Why did it seem some people were born blessed and others into adversity? It was an age-old question, and she wasn't likely to find the answer. Then again, the true answer lay in something she'd learned in Sunday school. God is in control. Of everything. Even the things that don't feel good.

She pulled her hair up and fastened it with a hair band. Something about the gesture felt like a transition from depressing thoughts to the work at hand. Refocusing on the Valentine's Day dinner, she ordered more red cloth napkins and hunted for the perfect art and font for the menus, which would be printed on heavy cardstock and placed on each plate. And here it was an hour until they opened and she'd forgotten to eat lunch. She stood, stretched, and walked out into the dining room. She'd make a sandwich then give Raquel a hand with rolling silverware and see how she was doing.

Raquel stood next to the corner booth where she'd sat in tears a few days ago. But this time she was laughing. And she was not alone.

Marshall Fredericks sat in the booth, holding out silverware in each hand. His brown eyes regarded Raquel with so much tenderness and affection that Hannah could almost imagine the dim corner glowing. It was so good to see the two of them happy. She kept her steps light as she walked toward the kitchen, not wanting to disturb the beautiful moment.

"We see you, Hannah." Raquel's smile was evident in her voice.

"I was trying to be discreet."

"No need." Marshall motioned her over. "I have a question anyway. Raquel said you have the menu figured out for the Valentine's Day dinner and you still have openings. Is that something you'd like to put out there?"

Hannah smiled at him. They'd come a long way since the first time he'd set foot in the Hot Spot and published a less-than-stellar review. She was upset at first, but his criticism had been constructive. Marshall had commented on the lack of firehouse-themed decor, which prompted Liam to show up with a box of memorabilia that he, his father, and grandfather had collected in their years as Blackberry Valley firefighters.

"If you're asking whether we'd like a shout-out in the *Blackberry Valley Chronicle* or by the Gourmet Guy, we'd be honored. I'm working on the print menus today. I'll send you one." She hesitated before saying the next thing on her mind. "I've been praying for your big decision. Whether you take the job or not, it must feel very rewarding to be offered a position with such a big-name publication."

"It does." Marshall gazed at Raquel and the light in his eyes dimmed a bit. His lips quirked up on the right. "We just have to see if it'll work for us."

"I feel for you guys." Hannah wished she had some wisdom to share. Instead, she told them about Linus Moss bequeathing his land to his true love in "perpertuity."

Marshall laughed. "That does put things in perspective, doesn't it? I don't know where Stone is, but Pike County is a good four hours from here on the interstate. How long would that trip have taken a hundred years ago?"

Raquel placed a rolled napkin in the basket in the middle of the table and sat down across from Marshall. "Even if they wrote letters, by the time news would reach either of them, it would be old. And if he was working the mines, poor Josephine was probably scared he wasn't coming back at all." She reached out and slid her hand over Marshall's. "You're right. It does put things in perspective."

Perspective. The word whispered in Hannah's mind as she walked into the kitchen. What if, instead of heading out for a four-day conference in Owensboro, Liam was going to Pike County to work in a coal mine? What if she couldn't simply pick up a phone and call or text him? What if she didn't have a ton of pictures of him on her phone she could look at any time she missed him?

Feeling much more grateful than she had the past few days, she stopped outside the kitchen doors, pulled out her phone, and typed JUST WANTED TO SAY HI AND— And what? This would be easier if they'd reached the point of saying those three little words out loud. Texting to say "I love you" was something most couples did, but it was too soon for that. Maybe she didn't need an "and." She backspaced and added a period. JUST WANTED TO SAY HI. That was enough.

She slipped her phone back in her pocket. As she put her hand on the swinging door, a tiny ding told her Liam had answered.

MISS YOU TOO.

Had he heard her heart in a simple hi? Her phone dinged with another message from him.

ARCHER AND I COMING FOR DINNER AROUND 9. HE GOT 2 MORE. GETTING WEIRDER.

Chapter Eleven

Hannah lined up five plates on the worktable and checked the order ticket. She'd spent the first half of the evening tag-teaming with Elaine, ushering guests to their tables and bringing waters. When the waiting area filled, she'd handed out menus and talked up their Friday night specials. Working wherever she was needed was one of her favorite parts of owning a restaurant. Now, as the kitchen clock crept closer to nine, she handled menial tasks, freeing Jacob to man the grill and fryer.

She set out what Jacob called "fixin's" on each plate and added color-coded plastic meat markers—red for rare, all the way to dark brown for well done. When Jacob said, "Now," it was her key to grab the buns he'd toasted on the grill and put one on each plate. She loved watching him pivot like a well-programmed robot, placing burgers on buns in rapid succession, then adding perfectly even portions of fries or onion rings to each plate, before ringing the bell for the server.

Dylan rushed in, lined three plates along one arm, and grabbed two in the other. Hannah had to laugh when she remembered him practicing this move with unbreakable plates before they opened. Gangly and clumsy, he'd just turned twenty when she hired him. Though she could have found someone more graceful and experienced, Dylan's winning smile and sense of humor had quickly charmed their guests. In spite of the cost of replacing drink glasses, she'd known he was a keeper within the first two nights. He'd come a long way, though there were still moments like this, when she prayed everything would make it to the table intact.

He grinned at them, turned around, and started to back through the swinging doors, then stopped. "Almost forgot. The fire chief would like a word with you, Hannah." He followed with a wider grin and a wink before successfully exiting.

"Go. I got this." Jacob pointed to the two tickets clipped to the ring above the table. "We're winding down, and who am I to interfere with true love?"

Hannah untied her apron and gave serious thought to tossing it at him. Instead, she just stuck her tongue out at him as she walked out.

She'd asked Elaine to seat Liam and Archer in her favorite booth. When things were slow, it was where she liked to hide out, doing paperwork while observing and making notes on what was working and what needed to improve. Raquel was taking their order. Thankfully, the joy on her face from her earlier time with Marshall was still there. She closed her order pad and pointed the end of her pencil at Archer and Liam. "They're a bit feisty tonight, so I'll turn them over to you."

"Great." Hannah sat down when Liam slid over. "All I need at the end of a long day is feisty firefighters." She leaned against his shoulder, and he pressed back.

"Hey. I like that," Liam said. "Feisty Firefighters. Next time we play ball with the police department, that should be our team name."

Raquel laughed, rolled her eyes, and walked away.

Hannah took a minute to give Liam a look she hoped conveyed all the sappy things she couldn't say when they weren't alone, then turned to Archer. "Two more, huh?"

"Yep." Archer picked up the jacket he'd laid on the seat and pulled out an envelope. By the thickness, she could tell it contained all six photos.

"So it didn't mean 'You owe me' after all?"

"I have no idea." He set one in front of her. "Got this yesterday. It was delivered to my aunt." He put a second beside it. "And this one was dropped off at Jump Start before they opened this morning. Which creeps me out. It's like this guy, whoever it is, knows all the people I know, and knows when I work and even where I get my morning coffee. I'm being stalked."

"It could be creepy. Or it could just mean somebody knows you really well." Hannah picked up the first photo he'd set down. Now that she was viewing them as letters, it was easy to see that the roof peak with gingerbread trim connecting two forty-five-degree-angle sides formed an *A*. The next, two arched windows side-by-side, was an *M*.

Liam tapped the second photo. "We're trying to think of what starts with an *M* that someone might think Archer owes them."

"If they're really spelling out a message one letter at a time, you'll know in a couple of days. And while it could be creepy, maybe it's as simple as 'You owe me a meal.'" A thought struck Hannah. "Or a match. Isn't that what they call it in racquetball?"

"We're back to Stan, huh?"

Hannah shrugged. "At the moment, we have Stan Carlson and Carrie Moore as very remote possibilities. Until you get more photos, they're our only suspects."

"Maybe I'll talk to Stan." There wasn't much conviction in Archer's voice.

Liam nodded. "I've always been a fan of the straightforward approach."

"Then we should probably use that with everyone," Archer pointed out. "You order from Sweet Caroline's regularly, right?"

"Right."

"Have you already put in your order for your Valentine shindig?"

"Yep. Did that last week." Where was this going?

"How about for Raquel's birthday party?"

"I need to call and order a few loaves of French bread. Why do you ask?"

"Perfect." Archer's despondency had vanished in a matter of seconds. "You need to order the bread in person."

"And I need to do that because…?"

"Because that will give you an opportunity to introduce yourself, ask her how she likes working at the bakery. You know, get chummy with her."

"And then casually insert your name into a conversation about French bread?"

Archer laughed. "Something like that." He nodded toward Liam. "You can confide in her about your disappointments in the romance department."

"Hey," Liam protested, chuckling.

"I'm hardly disappointed in the romance department right now," Hannah told Archer.

"Glad to hear it, though I'm not sure how. Anyway, then she'll open up to you about being ditched by someone who never actually asked her out."

"Wow. Is that how guys think women work?"

Liam nudged her arm. “I have to agree with Archer on this. Remember that woman you met at the grocery store a few weeks ago? The one who was standing in front of the ice cream freezer?”

Hannah closed her eyes. He had her there.

“It was fascinating,” Liam told Archer. “Here we are in the frozen food section on a Sunday afternoon. We’re each going to pick a pint of our favorite ice cream, and this woman walks up. She’s maybe in her midforties. She stands there and groans like this is the most important decision of her life. Hannah groans right along with her and says, ‘I know, right?’ The next thing I know, the woman is telling Hannah all about her impending divorce and what it’s doing to her kids. I walk off to find the hot fudge because it feels like a private conversation. A few minutes later, I come back to find that Hannah has her arm around the woman and is praying with her. It was amazing. I mean, how long would it take you to find out anything about a guy standing next to you buying ice cream?”

Archer narrowed his eyes as if he didn’t understand the question. “I don’t think it would even occur to me to try. Thanks for proving my point. It’s a strange thing, but it’s also very cool. It’s a gift.”

“And you’d like me to use that gift to interrogate your possible stalker?” Hannah asked.

“Well, when you put it that way, it sounds rather devious,” Archer protested. “All I’m asking you to do is give her an opportunity to share her feelings.”

“And if I find out she’s still holding a grudge, what do I do with that information?”

"I'll take it from there."

"Now *that* sounds devious," Liam said, clearly enjoying the idea of such an interaction.

Archer pressed a hand to his chest. "I am a sensitive man. I'll have you know I've let many a woman down with utmost gentleness."

"Many, huh?" Liam ribbed. "As in two?"

"Who's counting? The only one who really matters is the one who's currently holed up in a cabin in the woods, likely devising a way to let *me* down easy."

The upbeat mood evaporated. Hannah had never seen him look so forlorn. She wished she knew what to say to give him hope. She'd seen him with Bryn often enough to know Bryn was crazy about him. "I know Bryn doesn't have internet or a phone, but is there any way you could send her something? Can you get the address from her mom and send her flowers or an apology letter?"

Archer's brow furrowed. "I suppose I could. If her mom would give it to me. The one time I talked to her, I got the feeling she was protecting Bryn. She didn't seem to want to give out too much information."

"Is it possible her sole motive is protecting her daughter's chance to finally get her dissertation done and take a little time for R & R?" Hannah pointed out gently. "I ran into Bryn at the library last week, and she looked exhausted. When I asked how she was doing, she said she was feeling pretty frazzled from trying to balance work and volunteering with needing blocks of time to research and write. She isn't one of those people who can grab a few spare minutes here and there to work. She needs long stretches of uninterrupted time to concentrate. It makes sense that her mom would be protecting that time."

Archer rested his chin in his hand. "I understood when she wanted to get away to a hotel less than an hour away. But how do you work on a dissertation without internet? And she has until the end of April to get it done."

"When I talked to her, she said there was a new position opening up at the medical center in Bowling Green for someone with her degree. What is she going for, again?"

"PhD in Neuropsychology."

"Wow. That's so impressive. It sounded like she was pretty sure of getting the job, and she wanted to have her dissertation reviewed before it would start."

"That still doesn't explain why she has to be completely unreachable," Archer said. "I think she just wanted to get away from me because I can be so dense sometimes."

"Have you talked to Raquel about it? Other than on Tuesday, I mean. She's in a much better headspace today, and she and Bryn are close. I think she'd know if Bryn intended to end your relationship. Maybe she was upset when she left, but do you really think she was upset enough to call it quits?"

"I don't know. But it sure messes with my plans for Valentine's Day. Even if she's home by then, it will take some time to get back to where we were."

"What were you planning?"

Without a word, Archer swiped to a picture on his phone and held it out so Hannah could see it.

The photo was of an engagement ring. A thin platinum band with a marquise-cut diamond. It was Bryn's exact style.

So she'd been right about why he was working overtime. All of Archer's angst suddenly made sense. "It's gorgeous. You bought it?"

"Not yet. I've been saving up for a down payment on a house, and I don't want her parents to have to foot the whole bill for our wedding, so I've been setting money aside for that as well. With the extra shifts I've been putting in, I can finally get the ring, but now I'm not sure about anything. She doesn't know what I've been saving for, and I think that's part of why she's upset. I'm sure she's been feeling neglected with all my extra time at work, when it was hard enough for us to schedule dates as it was. I should have told her. I wanted everything perfect before I surprised her. I was going to show her dad the ring when I went to ask for his blessing. The perfect ring as part of the perfect proposal, enough money for her dream wedding, and a house where we could start our life together." He rested his head in his hands.

"That's all incredibly sweet," Hannah said. "Once Bryn hears what you've been planning, she's going to melt."

Archer answered with a snort. "Maybe. Or maybe I've already wrecked everything and am about to lose her. Which means everything I've worked so hard for means nothing."

"Let's not jump to such drastic conclusions," Hannah soothed. "Let's try asking Bryn's mom for the address of the cabin. I know Heather Reynolds. She and my mom were friends, and she's a very reasonable and kind woman. If you promise you're only going to write a letter and you're *not* going to drive up to Wisconsin, I bet she'd be willing to give it to you."

"I'm not so sure about that." His eyes suddenly took on a hopeful gleam. "But since you know her, maybe you'd be willing to talk to her for me. I don't trust myself not to say something stupid right now."

Hannah nodded before he asked. She had to do something to help the poor guy. "I'll talk to her."

Chapter Twelve

Saturday morning dawned with heavy, dark clouds shrouding the sun. Despite the dreariness, Hannah decided to walk to the library instead of driving. Armed with a notebook and pen in her purse and a large coffee with a liberal dose of caramel apple crisp creamer, she was ready to dig in. To make sure she wouldn't forget the decision she'd made last night, she set a reminder on her phone to go off in an hour. That was when she'd call Bryn's mother.

She waved at Evangeline as she headed to the back of the library.

Phyllis grinned when she entered. "Ready to hunt for buried treasure?"

"Literally or figuratively?"

"Maybe both. I did some studying after you left yesterday and found an obituary for Linus Moss. He died in a mine collapse on March 9, 1921."

"So that paper deeding his land to his sweetheart really was his last will and testament."

"It appears so."

Hannah couldn't explain the sadness that swept over her. Were the black smudges on the paper from Linus Moss handing it to someone as he took his last breath? Or had searchers found it after they uncovered his body? And his poor girlfriend. Or was she his fiancée? Had they planned to marry and live on his land, and then she was left to manage the property alone? "Did you find anything about Josephine Hamilton?"

"Maybe. There was a wedding announcement in the *Blackberry Valley Chronicle*. A Josephine Charlotte Hamilton married a man named Paxton Cromwell the Third on March 1, 1921 in Bowling Green."

"That's over a week before Linus was killed."

"I know."

"Linus's true love married someone else right before he died? That's a tough blow. I wonder if he even knew. Wouldn't you think he would have torn up that paper?"

"I know I would have." Phyllis motioned to the two boxes on the table. The file where they'd found the "treasure map" was still sitting on top of one of them. "Maybe you'll find some clues in there. I was tempted to go through it, but this is your mystery to solve. Just let me know if you uncover anything."

"I will." When Phyllis turned to walk back to the front desk, Hannah stopped her with a hand on her arm. "When I asked if you meant figuratively or literally digging, you said maybe both."

"Oh, right." Phyllis stepped over to the computer desk and picked up a printed page. "If that old plat map is accurate, and if I'm comparing it to the latest one correctly, I think that some of the land that was owned by Linus Moss is now part of King Farm."

The King Farm. Elaine Wilby's farm. "Which means we might have access to the 'dig here' spot."

"It just might mean that."

Hannah checked her watch, then pulled out her phone. She had no idea what they'd find if they went out to Elaine's farm. Was it possible the tree drawn on the map still existed? And what were the chances they could still recognize it after more than a century? "Elaine should be up doing chores. Let's see if she's up for a treasure hunt."

Hannah's call to Elaine went to voicemail, so she left a message.

Getting Heather Reynolds's cell number required some creative problem solving. Weeks ago, she'd heard Lacy's mom, Christine Johnston, mention that Heather was one of the volunteers on her committee for the Children's Health and Safety Fair. Christine was heading up the fair at the elementary school where she worked as the school nurse.

So Hannah had called Lacy. Of course, she had to answer all of Lacy's questions before she agreed to contact her mom to get Heather's phone number.

At last, Lacy texted Hannah the number. Hannah dialed it at once, only to realize when she got Heather's voicemail that she hadn't taken the time to come up with the right way to ask for the address of the place her daughter was hiding out to avoid interruptions.

But maybe there was an easier way. All she had to do was come up with a plausible reason why a woman with no children would show up at an event for children's health. When an idea hit, she saw an opportunity to, as her grandpa would have said, "kill two mosquitoes with one slap." Wouldn't it be nice of her to bring cookies to the hardworking health fair volunteers? And why bake from scratch when they had such a wonderful bakery right down the street?

She called Sweet Caroline's, then asked the woman who answered if they could set aside two dozen assorted cookies in two separate boxes for her to pick up. She had no idea whether she was talking to Carrie Moore or another employee, and she didn't want to ask. She couldn't think of a reason to ask for Carrie specifically without sounding like she had an ulterior motive.

Feeling like she'd done all she could toward solving two separate mysteries, she settled back and flipped to the next page in the folder. This one was a letter. With another pencil sketch. The drawing depicted part of what she assumed was a bridge. It was similar to the footbridge she and Liam had stood on three days ago, but this one was more ornate. Maybe it was the original park bridge that had been replaced at some point.

She turned it upside down, but this sketch didn't appear to represent a letter. The cryptic message beneath it said, *Though the creek separates us, we will be united when hands meet.*

Hannah repeated the words out loud. Why would a creek separate people? And who were the people? She picked up the next thing in the folder. A torn piece of what felt like newsprint paper, creased in several places as if it had been folded. No sketch on this one, and instead of back-slanted printing, the words were written in a beautiful, rounded cursive.

Dear Sir,

Please pick up your order at 7 a.m. tomorrow. It will be waiting for you at the back door.

Let me also say that we are very happy to have you as a returning customer, and we look forward to working with you well into the future.

Sincerely,

The Haley Mercantile Manager

It seemed an odd thing for someone to keep. And why were there no names? She supposed addressing a customer as "Sir" was customary back in the day, but why wouldn't the manager sign his name?

The next thing in the folder was a longer letter with a small sketch of two silhouettes in the lower right corner. A man facing a woman in a knee-length dress, holding both hands. What appeared to be a stream ran between their feet. It had to be another reference to the creek that separated them. Her lips moved as she silently read the words.

I'm feeling rather poetic this evening, my sweet. So much on my heart. So many words I want to say, but must save for tomorrow when I can whisper them in your ear. Is it wrong of me to admit I am tired of this game we must play? Tired of living in fear. There are times I simply want to grab you by the hand and run. I dream of taking you to some of the places I've seen. Imagine being able to shop in an open-air market or lie on a beach or break bread at a rooftop restaurant without looking over our shoulders. Imagine waking every morning without wondering if today is the day we will finally uncover the truth that will set us all free—or the day we will be caught and ousted.

Sorry to sound so morose, but playing hide-and-seek was fun when we were eight, laughing as we ran around the camp in search of hiding places. It is not so fun now that we are grown and should be living our own lives without concern for what our parents think. Ten years is far too long to be separated from my best friend.

I've learned some things today. It's funny how people will open up to a man in uniform. A group of school children took a tour today. While they were crawling around the engine, I had a good conversation with their teacher. She knew LM and JH and several of their friends. I have names. This is the most hopeful I have felt since we began our mission, and I can't wait to share the names with you in person.

Until the hands meet tomorrow night,

M

Until the hands meet. The first time she'd seen "hands meet," it had been paired with the drawing of the two people holding hands. Now she wondered. Could it mean the hands of a clock? Was it code for midnight, when the minute and hour hands met at the twelve? She opened her notebook, set it next to the letter, and started jotting down the things that had jumped out at her.

Who is "my sweet," and who is M?

What was the game, and why did they need to play it?

What were they afraid of?

Open-air market, lying on a beach, rooftop restaurant... where?

It didn't sound like anything that would have been in Blackberry Valley in…what year? Nothing was dated. But they knew when Linus Moss had died, and she was confident the initials in the letter referred to Linus and Josephine Hamilton. So, sometime around the 1920s maybe?

> *Caught doing what? (Hide and seek—hiding from parents)*
> *What would set them free?*
> *Man in uniform—engine. Steam engine? Train? Fire engine?*

Could *M* have been a firefighter? How far back did the firehouse's records go?

I have names. Names of people who had known Linus and Josephine? M used past tense. The teacher *knew* LM and JH. That could mean she still knew them, or they were no longer around. Or alive?

Hannah closed her eyes. She'd learned a few things, but for everything that fell into place, there seemed to be a handful of new questions. She wanted more time to comb through everything in the box. She was tempted to ask if she could take the folder home, but then she would be responsible for keeping it safe.

Amethyst had said she could take pictures. She snapped a shot of the letter from *M*, then started on the rest. The next was another drawing, part of a gazebo with fancy gingerbread trim that resembled stars. It seemed familiar, but she couldn't place it, like an echo from her past. She imagined standing in the center of it, twirling in a skirt that floated out around her. No. Not imagination. It was a memory. Tiny twinkling lights. And music. She was dancing along while staring up at the intricate trim around the top. Carvings of shooting stars. A chill shimmied up her arms.

She had been there. But where was there? She'd been back in Blackberry Valley for over a year, but she'd never seen anything like what she remembered. She swiped her screen and tapped on her father's name.

He answered on the first ring. "Hey, pumpkin. What's up?"

"Help me figure out something." As she told him what she remembered, a few more fuzzy details took shape. Candles. "I think it was Drew's birthday."

"His seventh birthday. I remember. It was at the Benton Mansion on Pine."

She closed her eyes and tried to imagine driving along Pine Street. "There aren't any mansions on Pine. Or anywhere in town."

Dad laughed. "It's the three-story red brick with pillars."

She knew the place. Well-maintained and beautiful, but it definitely didn't fit the description of a mansion.

As if hearing her thoughts, her father said, "It was the closest thing to a mansion in Blackberry Valley. Still is. I don't remember much of the story behind it. Built in the thirties, I think, by some guy who struck it rich. Oil, I think. I remember my grandmother talking about some kind of scandal or feud over the oil. Anyway, sorry to go off on a tangent."

"Tangent all you want. It's helpful. But how did we know the Bentons?"

"We didn't. The house was donated to the town sometime in the eighties. For a couple of decades, it could be rented out for parties. I think we rented the gazebo for Drew's party."

"Does the town still own it?"

"No. The upkeep was too much, so they sold it. Probably shortly after the party you remember. Carl Milburn and his wife own it now."

"Do you know if the gazebo is still there?"

"It was as of two years ago. I rewired it for them."

A flock of goose bumps raised the fine hairs on her arms. Had she danced in the same spot M and his sweetheart had met clandestinely? It felt as if their paths had crossed. "Thanks, Dad. I don't know what I'd do without your rabbit trails."

"Anytime, kiddo. Happy my ramblings are appreciated by somebody."

Chapter Thirteen

Blackberry Valley
March 22, 1921

Evangeline was awakened by a cold, wet nose snuffling around her ear. She opened one eye and peered at the dark purple sky through a hole in the barn roof. Not quite morning yet, but not as dark as it had been last night when she'd finally been able to flop down on a blanket covering a pile of straw. "Okay, Tucker," she whispered, "we can go outside, but be quiet."

She felt around for the rope and tied it to Tucker's collar, then stood. Straw stuck to her dress and the backs of her legs. She felt her hair and stifled a giggle. With straw poking out all over, she must look like a scarecrow.

Tucker scampered ahead of her toward a small door next to the one big enough for a tractor to drive through.

"Morning, peanut."

She jumped at the voice. "Pa. You scared me." And then she remembered. Pa was getting ready to go treasure hunting. "Can Micah and I go with you to find the ring?"

"I don't think so. But it's not going to take long. I saw the oak tree out in the pasture last night. All we have to do is dig."

She opened the door. Moon shadows danced around her feet. And then something skittered out from the tall grass. Tucker yelped and pulled the rope taut. "Only a rabbit, boy. No need to get all—" The rope snapped, and Tucker took off, darting for the rail fence enclosing the pasture. "Pa! Tucker got loose! He'll get trampled by the cows!"

"Stay here." Pa took off at a run. There was barely enough light to see him leap over the fence and charge across the pasture. A twig snapped, and her gaze shot to the left. Another figure scrambled over the fence. Mr. Benton. Evangeline's shoulders lowered. With two men hunting him down, Tucker would be safe.

But the next sound set her heart pounding. Mr. Benton was shouting bad words she'd heard around the mining camp, but had never heard from Micah's dad. Was Tucker hurt? Had he been trampled after all? Was he...?

She ran toward the fence and scrambled over, the rough wood digging into her bare feet. Scanning the moonlit field, she could make out the outline of several cows. Where were they? Tucker, Pa, and Mr. Benton?

A *thud* followed by a *crack*. Her father hollered, a sound full of pain.

"Pa?" There, under the big oak tree. He was sprawled out, half on the ground, half on a fallen tree limb. She ran to him and dropped to her knees. "Pa, are you—" Her words disappeared in a cry as the pale morning light revealed his left leg, bent in a way legs shouldn't bend.

Pa bellowed, this time not just in pain, but in fury. "Oren Benton, so help me, you'll pay for this!"

Chapter Fourteen

Hannah was dressing for work when Elaine returned her call. "Hi, Elaine." She put her phone on speaker and set it on her dresser so she could finish buttoning her blouse. "Did my message make any sense?"

"Not really. You want to know who owned part of my farm before my family bought it, and something about a tree?"

"Yes. Have you ever heard the name Linus Moss?"

"It sounds vaguely familiar. Why?"

The whole story was getting more complicated every time she repeated it. She shortened it to, "I saw some old maps at the historical society and when we compared two of them, it looked like part of some land that once belonged to a man named Linus Moss ended up being incorporated into King Farm. Is there a stream bordering your property?"

"Yep. Sugar Creek."

"By any chance, are there any really, really old oak trees near the creek? We're talking well over a century old." Hannah held her breath to wait for the answer. It was such a long shot.

Even though it was what she'd hoped for, Elaine's answer took her completely by surprise. "A few of them, actually. They're way on the western edge of my land, near the creek. I rent that part out as pasture, so I haven't been out there in years. A couple of those old trees had huge limbs that looked like open arms. We used to pretend they were alive, as if they could move around the way they do in fairy tales. I used to imagine one of them lowering its limbs like arms and inviting us to climb up. And there was an old headstone next to one of them. It was a great place for scary stories."

"What was on the headstone?"

"I'm not sure I ever saw an inscription. It was face down and kind of buried in the dirt, and I was always too spooked to try lifting it. Why the curiosity about the old trees?"

"One of the maps we found was hand-drawn, and there was a tree on it. It looks like it could have been drawn as a treasure map."

Elaine took a moment to answer. Hannah smiled as she imagined the shock on her face. "Treasure? As in X marks the spot?"

Hannah laughed. "More like O marks the spot, but yes." She told her about Linus's letter bequeathing his land to Josephine. "Have you ever heard the name Josephine Hamilton? Her married name was Cromwell."

"That one doesn't ring a bell. If I have time, I'll hunt through some of the old papers. This is so cool. Do you have a copy of the map? We have to go out there."

"Yes, we do." She checked the clock on her nightstand. She had just enough time to pick up cookies, hopefully have a conversation with Carrie Moore, and get to work on time. "How about tomorrow? I'll be home from church around eleven." As long as they were back in time for her to take the cookies to the health fair.

"Unfortunately, I can't. Blake's coming home and we're going to a concert. But I don't have any plans for Monday."

Hannah sighed. "I do. It might work if we could go early, though I hate to interfere with your chores."

"Buried treasure is a reason to get them done extra early. How about eight?"

"Perfect. Mind if I bring Liam?"

"Not at all."

Hannah wiped her palms on her black pants as she sat in the car in front of Sweet Caroline's Bakery. It was a silly thing to be nervous about. If Carrie was there, she'd simply introduce herself. It didn't have to turn into an interrogation. She wasn't on a time crunch to solve Archer's mystery.

As far as she knew, anyway.

She wasn't a fan of creepy stalker movies, but she'd watched a few in her younger years. Bitterness could cause a person to do awful things.

Still, that didn't mean Carrie had fallen into such a pattern of behavior.

With a deep breath for courage, she grabbed the door handle and started to get out of the car when her phone buzzed. Saved by the bell? She pulled it out and smiled at the screen. Dad. Maybe he'd talk her out of this. "Hi, Dad."

"Hi, sweetie. Do you have plans with Liam after church tomorrow?"

"No. He's helping with the health fair at the elementary school."

"Want to have lunch with your old man and your uncle, and then you and I can go on a field trip?"

"I'd love to. I think. Where are we going?"

"I talked to Carl Milburn. He invited us to come and look at the gazebo. He didn't say what, but he hinted that we might find something interesting."

"Fantastic. You're the best." She glanced up at SWEET CAROLINE'S painted in an arc across the bakery window. "I'll bring dessert and come prepared for a field trip. Love you."

"Love you too."

She got out of the car and pulled her jacket close to ward off the cold from outside as well as the clammy chill of nerves.

The first thing to hit her when she walked into the bakery was the aroma. She immediately felt her self-control and resolve to eat healthy surrendering to the lure of all things glazed and frosted.

The next thing she noticed was color. The walls and ceiling were covered with giant, fanciful cupcakes and doughnuts in shades of aqua, tan, and coral with splashes of purple.

"Good morning. Welcome to Sweet Caroline's. How can I help you?" A rosy-cheeked woman wearing a ruffled coral bib apron flashed Hannah a welcoming smile as she walked toward the low counter between two rounded glass display cases. Wispy platinum curls that had escaped a large teal bow at the base of her neck framed her face. Her name tag, clipped to the strap of her apron, had twisted around so the back was facing out.

"I'd like three blackberry turnovers, and I ordered two dozen cookies. For Hannah Prentiss."

"Hannah! I've been wanting to meet you." The blond woman held out her hand. "I'm Carrie Moore. I've been wanting to get over to the Hot Spot, but life just seems to get in the way sometimes. I hear such good things about your food, and I love that we can be part of making your customers happy."

"Carrie. Hi." Hannah grasped her hand. This woman did not look like a stalker. But she'd read enough whodunits to know that the perpetrator rarely resembled a stereotypical idea of a bad guy. Or girl. "It's so nice to meet you." Where to go from there? "How are you liking the new job?"

"Loving it. I went to culinary school and worked at a bakery in Knoxville for years, but when my mom got cancer, I quit to be here with her. My dad and my brother were both working, and sometimes a woman just needs her daughter, you know?"

Hannah's throat tightened. She did know. And she didn't want to ask the question she'd had to answer too often during her mother's illness. "Your mom...is she...?"

Carrie's smile widened. "She's doing great. Finished chemo a year ago, and so far she's cancer free. I'd planned on going back to my old job, but after working from home for two years, I decided I didn't miss the hubbub of the big city."

Another thing Hannah could relate to. "What were you doing from home?"

"I'm an online baking tutor for my alma mater. Working here three days a week gets me out of the house, and I still have time to help my family and keep teaching."

"Doesn't sound like that leaves much time for fun."

Carrie laughed. "You sound like my mother. I put in a lot of hours, but I do take time for friends."

"Are you dating?" She hadn't meant to ask that. At least not so early in their conversation. "Sorry. That's too personal."

"Not at all. In fact, I'll take any pointers you have to give. I hear you're dating the fire chief."

"I am. That was a total God thing. It's not always easy to meet the right kind of men in a small town." It was probably the kind of statement a judge would label "leading the witness." Or, in this case, a possible suspect.

"You can say that again. I've got some dating battle scars and stories to tell. One of them involves someone you know."

Before Hannah could encourage Carrie to go on, the bell over the door rang and a woman walked in holding the hand of a little boy who immediately planted his free hand against the glass in front of a tray of red-and-blue superhero cupcakes. Carrie excused herself, but held up one finger to let Hannah know their conversation wasn't over.

Hannah backed up and took a seat at a small, purple-painted table with two chairs, preparing to analyze any tiny changes in Carrie's body language or facial expressions if she told the gala story. In a college psychology class, she'd played with biofeedback devices that measured physiological markers like breathing, heart rate, and muscle tension. The more tense a person was, the faster the device would beep. By using relaxation and breathing techniques, they'd learned to slow their pulse rates. She wished she had something like that so she could tell whether Carrie was telling the truth or trying to hide something.

The woman paid for half a dozen cupcakes and walked out, her son bouncing with joy in anticipation of the sugar and food coloring that would make him even more hyper.

To Hannah's surprise, Carrie set two steaming cups on the table and took the other chair at her table. "Decaf," she said. "I'm due for a break. Guess I should have asked if you're a coffee drinker, and if you use anything in it if you are." Carrie laughed. "That was a convoluted sentence, wasn't it?"

This wasn't fair. Hannah wanted to be impartial. She hadn't been prepared for Carrie being so likable. "I am, and I don't mind it black every so often. Thank you." Hannah wrapped her hands around the warm cup.

"So, back to my dating scars. Or not-dating scars in this case." The corners of her mouth tipped up in a self-deprecating smile. "I seriously thought most of Blackberry Valley heard about this one. It just goes to show we have men of integrity in our fire department."

Unsure how to respond, Hannah simply tilted her head to one side, a gesture that had invited many confidences in the past.

"I can trust you not to repeat this, can't I?"

"Of course." She'd have to say enough to Archer and Liam to either prove or disprove Carrie's involvement. But she wouldn't repeat anything that would embarrass her, or Archer, further.

"I've always had a weakness for men in uniform. One in particular, though only from afar." Carrie squinched up her face. "Archer Lestrade." She gazed at Hannah, clearly waiting for a reaction.

Hannah nodded, hoping that her calm response displayed understanding rather than a lack of surprise, indicating that she'd already known as much. "Archer is one of the best."

"My thoughts exactly. Where I went wrong was sharing those thoughts with a mutual friend. She wanted to set me up on date with him, and I agreed. But nothing came of it, until one day our friend said Archer intended to take me to the chamber of commerce gala. I thought she was kidding, but he'd told her in person while he was ordering a corsage. She even followed up with a text, asking him what time he was going to pick me up. Only she didn't ask him when he was going to pick up Carrie. Instead, she used my nickname, because that's what she thought he was calling me." Carrie went on to explain about the car named Goldilocks, waiting for her date to arrive, then going to the gala alone—only to find the man she'd thought would be her date there with someone else.

"That must have been mortifying." Hannah didn't need to fake her empathy.

"It was awful. It wouldn't have been nearly so humiliating if my mother hadn't told half a dozen people I was going out with Archer. And if I would have given him a second to explain before lambasting him. And if I hadn't hung up on him like a jilted teenager when he called to try explaining again the next day." Carrie grimaced. "I don't think it dawned on me for weeks that it was really a hilarious mix-up worthy of a sitcom. Anyway, I owe a whole lot to Archer. I couldn't bear to show my face in town for the next few weeks, so I spent that time taking an online French pastry course from the Auguste Escoffier School of Culinary Arts. It brought a whole new dimension to my baking, and now I can put some of those new skills to use here. I should probably thank Archer in person sometime."

Genuinely interested, Hannah peppered her with questions about French cuisine.

When their cups were empty, Carrie said, "I could talk for hours about food. How would you feel about doing lunch sometime?"

"I would love that." And Hannah meant it, without even a hint of ulterior motive. She'd learned everything she needed to, unless Carrie was an incredible actress.

"Great. And back to your question about dating. There is someone I've seen a couple of times recently. If I get bold enough, I might ask him to accompany me to your Valentine's Day dinner."

"That would be wonderful."

"I'll try to convince my brother, Derek, and his girlfriend to come too. Though I suppose there will be quite a few firefighters there."

"There will be. Is that a concern, given your history?"

"Derek isn't too fond of them since his encounter with the fire department when he was working for your uncle."

"What—"

The bell above the door chimed. Carrie stood. "We'll continue this over lunch. I'll be in touch."

Chapter Fifteen

Grace Community Church was close to standing room only on Sunday morning. One of the elders opened the service by thanking God for times of waiting. The songs that followed all reflected that theme, and when Pastor Bob began his message by reading Romans 12:12—"Be joyful in hope, patient in affliction, faithful in prayer"—Hannah had to smile.

Patience. There it was again.

She glanced at Liam, sitting on her left, and he winked at her. Maybe this would be a theme of their relationship. She imagined working it into their wedding vows. "I, Hannah Prentiss, take thee, William Berthold, to be my wedded husband, to wait for you from this day forward, in fires and in windstorms, and to patiently share you with friends, family, and the community. I promise to always wear a smile and never whine as I wait for your return."

To be fair, Liam would get his turn. It would have to go something like, "I promise to keep the light on long past midnight when the last Hot Spot customers linger on a Friday night. I promise to attend the National Restaurant Association Show with you every year and never show that I am bored to tears…"

She tamped back a smile, but then Pastor Bob said something that hit like a splash of cold water. "To quote Elisabeth Elliot: 'To want what we don't have is impatience, for one thing, and it is to mistrust God. Is He not in complete control of all circumstances, events, and conditions? If some are beyond His control, He is not God.'"

Hannah's smile dissipated. *Lord, I never want to mistrust You. I know I can come to You with my wants, but please only give me the desires of Your heart. If Liam is the man you want me to spend the rest of my life with, I will trust you for the timing.* But as the silent words formed in her mind, she knew it would take time and discipline to truly embrace them.

"Yum." Uncle Gordon peered over Hannah's shoulder as she pulled a pan of Kentucky Hot Brown sandwiches from the oven. "You make these better than any restaurant in all of Kentucky."

Hannah grinned at him. "And you know how to butter someone up better than anyone in all of Kentucky."

Her uncle's laugh rumbled through the kitchen as he set a hot pad on the table for her. "Just want to be sure I'm in your good graces before the end of the month."

"What? My boxed cake isn't good enough for you?" Her dad turned from the sink with a spinach salad in his hands and an unconvincing expression of hurt on his face.

"Not good enough for turning sixty-eight. The round numbers hit me hardest. They deserve my niece's carrot cake from scratch." Uncle Gordon's tone was somber, but his eyes twinkled with mirth.

Hannah set the steaming pan on the table. Invented in the 1920s at the Brown Hotel in Louisville, Kentucky Browns were more like a casserole than sandwiches. She'd modified the original recipe slightly this time by using toasted slices of her dad's sourdough bread as the base. On top of that she'd piled thickly sliced turkey and roasted tomatoes, then smothered it all with a cheesy Mornay sauce. Finally, she'd broiled it until the cheese was golden and bubbling. She finished it off with more cheese and two slices of bacon on each.

After they took their places, her father blessed the food.

Then Hannah returned to the subject of her uncle's upcoming birthday. "You know I'll make you a carrot cake. And speaking of cake, Sweet Caroline's has a new employee. Do either of you know Carrie Moore?"

"I've met her," Dad said. "I met her and her mother at a cancer society fundraiser."

"She said her mom is doing fine now." Hannah didn't miss the shadow that crossed her father's face, or the quick glance her uncle shot him. Aunt Elyse had passed away two years before Hannah's mother. The two widowers took turns holding each other up. She waited a moment before addressing her uncle. "Carrie mentioned that her brother, Derek, worked for you. Do you remember Derek Moore?"

Uncle Gordon's brow furrowed. "Doesn't sound familiar. I did have a Derek Grayson working for me a few years back, though. He was a hard worker, but cranky and a bit reckless."

"How so?" Hannah asked.

"Well, one time we were installing a water heater. He was sweating pipes and caught some wall insulation on fire. He thought he'd put it out, so he didn't tell me. But when I was getting ready to light the pilot, I smelled something burning. He fessed up, and I called 911. The insulation was still smoldering in the wall behind the water heater. It could have been disastrous. The fire department had to tear out a huge section of drywall to make sure it was out, and my insurance had to cover it. That was Derek Grayson's last day working for me. We all make mistakes, but I couldn't tolerate him trying to hide it. That's dangerous in my line of work."

"That must be the same guy. I wonder if they have different fathers. Maybe he's Carrie's half brother."

"Now I remember," her uncle said. "He was her stepbrother. His father had just remarried, and Derek was none too happy about it. Might have been part of the reason he was so surly and careless."

"Do you happen to remember whether Archer Lestrade answered that call?"

"He certainly did. I remember him pointing a finger at Derek and telling him that if I hadn't called 911 the whole house would likely have been destroyed."

The Benton "Mansion" was indeed one of the stateliest old structures in Blackberry Valley. It was a two-story redbrick building with black shutters on the nine windows facing the street. Five dormer windows jutted from the roof. Hannah wondered if they were merely decorative or if the upper half-story was finished. The front door was flanked by white pillars and covered by a portico. A white-painted three-season wing on each end of the house gave it the symmetry popular in the early twentieth century. The place was a Colonial Revival house, if she remembered correctly from a class she'd taken in college.

Carl Milburn met them at the door. After Dad made introductions, Carl ushered them to a dining room with a colonial-style light fixture hanging over a gleaming cherrywood table.

"We're the third owners," Carl explained as he set several papers on the dining room table. "I don't know anything about the original owners other than the last name, Benton. I imagine the historical society might have some information. Guess we haven't been curious enough to research it ourselves. We found these in the attic, though." He picked up the papers and gave them to Hannah.

The pencil drawing of the Milburn house seemed similar to the drawings she'd seen at the library. At the bottom were the initials *MB*. Likely drawn by a member of the Benton family. Was it the same person who'd drawn the "Evangeline my Valentine" picture? Was M's last name Benton?

The next was a drawing of an old barn. The whole building listed to one side, and the roof was caved in like a swayback horse. A windmill stood behind it, drawn with such light pencil strokes that it was almost invisible, as if cloaked in fog. Or maybe cloaked in memory. It appeared to be a much older, and much more sophisticated, sketch of the same barn pictured on the yellowed paper she'd found in the box. She set it on the table and picked up the last paper. The gazebo. A familiar sketch, but drawn from a different angle than the first one she'd seen. Definitely by the same artist.

Carl pointed to the background. A grove of trees stood where the house was now. "This makes me wonder if the gazebo was built before the house." He stepped over to a sliding glass door that led to a flagstone patio. "Take as much time as you want and feel free to take pictures. Hope you find something to help solve your mystery."

"Thank you. I hope so too." Hannah walked out first then stopped to take in the scene. "Imagine what this looked like a century ago, Dad."

"Probably not much different."

Hannah nodded, easily able to picture the trees and grass before her back then. To say nothing of the creek that was almost dry in the middle of winter, but would rush over rocks in spring. That was an idyllic spot for a romantic rendezvous.

The grass crunched under their feet. The remnants of flowers and bushes, still dormant, surrounded the base of the gazebo that was enclosed with lattice. She walked up the two steps and immediately felt like a little girl again. She was wearing a short suede jacket over a midcalf full skirt, so she gave in to the nostalgia by twirling with her arms outstretched. The wool skirt belled out. Not quite as fluid as the one she'd worn to that long-ago birthday party, but it still made her feel a bit like a princess. When she stopped and laughed, she expected a funny comment from her dad. Instead, he was silent, frozen in place as he watched her.

And then she saw the tears on his cheeks.

He swiped at them, but didn't try to hide his emotion. "You're as beautiful as you were then." His voice was rough. "I wish your mom were here."

Her eyes stung. She stepped over and wrapped her arms around him. "Me too."

His arms closed around her. Her safe place. She was thankful that mascara smudges wouldn't show on his dark gray coat. After a long moment, she pulled back. "Ready to look for clues?"

"Let's do it, Detective."

They walked to opposite sides. It was clear that, as Carl said, many repairs had been made over the years. There were no signs of peeling paint, but some of the boards were clearly more weathered than others, the grain more evident from exposure to the elements. Several sections of gingerbread trim had been removed and the shooting stars replaced with scrolling vines.

"Over here." Dad was kneeling in front of a built-in bench. He'd lifted the lid, something Hannah wouldn't have thought of doing. She joined him on the cold planks.

Beneath the lid, there were words scrawled in black paint on the unfinished wood. *I'll be loving you.* Beneath that was a single word that appeared smaller, more slanted. *Always.*

Dad ran a finger across the painted words. "That's from an old song. 'Always,' by Irving Berlin. My grandparents used to sing it together." He closed his eyes for a minute, as if recalling a memory. Then his rich, deep voice reverberated off the ceiling boards.

Days may not be fair always
That's when I'll be there always
Not for just an hour
Not for just a day
Not for just a year
But always…

Hannah put her head on her father's shoulder as the lyrics replayed in her mind. Once again, God knew exactly what she needed. *Days may not be fair always. That's when I'll be there always.* Patience. She needed Liam to know that she could be flexible. She could be understanding when the things they'd planned didn't go the way they'd planned.

After a minute, she pulled away and pointed to the words. "So somebody came out here, lifted the lid, and painted 'I'll be loving you.' Intentionally hidden. It looks like 'Always' was painted by someone else, but with the same paint. The house was built in the thirties, but the gazebo may have been built before the house. The song is from the twenties. Could these words have been painted a hundred years ago and still be this readable?"

"Sheltered from the elements like this, sure." Dad bent down, then touched the hinge. "Actually, I don't think this board was attached when it was painted. Look at the top of the 'Ls' in the first line."

"The hinges cover them. So maybe it was painted by the person who built the bench?"

"Sounds logical."

Hannah sat down and crossed her legs, tugging her skirt over her knees. Cold air wafted up through the cracks between the floorboards, but she ignored it as she closed her eyes and imagined the secret rendezvous. Did "M" build the gazebo? Had he and Evangeline danced beneath the shooting stars?

Chapter Sixteen

Lacy's mom had done an amazing job of transforming the school gym into a fun-filled and inviting space for families. Carrying a windowed pastry box, Hannah walked under a bright CHILDREN'S HEALTH AND SAFETY FAIR banner. She'd waved at Liam as she crossed the parking lot. He was crouching down next to the ladder truck, at eye level with a preschooler, and she didn't want to interrupt. Besides, she probably needed to distance herself a bit from a situation that made her knees turn to jelly—Liam Berthold in uniform, talking to children.

Inside the gym, she searched for Heather Reynolds. She spotted Lacy's mom first. Christine Johnston stood at a booth beneath a sign that read FREE FIRST AID KITS. She was handing out ice packs, stickers, and small, zippered pouches in the school colors. When she spotted Hannah, she motioned her over, then stepped around the end of the booth and gave her a tight hug.

Hannah offered her the box of cookies. "It's my excuse for being here."

"Good thinking." Christine took an oatmeal cookie. "Lacy's in the kitchen manning the pizza oven."

"I'll go find her. But first—"

"You want to talk to Heather," Christine finished for her with a knowing smile.

"I don't want to take one of your helpers away from her job, but yes."

"It's not a problem. We have plenty of help today. Last I saw, Heather was behind the screen at the fishing booth." Christine pointed to a quilt made of several shades of blue with colorful fish swimming across the bottom. One child held a bamboo pole with a string attached. The end of the string dipped behind the top of the quilt. A line of children stood, waiting their turn.

"That game never gets old, does it? I remember playing it at Vacation Bible School when I was a kid."

"When we started planning this, it was one of my goals to show families how to have simple fun. Easy ways to engage children's minds and creativity without using screens."

Hannah did a slow scan of the room. A ball toss game, face painting, and photos with the school mascot, Black Beary. "You did well. Half the town turned out."

"You should have seen it around lunchtime." Christine tapped the box Hannah still held. "Sweet Caroline's donated these amazing cookies." She reached under the table for a small, empty wax paper bag. A sticker identified the former contents as caramel palmiers. "You would have loved them. They look kind of like mini elephant ears. Crisp and flaky with a hint of spice, and coated with caramelized sugar. They sold out in the first fifteen minutes."

"Sounds amazing. I had one of their blackberry turnovers yesterday. They have a new employee with French pastry training."

"No wonder those things were so good. So Lacy tells me you found some old love letters at the historical society."

"Yes. A lot of them, actually. But the ones I'm really interested in are from what appears to be a Romeo-and-Juliet relationship. They were adults, but hiding their relationship from their parents for some reason."

"Very romantic. You know, I've often thought of writing a book about Blackberry Valley love stories." She winked at Hannah as a family with three young boys approached the booth. "And I'm taking notes on modern-day romances too."

Hannah didn't bother trying to hide her grin from the woman who had been like a second mother to her. "Someday I'll tell you all the details." She waved as she walked toward the fishing booth, where she hoped to do a bit of fishing for information about Bryn Reynolds. She had to remind herself she wasn't here to interrogate Heather about Bryn's relationship with Archer. All she wanted was Bryn's address so Archer could write to her.

On the other hand, maybe it would be better if she wanted to send Bryn something herself. But what?

A care package. For survival in the Northwoods of Wisconsin while writing a dissertation. What could be more perfect?

While waiting for a pause in the line of kids at the fishing booth, Hannah peeked into the kitchen. Lacy held up one finger, opened an oven door, then said, "I'll come find you."

Hannah walked from booth to booth, offering cookies to volunteers, and getting a bit wistful. Next year her best friend would be one of the moms pushing a stroller around the health fair, gathering information about food allergies, first aid, bicycle safety, and dental care.

As if on cue, the mom-to-be popped up behind her. "Hi!"

"Hi yourself. You smell like pepperoni."

Lacy made a face. "Please don't say that word in my presence. It's going to be a long time before I crave pizza again. After about the fifteenth one, the smell was getting to be a bit much, but I held it together. Did you talk to Heather yet?"

"No. She's behind the fishing booth curtain. Now that you're here, we can do it together."

"What's your plan?"

Hannah told her about her care package idea. "How can she say no?"

"And then you're going to smuggle Archer into the care package?"

Hannah laughed. "Why didn't I think of that?"

An announcement came over the PA system, thanking everyone for attending the first annual Blackberry Valley Children's Health and Safety Fair and giving the dates for next year's fair. As vendors began packing up, Hannah and Lacy made their way to the fishing booth.

"Hi, Lacy. Hannah. How are you?" Heather clapped a hand to her forehead. "I didn't RSVP for Raquel's party. My husband and I will be there. It's so nice of you to do that for her, especially on such a busy day. Is there anything I can do to help?"

"Thank you, but I think we've got things under control. My chef has the menu figured out, and it's going to be pretty casual. Do you think Bryn will be back in time?"

"Definitely. She wouldn't miss it."

That was one piece of information that would give Archer some assurance. "How's she doing up in the wild woods all by herself?"

Heather shrugged. "All I know is the light stays on late into the night. The cottage is across the lake from my parents' house. They're keeping an eye on her but not bothering her. I hope she can get this done. She's been so stressed, trying to work and gather all her research and do justice to all her volunteer positions while wanting to spend time with a certain firefighter."

"He's missing her."

Heather's smile was sympathetic. "Poor guy. Is it wrong for a mom to think that maybe this separation will move things along a bit, if you know what I mean?"

"Not at all. I have a feeling he's thinking along those lines." It wasn't her place to hint at Archer's misgivings, nor at his plans. She changed to a safe lane. "Is there a way I could send Bryn something? Lacy and I thought it would be fun to put together a Northwoods survival care package."

"What a nice idea. She would love that. I can give you my parents' address. They have promised her they won't be helicopter grandparents, but I know they've dropped off some goodies here and there. I'm sure they'd be happy to do it again."

Hannah took out her phone and opened Bryn's contact file then handed it to Heather.

As Heather typed, Hannah took a steadying breath. "Someone has been delivering photographs to Archer this past week. Do you know anything about that?"

"Photographs?" Creases formed between Heather's eyes. "What kind?"

Hannah described them, and Heather shook her head. Unless she was a superb actress, she didn't know anything about them.

"Do you think it's some kind of joke?" Heather asked. "Archer and Colt are always pulling these ridiculously juvenile pranks on each other. Silly stuff like sugar in saltshakers. A few weeks ago, Archer signed Colt up on a dating app for meeting women who love bacon."

Hannah laughed. It wasn't the first time Colt's name had come up in connection to practical jokes, and he was known around town as a superior bacon cooker. "I guess we'll have to consider that a little more seriously."

"That would be my first guess." Heather seemed to study Hannah's face. "But you're worried about it, aren't you? Do you think it's something more serious?"

"Archer seems to think it's possible that someone is sending him a threat or a warning."

"I can't believe Archer Lestrade would have a single enemy. Everybody loves him."

Except for the people he's aggravated just by doing his job. But she didn't need to share that worry with Heather.

"Was everything good between Archer and Bryn when she left?" Lacy asked.

Hannah gave her a pointed look.

Heather grimaced. "I probably shouldn't say this, but I do sense I'm not the only one getting a bit impatient that Archer hasn't proposed yet. He's a conscientious guy, and I'm sure he wants to have all his ducks in a row before they move on to the next step, but it's starting to feel as if he's dragging his feet. Anyway, it's their business. To answer your question, I think they're fine."

"Good." It was all Hannah could think to say. "We should let you get things packed up here."

"It was good talking to you, and thank you for wanting to do something nice for Bryn."

Though she would have loved to tell Heather about the picture of the engagement ring Archer had shown her, she simply thanked her for the address, and they walked away.

The firefighters were packing up when Hannah walked out of the school. Liam waved her over and she slid into his arms for a quick hug. "How'd it go?"

"It was fun." Liam straightened a stack of brochures and set them in a box. "We saw a couple hundred kids. But I'm all yours now, and I'm starving. There's some pad thai calling my name. How about an early supper and a movie at my place?"

"Sounds—"

"Did I hear someone say they're starving?" Lois, one of the department dispatchers, held out a familiar bakery box. She offered the spicy, brown sugar and butter-scented contents to Hannah first. "Caramel palmiers. Some woman handed them to Archer. He insisted they were all for him, but he's reluctantly sharing." She grinned at Liam. "Aren't they amazing?"

"I haven't had one yet."

"I heard about these." Hannah lifted one from the box and took a bite. "Heavenly."

Liam took the last cookie, thanked Lois, and took Hannah's hand in his free one. He took a bite as they walked to her car, and Hannah laughed at his expression. Pure bliss.

As she drove to the Thai restaurant, she told Liam about her brilliant plan to send a care package to Bryn. "My original thought was to have Archer write a letter to go along with it. I did that once when I ordered a care package sent to Drew when he was in college. I just emailed the letter, and they copied it out and stuck it in the basket. But then I got to thinking that Heather might not like the idea of Archer interrupting Bryn, even with a letter, and I didn't want to be deceptive."

A wheezing sound from the passenger seat grabbed her attention. Liam's face was blotchy and puffy. His hand rose to his throat. His fingers seemed to be swelling before her eyes.

"I think. I need. To go—"

"To the hospital. We are on our way right now." Hannah stomped on the gas pedal and turned right instead of left without stopping at the stop sign. *Lord, help. Please.*

Chapter Seventeen

Hannah slowed at the next four-way stop and shot a glance at Liam. When they locked eyes, he gave her a half smile that stretched his skin and had to be painful. "I'll be fine," he whispered, voice tight and low.

She blinked hard, not allowing tears to blur her vision. Even now, in the middle of a life-threatening crisis, he was trying to reassure her.

"Almost there."

The red neon letters spelling out EMERGENCY brought a flood of relief. She pulled up beneath the carport, shut off the car, ran around to Liam's side, and yanked the door open. In the bright overhead lights, his face was ghastly white. *He's still breathing.* And now they were here. Safe. But the self-talk didn't calm her racing pulse.

Liam braced himself against the top of the car door and she dipped under his arm. As the glass door slid open automatically, a security guard rushed out with a wheelchair. In seconds, they were hurrying toward the desk.

Hannah ran in front of them and stopped at the reception desk. "This is Liam Berthold. He's having an allergic reaction."

The woman stood, the picture of calm and competence. She picked up a phone and spoke into it, then walked out of her cubicle. "Well, Chief, you got tired of always coming in the back door, huh?"

She thanked the guard and pressed a large silver push button that opened two double doors. "We'll take good care of you." She wheeled him into a glass-walled room.

A nurse in pink scrubs covered in red hearts followed. Since no one stopped her, Hannah did too.

The receptionist patted Liam's shoulder. "Lauren's new, but she's good. Don't be too hard on her." She locked the wheelchair. "Lauren, meet our fire chief, Liam Berthold. He's one of BV's finest. Treat him like royalty."

"We'll roll out the red carpet." The nurse helped him out of the wheelchair and onto the end of a paper-covered table. She motioned to a chair in the corner, for Hannah. "Wife?" she asked.

"Girlfriend."

"Okay with her staying?" Lauren asked.

Liam nodded, and again shot a reassuring smile Hannah's way.

Hannah sank onto the chair and let out a long breath. A wave of dizziness hit her, and she took two more slow breaths until it passed.

A young woman with bright red hair in a messy bun came in with a laptop on a rolling cart. A name tag on a lanyard said she was from the admissions office. She asked Liam for his full name and birth date, then fastened an orange bracelet on his wrist.

Hannah hugged her purse to her middle as she watched the nurse work with efficient speed, listening to his breathing, taking his pulse, blood pressure, and slipping a pulse oxygen monitor on his finger. She shined a light into his eyes and mouth and examined his hands, all while asking him questions. "Any known allergies?"

Liam shook his head.

"He'd just eaten a cookie," Hannah added.

The nurse nodded. "That's a likely culprit, but occasionally we see delayed anaphylaxis, so it could have been something you ate or came in contact with earlier."

A woman wearing a white coat walked in. Probably in her fifties, curly salt-and-pepper hair, glasses on a chain. She greeted Liam like an old friend, then turned to Hannah and introduced herself as Dr. Weston. The nurse filled her in on all of Liam's symptoms.

"We'll get an IV in and give you a dose of epinephrine, then keep an eye on you for a couple of hours. It'd probably be a good idea to put in an order for an EpiPen and schedule you for allergy testing."

Hannah closed her eyes as they administered the injection and inserted the IV. When she opened them again, Liam was sitting farther back on the table with a pillow behind him. The nurse handed him the call button and said they'd check on him every few minutes.

Liam reached out, and she took his hand. It felt like a rubber glove filled with water. She scooted her chair closer and bent her head to press her lips against his tight, warm skin.

"You're my hero," he rasped.

"But it could have been…" She couldn't let herself go there. "If we'd stood around at the school for just a few more minutes, you would have had a whole team of trained heroes."

He shrugged one shoulder. "None of those guys are as pretty as you."

She laughed and kissed his hand again. "'Pretty' shouldn't be your first prerequisite when your airway is closing."

"I knew I was in good hands."

"When's the next CPR class? I think I might need a refresher course if I'm going to keep hanging out with you."

"'If?'" The gleam she loved had returned to his eyes.

"Because. Not if."

He tried to wink with his swollen eye, and it made them both laugh. "I could give you a good deal on a private class." One eyebrow rose up and down, making his puffy face look pathetically comical.

"I think they gave you more than epinephrine. You're getting goofy."

"Goofy for you."

She laughed. This man. She shot a prayer of gratitude heavenward. Her next breath shuddered. If she hadn't gotten him here in time… If he had… She scrambled for a quick subject change. "Has Archer received any more pictures?"

Liam nodded. "When I dropped him off after we got home from Cave City, there was an envelope under that old-fashioned door knocker he put on his front door. It was a picture of a newel post." He stopped to catch his breath, but his voice was getting stronger with each word. "It's probably a small *i*, although we weren't sure. The background was blurred, so no idea where it was taken. Then this morning when we got to the school, a woman wearing a volunteer name tag for the fair came up and handed him another envelope, saying it had been left in the volunteer room. It was a photo of one of the new braces they put under the park bridge. Clearly an *L*."

She took a moment to remember the letters in order. "So now we have U-O-M-E-A-M-I-L. If we're right about it spelling something, it could be 'You owe me a mill.' Mill could stand for million, right?"

"Guess it could."

The glass door slid open. A woman in teal scrubs ducked her head around the curtain. Hannah recognized her. Jan Martinez was a frequent Friday night customer at the Hot Spot. "Hi, Chief. I'm the person no one wants to see."

"Hi, Jan. Always happy to see your smiling face. Just not your needles and tubes."

"Sorry." She shrugged then turned to Hannah. "Tell Jacob he outdid himself Friday night. Whatever he tweaked on the Candlelight Chicken made it even better than before, and I didn't think that was possible."

"Maple-cured bacon," Hannah said. "But don't tell him I shared his secret."

Jan mimed zipping her mouth closed. "My lips are sealed."

In the space of that brief interchange, Jan had tied a tourniquet around Liam's upper arm and was now preparing a syringe.

"What's this for?" Liam asked.

"Dr. Weston wants to be sure we're dealing with an allergic reaction before releasing you. There are other things that can cause similar symptoms."

"Other things?" Hannah asked, her pulse skipping. She told herself she was overreacting. They were simply being thorough, and she should be grateful for that.

"Viruses and such."

And such. Maybe it was being here, in the same room and same chair she'd sat in more than once with her mother, that caused her anxiety to spike. Tests and hope and more tests and disappointment. Devastating news followed by the lure of a new treatment that didn't work. She could feel all the roller coaster emotions returning. *Please, Lord…*

The snap of the tourniquet being released, followed by the sound of a vial being capped signaled to Hannah that it was okay to look up.

Jan pressed a wad of cotton to the crook of Liam's arm, then fastened an adhesive bandage over it. "All done. I'll take my needles and tubes and leave you two in peace."

"Have a good day, Dracula."

"See you later, Chief. Keep him in line, Hannah."

"As if." Hannah narrowed her eyes at Liam as Jan ducked through the curtain. "Like anyone could control you." When he grinned back with feigned innocence, she stood and took a closer look at him. "How are you feeling? The swelling has gone down a lot in the last couple minutes."

"I can tell. I don't feel like I want to scratch my face off anymore. Hope they don't keep me overnight. We have places to go and things to see tomorrow."

Tomorrow was Monday. She had the whole day planned, down to what she was going to wear. But none of that mattered now. Yet she knew better than to tell this man who had worked so hard with her to come up with a solution for their busy schedules that she thought they should cancel their plans. They'd wait and see what the doctor said.

When the test results came back.

What if it wasn't an allergic reaction? "What do you think they're testing for?"

"Oh, you know, dengue, schistosomiasis, leprose, trypanosomiasis, food poisoning." He shifted on the table, raising up on his left elbow.

"What? You're scaring me. What are you thinking?"

"The cookies."

"Yes. There was probably something in them you're allergic to. You can suddenly be allergic to something you never were before. Lacy used to love apricot jam, but one day she ate it and broke out in hives."

"But what if..." He closed his eyes.

"What are you thinking?" she repeated.

His eyes opened. A crease formed above his nose. "The woman who brought the cookies. She walked right up to Archer, opened the box, and handed him one. But he'd just finished recoiling a hose after showing it to some kids, so his hands were dirty. He held up his hands and said he'd have it later. She left it on the table for him. What if that particular one was meant for him, and what if it was put back in the box?"

"You're not implying the cookie could have been..." She couldn't even say the word. It was too preposterous.

Liam's gaze bore into her. "Do you think Carrie Moore sent Archer dangerous cookies?"

"Absolutely not," Hannah answered at once. "We had a good talk yesterday. She's a wonderful person. She told me about the mix-up over the gala, and she laughed about it. We even planned to get together for lunch." She sat back in the chair with a thud as all her energy seeped away. "What if she played me?"

Liam gave a long sigh. "I think we'd better call Archer."

Chapter Eighteen

Blackberry Valley
March 23, 1921

"No! You can't! I won't! It's not fair!"

Curled on her blanket in the corner of the barn, Evangeline sobbed. She stared at the pictures she'd nailed to the timbers behind her, trying to make this corner feel like home. They were pictures Micah had drawn of Suzy and Betsy and their school. The pictures made her cry harder. She hugged Tucker so tightly he whined, then wriggled out of her arms. "Micah is my best friend. My only friend now. Just because you and Mr. Benton had a fight doesn't mean—"

"A *fight*?" Pa pounded his fist on the arm of the rocking chair he'd made for Ma then pointed to his leg, propped on a hay bale and wrapped tight in Ma's shawl. "A fight takes two people. This was an ambush. He attacked me. He. Broke. My. Leg." His voice rose to a level Evangeline had never heard before. "Do you realize what that means? How can I plow, or plant, or build us a decent house? I can't go back to mining. I can't do anything. And now he's accusing me of stealing the ring."

Not bothering to swipe away the tears dampening the front of her dress, Evangeline hung her head. Pa hadn't taken the ring. He'd only been trying to save Tucker. Why wouldn't Mr. Benton believe him? They'd been friends since they were boys. Didn't Mr. Tucker know Pa never, ever cheated anyone?

Yesterday morning, she and Ma had dragged Pa to the barn on a blanket. Then Ma had asked her to help hold him down while she pulled on his leg to set it. Evangeline had cried and begged her to ask Mrs. Benton to help instead, but Pa had refused. It was the most awful thing she'd ever had to do. Ma had worked with the doctor back in the camp, so she knew how to set bones and bandage wounds, but just the thought of anyone being in pain made Evangeline sick.

Pa had been so angry all day, but by suppertime she'd heard him say he understood why Mr. Benton might have thought he was trying to get a jump on the treasure. He said they'd have a talk in the morning.

But then, shortly before nightfall, they'd heard Mr. Benton swearing again, right before he shoved open the barn door and stormed in to accuse Pa of stealing the ring. He and Micah had dug up the box buried under the oak tree without Pa. The only thing in the box was a little carved pig.

Evangeline thought for a while. How would she feel if someone had done that to her? When she closed her eyes and tried to imagine Micah or Suzy or Betsy hurting her then accusing her of stealing and lying, the tears started all over. "I'm sorry, Pa. I understand. I won't"—her voice cracked and she could hardly force out the next words—"I won't ever talk to Micah or any of the Bentons ever again."

Chapter Nineteen

By noon on the day they were supposed to spend in Hopkinsville to celebrate Valentine's Day, Liam was sprawled on his couch surrounded by Archer, Colt, Raquel, and Jacob. His "and such" blood tests had all come back negative, and he'd been released shortly after midnight with an EpiPen and orders to rest for the remainder of the day, and to avoid anything he'd eaten in the previous forty-eight hours. Until he had a chance to be tested for allergies, they couldn't be too careful.

Hannah massaged her lower back. Unwilling to leave him alone, she'd spent the remainder of the night on Liam's couch. Now, as she watched the group gathered in the living room from the kitchen, where she warmed up chicken soup, her heart filled with gratitude.

Just to be on the safe side, while waiting for Liam's discharge, they'd made a list of everything he'd eaten on Saturday and Sunday. He and Archer ate granola bars and apples on their way to Cave City and had packed their own lunches—ham sandwiches on wheat bread and a bag of potato chips. They'd stopped for supper, when Liam had eaten a Caesar salad, steak, and a baked potato with sour cream. Yesterday had been cold cereal and milk for breakfast, pizza for lunch at the health fair, and then the infamous French cookies.

Hannah had looked up the recipe for caramel palmiers. The usual flour, sugar, butter, plus cardamom and cream cheese. Much to Liam's chagrin, Hannah had concluded that, for a couple of days, he needed to avoid all grains, nuts, dairy, eggs, cardamom, tomatoes, apples, pork, and potatoes.

Liam had called Archer from the hospital, and Archer had told Colt. They were both working a twelve-hour shift, but they had come over in uniform, pagers at the ready. Hannah had called Lacy to ask her to pray. Lacy had stopped at Jump Start early that morning and told Zane, the coffee shop owner and also Jacob's brother. On her way out, she'd run into Raquel. Lacy had also texted the church women's group. For her part, Hannah had called Elaine to tell her they couldn't go out to her farm. Naturally, Elaine asked why, and Hannah told the truth. Then she'd called her dad and Liam's grandpa. It wouldn't be long before the whole town would be at Liam's door bearing food gifts.

Hannah listened to the laughter in Liam's small living room and couldn't help but compare this outpouring of support to the circle of friends she'd had in California. Once, when she'd sprained her ankle and had to be off her feet for several days, one friend sent a meal via delivery, and another a lavish bouquet. None had come in person.

Thank You, Lord, for bringing me back home.

The joking had died down by the time she carried a tray out to Liam. They were talking about the French cookies.

"What could she have used?" Jacob asked. "Did it taste funny?"

"No. It was delicious."

"Cyanide." Archer sat on the floor, his back against the end of the couch. His face was pale. "Cyanide sometimes smells like bitter almonds. It could easily be disguised in a cookie."

Raquel, sitting on the edge of the recliner seat, gasped. "I saw that on a murder mystery show once."

Jacob tapped on his phone and read what he'd found. "Early symptoms usually start within minutes. They include elevated heart rate, shortness of breath, headache, dizziness, and vomiting. After that, seizures, and all your systems start to shut down."

"That's kind of different from your symptoms," Raquel said, looking at Liam. "I mean, yours was serious. If you hadn't gotten to the hospital your airway could have—" She stopped and grimaced when Hannah froze three feet from Liam. "Sorry. That must have been so scary. I'm sure you don't want to relive it."

"I'd rather not." Hannah waited for Liam to scoot into a sitting position then set the tray on his lap.

"Thank you," he said, giving her a look that said as far as he was concerned, she was the only woman in the world. It threatened to melt her composure.

For hours now she'd been fighting to hold all the what-ifs at bay. Tonight, alone in her apartment, would be the time to let it all out and have a good cry. For now, she needed to keep it together. "You're right, though, Raquel. He had a pretty classic allergic reaction. It doesn't sound like poisoning."

"What if there was just a miniscule amount of cyanide in the cookie?" Archer asked. "Couldn't that have caused you to be sick, but not die?"

Liam lifted both hands, palms up.

"And you've never had a reaction like that before?" Jacob asked.

"Never."

"I have." Archer rubbed his stubbly chin and shot Liam a baleful look. "In eighth grade I had a hardboiled egg-eating contest with some friends. I ate nineteen."

Raquel made a gagging sound. "Sorry. Can't stand them. Go on."

"And I broke out in gigantic hives. The doctor said it might be temporary, or the next time I ate them it could kill me. I avoided them for years. Now I can eat eggs with no problem." His wide-eyed gaze swept the room. "Winter knew I had that allergy. What if she told Carrie?"

The room grew pin-drop silent.

Liam broke in with a laugh and a referee's "time-out" gesture. "Wait. That's crazy. *We're* crazy. If Carrie purposely delivered something made with eggs to you, wouldn't she know you were avoiding them at all costs? And it would be a pretty wild coincidence if I had an allergic reaction to something you're allergic to."

Hannah shook her head. "I looked up the recipe for those cookies. There are no eggs in them."

Archer's face scrunched and a sheepish grin crinkled his tired eyes. "You're right. That was a dumb thought." His smile morphed into a frown of consternation. "I guess that brings us right back to poison."

Hannah chimed in. "I met Carrie. I've been thinking back over our conversation, and I absolutely don't believe she would have done anything like that."

Three pagers went off at once. Archer and Colt jumped up, waving at Liam to ignore his pager. "Stay put, Chief," Archer said with a grin. "We'll keep you posted." With that, they ran out the door.

As soon as Liam got word that the car fire on Vine Street was under control, he slumped back on the couch and fell asleep. He'd made a three o'clock appointment for allergy testing, so he had an hour to catch up on missed sleep. Jacob had headed out shortly after Archer and Cole, leaving Hannah and Raquel alone. As Liam snored softly in the living room, Hannah made tea, and they sat at the small kitchen table talking in hushed tones.

"How are you doing?" Hannah asked, stirring a dollop of honey into her mug. "I need to hear about someone else's problems."

"No, you don't. We're at a standstill. I did what you suggested. I was almost completely honest with Marshall about how much I'll miss him, but I said I want what's best for him. He said that what's best for him right now could be best for *us* in the future." Her cheeks pinked as she smiled.

"That says a lot about how serious he is regarding the relationship."

"That's what I'm telling myself. Along with reminding myself he's worth waiting for." Her eyes shimmered, and she blinked fast. "Let's change the subject. What's the latest with Archer's mystery?"

Hannah showed Raquel all the pictures she had and told her about the last two. As soon as Archer had walked in and seen that Liam was okay, he'd showed them his latest photo. Another *L*.

"Our current theory is that it means, 'You owe me a mill,' as in million."

"Any way that could tie in with the bakery lady?"

Hannah blew on her tea, giving herself a moment to try fitting the pieces together. "I don't think so. But she gave me something else to think about." She told Raquel what she'd learned from Uncle Gordon about Carrie's stepbrother. "It's most likely another rabbit trail. I'm beginning to think we're on the wrong track about everything. But here's the other mystery." She showed Raquel the picture she'd taken of the sketch of the Stanton Building window, then compared it to the first photo Archer had received.

"Whoa. They match. But the drawing was done a hundred years ago?"

"Yep."

"So someone was inspired by the sketch and started taking pictures that make letters?"

"Possibly." Hannah broke a muffin in half. "Except that the display at the library wasn't up until after Archer got the first envelope."

Raquel pressed her lips together. "That should narrow down your suspects, right? Who put up the display, and who donated the Evangeline valentine?"

With all that had been going on, she'd let those questions fall by the wayside. "I think we need to let go of all of our theories and start over from the beginning. After Liam's appointment, maybe we'll stop by the library. Speaking of the library, the same person who made the Evangeline valentine also wrote some other letters." She'd snapped pictures of a few of them on Saturday, but hadn't read them yet. "I'm going to print these so we can read them easier. Do you have time?"

"For sappy old love letters? Definitely."

Hannah checked on Liam as she tiptoed through the living room. All trace of swelling was gone, and he slept soundly. She walked down the hall to his office and sent the letters from her phone to the printer.

As the printer softly whirred, she scanned the room. She'd only been in this room a couple of times, when her office printer had broken and he'd let her use his to print out invoices. The room reflected Liam perfectly. The walls were crammed with firefighter memorabilia and group pictures from years gone by, taken in front of the building she now owned. A shadow box filled with Blackberry Valley Fire Department patches dating back to the late 1800s when the station was built. Grainy old framed photos with captions identifying Liam's grandfather. Newer pictures that included his father. A wall of shelves held several old metal helmets, a brass hose nozzle, a rusted water bucket, and two lanterns.

She stopped in front of a picture of Liam at his graduation from the Fire Academy of Kentucky. He stood between his father and grandfather, all in dress uniforms. All three beamed with pride. She couldn't help the question that rose in her mind. Would there be another generation of Berthold firefighters?

She picked up the sheaf of freshly printed pages and walked to the kitchen. She'd made two copies of each letter. There were no dates on any of them, so she had no idea what order to stack them in. She handed a sheaf to Raquel. Hannah had just settled into her chair and picked up her teacup when her phone buzzed with a text from Lacy. I'M IN TOWN PICKING UP CHICKEN FEED. I PACKED A GOODY BASKET FOR YOU AND YOUR PATIENT. CAN I STOP BY?

Hannah showed the message to Raquel.

"Guess you better print off more copies." Raquel pushed back her chair. "I'll heat up more water."

Hannah answered Lacy with YES! RAQUEL IS HERE. COME READ OLD LOVE LETTERS WITH US. She added the code for the front door and told her she'd leave the apartment door unlocked because Liam was sleeping.

The answer came in seconds. A thumbs-up emoji.

By the time Hannah had made another set of copies and the teapot came to a boil, Lacy walked in, carrying a wicker basket lined with a linen napkin. Hannah took out one thing at a time. A jar of homemade strawberry jam and one of home-canned pear sauce, a box of grain-free crackers, a lemon, and a jar of something gooey and orangey-brown.

Hannah picked up the last jar and gave Lacy a questioning look. "Whatever this is, I'm not sure I can make him eat it."

Lacy laughed. "It's an anti-inflammatory tea. Turmeric, fresh ginger, cinnamon, and honey. One tablespoon to a cup of hot water, then add a squeeze of lemon. It'll cure anything."

"Even a broken heart?" This from Raquel, who'd taken her eyes off the letter in front of her just long enough to greet Lacy. "Listen to this." She picked up the page, and Hannah and Lacy sat down to follow along.

Dearest Micah,

"Micah!" Hannah waved her hand in apology when her friends jumped. "So far I've only identified him as 'M.' And I'm thinking his last name might be Benton." She told them about what she and her dad had seen at the gazebo. "Is it signed by Evangeline?"

She glanced at the bottom. It was signed with an *A*. So it hadn't been written by Evangeline. A wave of inexplicable sadness drifted over her. So many possible scenarios came to mind. Micah Benton might have had several relationships. Evangeline might have been only a passing fancy. Had he been serious about "A"?

She bent over the letter once more.

> *Once again, I write a letter I cannot send, but writing to you is better than putting all my thoughts in a diary. I pretend, as I write, that someday someone will confess to taking Mr. Moss's ring and our fathers will once again be friends—*

Hannah jabbed a finger at the word *ring*, startling her friends once again. "That must be the ring on the map Linus Moss drew. The buried treasure." She gave Raquel and Lacy a quick summary to make sure they were caught up on the details. "The map was in the same folder as these letters. I'm convinced that somehow Micah and this 'A' person, and maybe Evangeline, are connected to the ring."

"And their fathers are feuding." Lacy's eyes sparkled as these new clues started shifting into the bigger picture. "That explains the Romeo-and-Juliet thing."

They read on.

> *...and then I can give you all of my words in a box tied up with a blue ribbon. My heart in a box.*

You cannot know how wonderful it was to see your face again, up close and not from my hideaway in the oak where I spy on you and your family. Nor can you know how heart-wrenchingly horrible it was to pretend I did not want to see you anymore. I pray you understood, and that I did not ruin our chances of being together again someday.

I am in a mood today. You walked in here just a day after I learned that Margaret McRay is getting married. She is sixteen, only four months older than I am.

"She's so young," Raquel said. "I was picturing them older."

"You sound disappointed," Lacy said.

"I guess I was identifying with them. They were forced apart, kind of like Marshall and I are going to be. I suppose it sounds silly to admit I was hoping for some encouragement from their story. But if this is a teen infatuation and not a mature relationship, it changes how I see them."

Lacy raised her right brow. "Shakespeare's Romeo was sixteen and Juliet was only thirteen."

"Yes, but—"

"Did you see the sixties version of Romeo and Juliet?"

"Yes." Raquel gave a wistful sigh.

"Hannah and I watched it together. I remember agreeing that if we ever found a guy like Romeo, we'd rather have a few stolen moments with him than a lifetime with someone who didn't make our toes tingle."

Hannah sputtered a laugh. "We said that?"

"I think we were fifteen at the time."

"That explains a lot. But I agree. I mean, we all know people who settle for relationships that aren't great, and here we are"—Raquel pointed at Hannah and then back at herself—"with amazing guys, but we're whining because we can't see them as much as we want. We need to start thinking like Juliet."

"But hopefully with better communication skills, so that the relationship doesn't end in disaster," Hannah said, recalling the end of the tragic play.

"Right." Raquel pointed to the paper in front of her. "Back to Micah and maybe Evangeline."

In truth, I think that is far too young, but it makes me sad. She is so happy, and here I sit, longing for someone I really only knew when I was a child.

I pray for you every night. I pray about us, even though, for all I know, you may have a girlfriend. Though I do hear things about you often and have heard no rumors of romance. Then, yesterday, in the few minutes you stood before me, I knew that, if nothing else, you still see me as your dearest friend. For that, if nothing else, I will be eternally grateful.

Good night for now, my dearest friend. I will write again soon and dream of the day I will hand you the box tied up in a big blue ribbon.

"Poor girl." Lacy picked up the next letter then glanced at her watch. "Neil is meeting me at my OB appointment in an hour. I hope we can get through all of these."

"Liam has an allergist appointment at three," Hannah said. "That should give us enough time, and there are more where these came from. I wish they had dates. It will be confusing to read them out of order."

Raquel propped her chin in her hands. "I just hope there's a happy ending."

"Me too," Hannah said. And she wasn't only referring to the century-old romance.

Chapter Twenty

Blackberry Valley
January 28, 1931

"I'll let you know as soon as he finishes it, Mrs. Buchanan." Evangeline waved at the woman who'd walked into the mercantile with her nose a bit too high, but walked out with something closely resembling a smile. It was the third day in a row Annabeth had come in to inquire about the hope chest Pa was making for her granddaughter.

Evangeline had heard the gossip. Annabeth Buchanan had grown up dirt poor like so many others in town, but she'd met and married one of the wealthiest men in the valley. People talked about it like it was a real-life Cinderella story. Nowadays, things were different. Though everyone knew she and her husband had lost most of their wealth in the stock market crash, Annabeth still carried herself as if she were the queen of Blackberry Valley.

Evangeline watched her wave to someone across the street and felt a twinge of pity that the woman still felt the need to keep up the façade, even though the drop waist on her saggy gray dress was five years out of style, her cloche hat was now shapeless, and the cuffs on her black wool coat were frayed.

As Annabeth stepped toward the Franklin runabout driven by the butler the Delaneys had employed since they'd married back in the eighties, Evangeline whispered, "You'd be so much happier if you just admitted you were struggling like the rest of us."

But did her family really fit the description of struggling? Business was down and money was scarce, but compared to those first few years after what, for the sake of the younger ones, they called Pa's "accident," life was good.

A truck pulled up in front. Around the fading HALEY'S MERCANTILE sign painted across the window, she watched her brother heft a burlap bag onto his shoulder, then lift another with one hand and prop it on his other shoulder. She ran to the door and flung it open for Isaiah.

"Potatoes and apples from the Wilsons," he said, barely winded. "It's the last from their cold cellar." His gaze roamed the space. "Store empty?"

"At the moment. Why?"

He slid the bags onto the floor in front of the counter. "Got some pumpkins too." He winked at her. "Maybe pie for Sunday dinner?"

That wink. She hadn't been able to say no to him since she was twelve. Since he'd stepped up and become the man of the house as a skinny ten-year-old, felling trees, planting a garden. Together, under Pa's direction, she and Isaiah and Ma had built a sturdy little cabin in time for the first winter. Pa had finally come out of his dark place about the time he could start putting weight on his leg again. Without money for a doctor, it hadn't healed as straight as it should, but he could walk. When Ma was expecting again, he'd made a cradle for the baby. That was the beginning of a whole new life. He'd made another and taken it to the mercantile. It had sold the same day, so he'd started taking orders for tables and chairs and dressers. People for miles around wanted the things he crafted by hand.

When Evangeline turned fourteen, she'd gotten a job at the mercantile, and now, eight years later, Pa owned it, and she lived in the apartment upstairs and managed the store. Yes, it had been a struggle, but life was good.

Isaiah dragged in a bag of squash and pumpkins. "I'm going to hang out in front for a bit. See who I see." He grinned like the proverbial cat who ate the canary.

"Expecting someone special?" she teased.

"Maybe. Might stop at the Martins on the way home to see if they got any of Mrs. Martin's canned sweet corn left."

Evangeline laughed. "Might stop at the Martins if you don't run into that special someone in town?"

He shrugged and winked. "You'll see."

"Might as well just admit it's not the Martins' corn you're sweet on, little brother."

His tan face pinking, Isaiah straightened his cap and waved. "You have a 'specially nice day, Sis. Be extra nice to the customers."

He was being strange, even for Isaiah. Maybe that was what love did to a person. She wouldn't know.

"Maybe I'll bring a guest to eat that pie you're gonna make for Sunday."

Another seat at the table. If Isaiah was going to start officially seeing Audrey Martin, it wouldn't be long before they were married, and then there'd be littles. She would rejoice with them. And yet, she was the oldest. Was it wrong to long for a bit of the happiness she saw on her brother's face?

Chasing away the thought with a shake of her head, she went back to doing inventory on the bolts of fabric on the shelves behind the counter. "Unbleached muslin," she said out loud as she penciled it into her ledger. It was by far the cheapest, and a step up from the flour sack cloth many women were using. She rested her hand on a light blue cotton with white flowers dancing on green vines. "And more of this."

"More of what?"

She turned at the masculine voice, her usual greeting at the ready. "Good afternoon. How can I help—" Her mind went blank. She gripped the edge of the counter.

"Hi, Angel."

Only one person had ever called her that. Since back when they were six and he'd watched over her shoulder as she struggled to write her name for the first time. "There's an angel in Evangeline!" he'd shouted, earning a rap on his shoulder with a ruler from Miss Goodnight.

That one person now stood three feet away from her. Her lips formed his name, but no sound came out. She drank in his tall frame. He had to be at least a foot taller than he'd been six years ago when he snuck into the store and handed her a picture he'd drawn for her. Six years and a million regrets ago. She'd told him to leave then. Told him she didn't want anything to do with him or his family. And then she'd run to the back room and cried until she couldn't catch her breath.

She felt just as breathless now, staring up into eyes the color of a summer sky. How, after what she'd done to him, could he look at her like that? Like only he had ever looked at her. She fought for a breath and finally managed a whisper. "Micah."

Chapter Twenty-One

Liam reported that a red spot on his arm already felt itchy by the time they got in the car after his appointment for allergy testing. To keep his mind off the discomfort, Hannah asked him about Archer's latest theories on his mystery photos.

"Archer made a list of people who might think he owes them something. The last three letters make some of the names pretty absurd. I don't think he's ever done anything to make anyone claim he owes them a million dollars." Liam pulled out his phone. "There was the kid with the bike, but he checked into that. The dad's insurance covered it. There's still the jewelry store fire. They did lose a chunk of money, but there again, they had good insurance. He was in that fender bender a few weeks ago. The woman who ran into him was totally at fault, but she tried to claim he hadn't used his turn signal. Even though there was a witness who said he had, and he wasn't charged with anything, the other driver might still be angry."

"That's a whole lot of work to go through just to—what? Scare him? If someone is trying to threaten him, why wouldn't they give a better clue as to what they're threatening and what they want? Hurting his reputation, suing him, blackmail, bodily harm, something."

Liam grinned. "You watch too much TV."

"My favorites are educational."

"And unrealistic."

"You're not going to talk me out of them. Because of watching forty-six episodes of a fire department show, I now know all about the thrilling drama and romance in a firefighter's life."

Liam sputtered. "Romance, huh? I spent four hours doing paperwork on Friday. I'd like to see that in one of your shows."

"Don't you dare spoil it for me." She shot him a look of feigned defensiveness.

"I wouldn't dare introduce reality into your fantasy world, my dear."

"Back to the mystery. What if 'mill' doesn't stand for million? What if it's an actual mill?" Hannah pulled into the library parking lot. "I remember Dad telling me about a fire at the feed mill a few years ago."

"I hadn't thought of that. But it was at least two years ago, and I don't remember any complaints filed. I'll check into it, though."

Hannah shut off the car. "There are other kinds of mills. Lumber mills, steel mills, woolen mills. Paper, cider... Treadmill! He belongs to a gym, right? Did he ever break their treadmill?"

"A million-dollar treadmill?" Liam looked at her with a deadpan expression, but she could tell he was working hard not to crack a smile.

"Right. How about a coffee mill? That's it! I read about a big chain coffee shop that evacuated all their customers when they smelled smoke and burnt plastic. There was a fire *inside* a coffee grinder. Archer goes to Jump Start every morning. What if they had a coffee grinder fire when Archer was there and—" She didn't know where to go from there with her intentionally ridiculous story.

"And Archer let it burn?" Liam finished for her. "You do realize we are in the business of putting out fires, not exacerbating them, right?"

She blew out an exaggerated sigh of defeat. "I really thought I was onto something." She smirked at him. "What else could 'mill' stand for?" She pulled her phone out of her purse and typed in *MILL acronym*. A long list popped up. "'Manufacturing Industry Learning Lab, Millers Improving Local Lives, Motivating Individuals for Learning and Living.' These are all boring." She scanned toward the bottom of the list and laughed. "These are much better. How about 'Monsters in Lake Louise,' 'Misery Island Little League,' or 'Murderers in Louisiana Lore.'"

Liam's patiently indulgent expression made her want to keep going.

She put her phone back. "Or, let's see. 'Mice Irritating Lacy's Lambs.'" That earned a laugh, and she nudged him with an elbow. "You think of one."

He closed his eyes. After a moment, a slow smile sent lines fanning around his lashes. "Madwoman Instigating Liam's Laugh." With a full grin on his face, he winked at her, then shook his head and opened the car door.

When Hannah reached the passenger side, he reached out and pulled her into a one-armed hug. "That's something else I like about you."

"What?"

"You make me laugh. Even when I don't feel like it."

Evangeline Cooke greeted Hannah and Liam when they walked into the library. "Back for more sleuthing?"

"Maybe. Do you know who set up the valentine display?"

"Unfortunately, I wasn't here. Did you ask Phyllis?"

"I asked Amethyst. I know she helped, but I don't know who else was involved. We've gone off on so many rabbit trails that I forgot to follow up on that with Phyllis." She folded her arms as she looked over at Liam, who was intently reading an old love letter.

"Think he's taking notes?" Evangeline teased. "He wouldn't be the first. I've seen a couple of men take pictures. Some lucky women are going to get some flowery messages this year."

A woman with a toddler on her hip approached the desk, so Hannah walked over and joined Liam. "Evangeline is wondering if you're taking notes."

He laughed. "As if I need help. What could be more romantic than a guy who wants you right by his side when his airway's closing up?"

"True. Nothing thrills a girl's heart quite like a guy in anaphylactic shock." She nodded toward the historical society, and he followed her to the back of the library.

Amethyst was covering the desk again. Hannah introduced Liam to her, then asked when Phyllis would be in.

"She's at an eye doctor appointment. Should be back any time now. Did you figure out who Evangeline's valentine was?"

"Not yet."

"I've been reading some of the letters. Whoever they were, they were up to something." Amethyst bent and pulled the file folder marked *Haley* out from under the counter. She opened it and handed a piece of paper to Hannah. This one appeared to have been folded many times over, much like one of the other letters she'd found in the folder. Only a few lines, and no greeting at the top, but the now familiar "M" was at the end of the page. And another sketch in the bottom right corner.

A sketch of a full moon reflected off a river, and in the foreground, a bit of a roof line and a series of intricate spindles interspersed with shooting stars.

"Is that…?" Liam asked.

Hannah nodded. She'd told him about the words she and her father found under the seat in the gazebo. She held the letter so they could read it together.

Full moon tonight, and I'm in need of someone to try out the new dance floor. And then, when hands meet and all is still and quiet, we can take a ride with a spade and a prayer. May we find our future tonight beneath the welcoming arms.

M

Liam sighed. "A spade and a prayer? Are they playing poker? Or burying somebody?"

"They're *un*burying the treasure," Amethyst said. "Don't you think?" she asked Hannah.

"It sure sounds like it. So they were meeting at the gazebo, then riding—that could have been a horse or a car, I suppose—to someplace at midnight."

"Whose 'welcoming arms?'" Liam asked.

Hannah searched her memory. The phrase reminded her of something she'd heard just recently.

"Not a who. A what. The tree, right?" Amethyst bounced on her heels. "The tree on the treasure map."

Of course. She must be more exhausted than she'd realized. "Elaine said she and her brother used to play on an old oak tree that sounded like it might be the one on the map. She said she always imagined it was alive and inviting them to climb up."

"Inviting. Welcoming." Liam rubbed his chin. "Sounds probable."

"Here's another one." Amethyst picked up another note. Same paper, same multiple folds.

> *Don't despair the lost years, my angel. God's timing is perfect. Maybe if we had not been apart, we would be taking each other for granted by now. We would not be savoring every stolen moment. Two more nights, and we can test our theory. Have you stopped to imagine the rejoicing if we discover they have both been wrong all these years?*

Hannah set the letter back on the table, and Amethyst said, "I wonder if 'two days' means this one was written two days before the one about the full moon."

"Could be," Liam answered. As he and Amethyst speculated about what the theory could mean, Hannah was stuck on the line, "Maybe if we had not been apart, we would be taking each other for granted by now. We would not be savoring every stolen moment." Though she and Liam didn't need to sneak around, it often felt like all they had were stolen moments. And she did savor them. If they had all the time in the world, she probably wouldn't treasure their time together quite as much.

"Hannah?"

She blinked at Liam with an apologetic smile. Thinking about savoring stolen moments when he was standing beside her was silly. "Sorry. What did you say?"

"I asked if we could still go out to King Farm today."

She pulled back her sleeve and noted the time. "Not a lot of daylight left and"—she covered a yawn—"I was going to say you're probably tired, but I might be talking about myself." At that moment her phone buzzed. A text from Archer.

How's the patient? I'll pick up allergen-free supper and take a shift babysitting when I get off at 6.

Hannah showed the message to Liam.

Liam scowled. "I don't need a babysitter, but I know you won't go home and rest if I don't give in."

She was about to argue, falsely, when Phyllis came through the door. "Hi Chief, Hannah. What have you learned about Evangeline and her valentine?"

"I think we've figured out that 'M' is Micah Benton."

Phyllis's smile brightened. "The last of the Bentons left the valley a long time ago, but there may still be descendants. I know we have some information on the family. I can do some digging unless you want to do that yourselves."

"This is going to be a busy week for me. If you have time, that would be great." Hannah tapped the folder. "What I really came in for is to find out if you knew who donated these. My dad said there used to be a Haley Mercantile in town."

"Yep. It operated from right after the Civil War until sometime in the forties. Then the building was bought by Oscar Stanton and became the Stanton Bank. I did look up who brought in the letters.

Sorry I forgot to let you know. They're just on loan. They were in a box Kathryn Hobart brought in when she moved to Bowling Green a few years ago. Do you know her?"

Hannah shook her head.

"She's in a nursing home, but I can try contacting her to see if I can figure out what their connection is to the Haley family."

"And the Bentons."

"Definitely."

"Thank you. I'm also wondering who helped put up the valentine display. I'm trying to figure out who might have seen the drawing of the Stanton Building window."

"That was just me and Amethyst and Lorelai Dawson. She's so gifted with putting things like that together. You go to her church, don't you?"

"Yes." Lorelai was Pastor Bob's wife. She worked part-time at the antique store and was, as Phyllis said, gifted at interior design. What she was not was someone who would send Archer Lestrade mysterious photographs.

"That sounds like a dead end to me," Liam said, expressing her thoughts perfectly. They said goodbye to Phyllis and Amethyst and left.

On the way to the car, Liam said, "I keep thinking I've seen the name Micah Benton somewhere, but I can't place it."

Hannah thought for a moment. "There was a mention of children crawling around an engine in one of the letters. I meant to ask you about it. I wondered if it could have been a fire engine."

He smiled. "So we might have more in common with this couple than we know. I'll check our records." He reached for the passenger door handle. "Now take me home so you can get some rest."

"I can stay until Archer—"

Liam held up a hand. "No arguing. You need to go home and start planning for the next time we can spend a whole day together."

"And when will that be?"

"Next..." He stopped, folded one arm across his chest, and tapped his chin. He winced. "I don't know. But there will be a next time."

Hannah stepped away from him to hide the disappointment she was sure was evident on her face. As she opened her car door, she recited, "savor every stolen moment." It might be all they'd have for the next two weeks.

Lord, help me savor instead of simmer.

Chapter Twenty-Two

Four days to Valentine's Day. Approximately one hundred hours to have everything set for a birthday party and a culinary extravaganza.

Hannah sat in her office a few minutes after noon on Tuesday and stared at the list she'd recopied. She crumpled the old one with its scribbles and arrows and underlines. The new one was shorter. She'd finished the menus and printed them on heavy linen-textured cardstock. The Hot Spot logo nestled inside a stylized heart gave just the right pop of color on the otherwise black-and-white page. It had felt good to cross that off her list.

The red cloth napkins had arrived. She'd take them home tonight and iron them. The narrow table she had set up behind her desk was laden with decorations. She couldn't wait to string tiny red lights around the whole perimeter. Along with the heart-shaped fairy lights she'd placed in crystal bowls for centerpieces, the dining room would be filled with a romantic glow, setting the perfect ambiance.

She switched to another tab on her laptop and opened Marshall's blog. *The Gourmet Guy* had featured the restaurant yesterday with a blog post titled, "The Hot Spot Will Be Cookin' on Valentine's Day." It was a beautifully written piece with phrases like, *Chef Jacob brings a touch of class and sophistication to down-home comfort food, and the waitstaff instantly make you feel like you're part of the Hot Spot family. A string trio will serenade you and your special someone as you savor a meal you'll never forget.*

Marshall's ebullient words had caused their voicemail to fill with reservation requests. As it stood now, they could probably squeeze in three or four more couples, but that was it. From four to ten on Saturday night, the dining room would be full.

Clicking back to the row of open documents, she scanned the guest list for Raquel's birthday. Hannah had invited thirty-four people. Twenty-seven planned to be there. She went through her list for the party. She'd chosen teal and silver for the theme colors, a combination Raquel enjoyed and had nothing to do with the traditional Valentine's Day hues. She had disposable tablecloths for the food table, and she'd found a silver box to use for birthday cards. Elaine was picking up balloons. Jacob had assured her several times that it wasn't too much work for one day. She'd already printed out the check for a bonus for his double-duty day.

Standing, Hannah stretched. Her stomach told her the toast and coffee she'd had at six that morning needed reinforcements. She'd been up early because she'd gone to bed at eight. The full weight of all that had happened since Sunday afternoon—and what could have happened—hadn't hit until she'd walked into her apartment. She'd barely had the energy to heat a can of soup and brush her teeth before falling into bed.

When she walked into the kitchen, Jacob had a sandwich already made for her. It almost brought tears to her eyes. "You're the best."

"It's why you pay me the big bucks."

"If I had to pay you what you're worth, I'd go broke." She took a bite of the cranberry chicken salad sandwich, closed her eyes, and hummed with delight. As she swallowed, her phone rang. Lacy. Always a welcome interruption. “Hi, Lacy. What’s up?”

“How’s Liam?”

“Back at work. He texted this morning and said he felt fine.”

“Good to hear. I know your brain is on overload this week, but I was wondering if you’d thought any more about a care package for Bryn. Or was that merely a ruse to talk to Heather?”

“Well, it was partly that, but we should actually do it. Thank you for reminding me. I did research some ideas while we were sitting in the ER. I found a woman near where Bryn is working who hand-delivers custom-made gift baskets.”

“Perfect. Hey, I just made snickerdoodles, and I’m taking some to Neil. Do you have time to meet me at Legend & Key? I’ll make us some tea.”

Time wasn’t something she had a lot of, but savoring stolen moments worked for friends too. “How soon?”

“I can be there in ten.”

“That works for me.” Hannah hung up and chatted with Jacob as she finished her sandwich, then took her plate to the sink and told him she’d be back before three. On her way out, she stopped to grab the mail. Two bills, a restaurant magazine, a letter addressed in crayon from a little boy who’d celebrated his eighth birthday at the Hot Spot—and a manila envelope wedged behind the mailbox. An envelope with no address. Only a name.

Archer Lestrade.

Hannah drummed her fingertips on the envelope, which sat on the small round table between two wingback chairs she and Lacy occupied in front of the bookstore's fireplace. The scents of jasmine tea and the cinnamon-sugar sweetness of snickerdoodle cookies mingled with the slightly musty tinge of old books and the fresh ink and paper smell of new ones. An inviting combination.

"If it's another 'I,' it could still be spelling out 'million,'" Hannah pointed out.

Lacy nodded, then continued sipping her tea. Her eyes narrowed the way they often did when she was deep in thought.

"What are you thinking?"

Lacy rested a fingertip on Archer's name. "This font. It's unusual. Is this the same as all of the other envelopes?"

"Yes." Hannah repeated, "What are you thinking?"

"A few years ago I tried learning some new lettering for addressing our Christmas cards. Something this fancy takes time, more time than I wanted to put into it. And look at the top of every *R*."

Hannah picked up the envelope and studied the strokes. An upsweep followed by a thin tapered downward curve. "They remind me of little birds."

"That could be a signature mark. Something unique to the person who wrote this."

"Archer didn't seem to recognize it." It was a clue, but where to go from here? They sat in silence for several minutes. Finally, Hannah gave up on going any further with the lead for the moment. "Okay, on to the care package. I texted the woman who makes and delivers them. Her business is called Blessings & Bliss."

"I love that."

"Me too. It's not just a business. It's a ministry too." She found the site on her phone and showed it to Lacy.

"Bryn asked me once if I made goat-milk lotion. That led to a long conversation about natural skin-care products." Lacy pointed to a picture of a box filled with bottles of lotion, shower gel, and a vanilla-scented candle. "I think she'd love something like this."

"I agree. And the woman only lives twenty minutes from—"

"Is that another photograph?" Neil walked toward them carrying a stack of books.

Lacy smiled up at him. "It was stuck behind the Hot Spot mailbox."

"What's this one?"

Hannah shrugged. "I don't know. I tried to get in touch with Archer but they're out on a call."

"So you two are trying your powers of X-ray vision to look at it without opening it?"

"Yep." Lacy lifted her cup. "Although we do have an electric teakettle in the back."

Neil shook his head. "Unfortunately, the store has a code of ethics that doesn't allow for being an accessory to a crime. Opening mail not addressed to you is considered mail theft or tampering with correspondence, punishable by up to five years in prison. Even if you steam it open and re-seal it so no one can tell."

Hannah gaped at him. "And you know this how?"

Lacy shook her head. "He took a corporate law class in college. He doesn't let me get away with anything."

"But it wasn't delivered by the post office." Hannah turned the envelope over. "So it's probably perfectly legal for me to steam it open." She drummed her fingers on the table. "But I won't. It's addressed to Archer, so he should be the one to open it."

"If the photos aren't coming by mail, how is it possible no one has seen who's delivering them?" Neil asked.

"Good question." One Hannah should have given more thought to.

"Do you have security cameras in front of the restaurant?" Lacy asked.

"Unfortunately, no."

Neil set down the stack of books, pulled a chair up to the small table, and joined them. "You need to find an eyewitness." He pointed to the envelope. How many of these has he gotten so far?"

"This one makes ten."

"And they've all been delivered to different places?"

Hannah nodded. "One was under the windshield wiper on Archer's truck, another under a door mat. A couple behind or near mailboxes."

"At different times of the day?"

Hannah took a minute to think about that one. "I'm not sure. I think most were dropped off during the night, although Archer found the one on his truck when he came out of work. But he starts his shift at six in the morning, so it could have been put there before the sun came up."

Neil leaned on his fist. "What time did you find this one?"

"When I got the mail a little after noon."

"Is Greg Schmidt your mail carrier?"

"Yes."

"He's ours too. I've known him since we were kids." Neil pulled out his phone. He stopped with his finger suspended over the screen. "Just a warning. He's a talker. Guy loves his stories."

"I've heard some of them."

Neil scrolled and tapped. "Hey, Greg. It's Neil Minyard. I'm here with Hannah Prentiss and Lacy. Hannah has a question for you. I'm putting you on speakerphone."

Hannah asked if he remembered seeing a large envelope behind her mailbox.

"Yeah. I pulled it out because I thought it might have been outgoing. But I wasn't sure, so I put it back in case it wasn't. You usually address your outgoing mail completely. Is that one of those mystery photos Archer Lestrade has been getting?"

"Pretty sure it is. We're trying to figure out if they've been delivered at the same time every day."

"Oh, I can help with that. There was one at the Lestrades' house under the welcome mat a few days ago. I usually get there by eight thirty. I looked at it in case it was something to be mailed, but I left it since it was addressed to Archer. And let's see, there was one more at the fire station. That's not on my route, but I heard one of the other carriers say he saw it. There's been a lot of talk about who's delivering these. The one on your mailbox was there when I passed at about quarter to seven on my way to work this morning. I suppose most people wouldn't notice something like that, especially when it's still dark out, but I pay attention to details. I stopped a robbery once, you know."

Hannah did know. She'd heard Neil's version several times.

Lacy repressed a laugh. "You're my husband's hero, Greg."

"I bet Hannah hasn't heard the whole story, and I'm certain she hasn't heard it directly from the horse's mouth. So, two years ago, I was walking my route before the sun came up, and I saw this guy all dressed in black using a crowbar on one of the windows at Legend & Key. Why anyone would want to break into a bookstore is beyond me, but there he was. I hid around the corner and called the sheriff. They got there in about six minutes and caught the guy red-handed."

"That's incredible," Hannah said. She had indeed heard the full story from Neil, but that was all right. "Thank you for telling it, and for letting us know about the photos."

"My pleasure. I'll talk to you folks later."

Neil ended the call.

Hannah rubbed her temples. "I'm not usually up before dawn. Definitely not this time of year. But last spring, before we opened, I was going for some early morning walks. There were a couple of people I'd pass every morning like clockwork. Jack Delaney was one." The editor-in-chief of the *Blackberry Valley Chronicle* was a frequent Hot Spot patron. "He was training for a triathlon. I wonder if he still runs."

Neil shook his head. "I can't quite figure if early risers like that are amazing or not quite right in the head."

"I agree," Lacy said. "As much as I love our animals, it takes some serious psyching to get myself out the door to feed them when it's still dark this time of year. I'd never be motivated to do it if lives weren't at stake."

"One way to find out if he's still running." Neil pointed to Hannah's phone.

She hesitated. Jack was a busy man. But after a moment, she picked up her phone and found the number for the *Chronicle*. When she got through to Jack, she said, "I have a quick question. Any chance you ran past the Hot Spot this morning?"

"Sure did. And actually, I was going to call you today."

"You were?"

"Yes. But you go first."

She explained about the envelope. "Just wondering if you might have seen anything."

"That's why I was going to call you. I think you've just confirmed one of our suspicions."

"Our?"

"Pippa knows Archer, so she's heard all about the photographs. She told me about it because she's thinking of asking him if she can write a story about his mystery."

Hannah wondered what Archer would say to that. Pippa Nelson was a good reporter. If this turned out to be something fun like their treasure hunt theory, it would make for an interesting read.

"She's also a runner, and the morning one of those envelopes was delivered to Archer's aunt's house, she saw an orange SUV near there, and she's seen it a couple of other times. She told me to keep a lookout for it, and this morning, a little after five, I saw an orange Range Rover parked across from the Hot Spot. The driver was walking away from your place, wearing a dark hoodie. I saw the envelope stuck behind your mailbox."

Hannah's pulse quickened. "Did you get a look at his face? Or maybe a license plate number?"

"Unfortunately, it was too dark. I'm no car expert, but I owned a Rover once. I know that to get that particular burnt orange color, there would have been a hefty up-charge, so there aren't many of them. I'm guessing it was three or four years old."

"Any bumper stickers, parking stickers, or dents that would make it identifiable?"

"I only saw the driver's side and the back, and not very clearly, but I didn't notice anything like that. Wish I could be more help. I'll keep watching for it."

"Thank you," Hannah said, taking in Neil's and Lacy's excited expressions. This is the best lead we've had so far. If Archer knows someone with an orange Range Rover, this mystery may be solved."

Chapter Twenty-Three

Blackberry Valley
January 28, 1931

"I knew why you told me to leave." Micah sat on one of the upturned buckets next to a small, square chess table in front of the window. "I was crushed until I saw your pa walk in right after I left. Then I knew you were merely acting cruel and heartless just to spare me."

Hands shaking, Evangeline turned over the Closed sign, then rushed to pull down the shade to cover the front window. "It was the hardest thing I ever did. I didn't know what he'd do to you. Or me. I still can't think about it without—" She stopped, trying to catch her breath.

"Let's not then. Let's think about now. We're adults. They can't control our actions anymore."

Evangeline hugged herself tightly. "I wish that were true. You've been gone a long time, Micah." Though she hadn't seen him in six years, she'd heard things. She knew he'd enlisted in the navy at sixteen, probably lying about his age, and had spent time in Panama and

Nicaragua. She knew he'd gotten a job working for a New York magazine, traveling around the world to sketch people.

His life had taken such a different course than hers. His deeply tanned skin and sun-kissed hair gave evidence that he hadn't been back long. Why had he returned to Blackberry Valley?

She didn't want to burst his bubble, but he needed to know how things were. "They're still as angry as ever. My father won't sell Benton produce, so yours set up that stand where he's undercutting our prices. We only have three cows, but during the drought, when the creek ran dry, your father wouldn't allow us access to your spring. And now that they've found oil on your land and your pa's planning to build a big, fancy house in town, my pa's even more resentful. The gap between our families is just widening."

"I was afraid of that."

She dropped onto the bucket across from him and picked up a pawn. "It's still so ugly, Micah. I live upstairs here, but if Pa finds out we were together, he'll kick me out of my apartment. I'd likely lose this job and wouldn't be allowed in his house." She had to ask. "Why did you come back? Is it because of the oil? Are you joining your dad in his new business?"

Micah's jaw tightened. "No. I can't. I won't. I'm still working for a couple of magazines, and I'm applying for some part-time jobs. The auto shop and the firehouse. And as to the first part of your question, I'm here because of you."

His eyes bore into her soul, and she couldn't breathe.

"I got here yesterday. Pa hasn't talked to me much. He's still mad that I left. But I couldn't take all the bitterness anymore. All the time I was gone, I kept praying things would change."

"I've been praying the same right here. Ma's health is bad. I know it's from all the stored-up hurt. It about killed her not to be there for your ma when she lost the baby years back."

Micah clenched his fists. When he looked at her again, there was fire in his eyes. "Do you think your pa took that ring?"

"No. And I don't think yours did either. They're both—well, they *were* both good men. I've said over and over that someone must have taken it before we ever got to the farm."

"I agree." The fire in his eyes gleamed brighter. He slapped the table. "It's up to us to end this."

"How?"

"By finding out what really happened to the ring." He lowered his voice and looked to his left and then to his right, as if there were spies lurking behind the dry goods or jelly jars. "And I have an idea how we can do it."

Chapter Twenty-Four

I'll deliver it tomorrow if I can get it put together and get out before the storm hits.

After Hannah read the text from the Blessings & Bliss lady, she checked the weather for Pittsville, Wisconsin. Sure enough, a wall of green was creeping across Minnesota, predicted to descend on most of northern Wisconsin in the form of freezing rain in the next twelve hours. The roads up there could be covered with ice before dawn the following morning. The high temperature over the next three days was only thirty-five. Starting Friday, that part of Wisconsin would be blanketed by up to ten inches of snow.

Hannah hoped Bryn would still be able to make it back by Saturday. Maybe if she got the basket and read the note Hannah had emailed to include in the basket, she'd get in her car and beat the worst of the snow. Archer might be upset with Hannah if he found out what she'd written, but somebody needed to let Bryn know he was miserable without her.

As if on cue, a text popped up from Archer.

Long day. House fire. Have an idea about the SUV. Colt? Open the envelope. Another "I"?

The short, choppy sentences indicated he was probably exhausted.

Hannah rushed into her office and used a letter opener to slit open the envelope. A photo tumbled onto her desk. A picture of the trim between two arched windows. It was familiar, but she couldn't be sure. She scurried into the dining room, smiling and greeting familiar faces as she made her way to the front window, hoping to find what she was looking for while there was still enough light.

There. Just down the block. There were four double-arched windows on the second floor of the red brick building that housed Blackberry Blooms. She hurried back to her office and answered Archer.

Nope. A "Y" on the flower shop building.

Weird.

Yep. Know anyone named Milly?

No. "You owe me a Milly" doesn't make any sense. Think we're off base. Chief and I will be in for supper. Colt's not working, but I'll try to find him and drag him along.

When Archer and Liam came in around six thirty, Colt was not with them. Hannah seated them, then sat next to Liam. Dylan took their orders, and Hannah asked for a cup of decaf. Then she handed Archer the envelope.

Liam slipped his arm around her shoulders. "It was smart of you to think of asking Greg."

"That was Neil's idea."

"Well, it was smart of you to follow through on it, and even smarter to talk to Jack Delaney as well."

Hannah laughed. "You're scraping the bottom of the barrel for compliments."

He grinned at her. "Those might have been lame, but I can come up with a ton that aren't. You are exceptionally pretty tonight. Your smile lights up the room. You have the—"

A cough interrupted him. Archer looked ready to bolt or be sick. "You two want to be alone?"

"Yes," Liam answered in the same tone. "But being the magnanimous people that we are, we'll allow you to stay."

Archer rolled his eyes. "Who needs enemies when I've got friends like you?"

Hannah loved the banter these two could keep up for hours on end, but she couldn't sit there all night. "Do you have any connection with the flower shop? Did you let their flowers burn? Cause a tree to fall on their building? Date the owner?"

A sheepish look crossed Archer's face.

"You didn't."

He shrugged. "I may or may not have gone out with Winter Bronson a few times."

Hannah glanced at Liam. The look in Liam's eyes told her that he'd already known about it.

"Wait. So Winter tried setting you up on a date with Carrie, then, after that huge misunderstanding that humiliated Carrie, Winter went out with you?" Hannah asked, incredulous.

"No. Do you really think I'm *that* insensitive?" Archer held up a hand. "Don't answer that. Winter and I had been friends for years, and we decided we should see if there could be something more. After two dates we decided we're better off as friends. It was after that that she tried setting me up with Carrie. You know I haven't had eyes for anyone else since I met Bryn."

"That's true. And you're sure Winter felt the same way you did? It's been my experience that when one person says they just want to be friends, the other tends to say they agree even if they don't." She grinned at him. "I think we've found the theme. Winter and Carrie, and who knows how many other women, have banded together to show you the error of your ways. Did you also date someone who worked in the Stanton Bank building?"

"No." The sheepish look returned. "The daughter of the guy who used to run the antique shop doesn't count, does it?"

Hannah couldn't hold back her laugh any longer. "Did you humiliate her too, Romeo? Give her a reason to buy an expensive outfit and then ghost her? If we hadn't just eliminated the million-dollars idea, I could have believed it might be a reasonable figure if you add up all of the broken hearts you've left in your wake."

Archer cleared his throat. "Okay, in all seriousness—"

Liam snorted. "As if you're capable of all seriousness."

Archer rolled his eyes and made a point of lasering in on Hannah and ignoring Liam. "I'll have you know that Margie Brown, the daughter of the antique store owner, ditched *me*. Some nonsense about firefighters working crazy hours. Can you believe it?" He smirked at Liam. "Now, can we get off the topic of my exes and get back to the important stuff? Colt's parents own an orange Range Rover. What else did Delaney tell you? There's one specific detail that would tell me if it's theirs or not."

"I think I already told you everything he said. He called it burnt orange, three or four years old, with no stickers or other markings. What detail would you be looking for?"

"Colt borrowed his parents' Rover when he helped me move into my apartment. The driver's side mirror is bent, caused by *someone*"—he cast a pointed look Liam's way—"leaning my bed frame against the side of the car and not making sure it was going to stay where he put it."

"Hey, free labor doesn't come with any guarantees," Liam protested.

"I bought you pizza," Archer argued.

"Honestly, you guys." They reminded her of the children in a Sunday school class she'd taught in LA. "I called Jack at the paper. I don't have his personal number. Do either of you?"

"I think I do." Liam tapped on his phone. "Got it." He pushed the speaker button and slid it over to Archer.

After explaining why he was calling, Archer asked if he remembered seeing anything unusual about the driver's side mirror. "Did it look crooked?"

"Sorry. It was too dark to pick up on any details. Wish I'd thought to take a picture. One thing I don't think I mentioned to Hannah was that the guy in the hoodie was short. I'm just guessing, but maybe five-six or so."

"Thanks. Every little bit helps."

"I'll keep my eyes open, and Pippa's on the lookout too. Has she talked to you yet?"

"No." Archer frowned in confusion. "Why would she want to? Oh. She wants the scoop on my mystery, right?"

A chuckle came through the phone. "Would you mind? People are talking about this. It would make a great human-interest piece. Assuming it all ends well, that is."

Archer gave a wry smile. "Might be even more interesting if it doesn't."

Jack's laughter boomed through the speaker. "You could be right."

When the call ended, Hannah said, "Have you talked to Colt today?"

Archer shook his head. "Left a voicemail. I think he and a buddy went up to Cave City. He seemed jealous when we told him what a great time we had kayaking on Saturday."

"Can you call his parents?"

"I tried. You'd be impressed by what it took to find where his dad works. I remembered Colt saying he was a plumber, and that got me thinking that since your uncle is a plumber they might know each other, so I got your dad's number from Liam and he gave me your uncle's number, and he knew Mr. Walker. But when I called his company, they said he was out on a job and wouldn't give me his cell number. I left a message for him to call me, but I don't know if he got it."

"I'm impressed. If you ever get bored with fighting fires and getting cats out of trees, I bet Sheriff Steele would take you on as a detective."

Archer stroked his chin. "The idea of a different boss does have an appeal."

"As does the idea of hiring someone who actually does his job instead of just breaking hearts and solving mysteries with my girlfriend," Liam retorted.

Dylan brought their food, and Hannah stirred a packet of sugar into her coffee while the men took their first bites. Her comment about cats stuck in trees got them off on a tangent of pet-rescue stories. She waited until they'd scarfed down their food in record time while keeping the conversation flowing, a skill she assumed they'd honed on the job.

When Archer crumpled his napkin and pushed his plate aside, she brought them back to the mystery. "You said you thought we were off base to focus on the pictures as letters. What's your next theory? Assuming I'm wrong about all your exes ganging up on you, that is."

"Funny," Archer deadpanned. "I think we should go back to the places they were taken. We've been looking at recent history, the people who own the businesses now, or people I've had some interaction with recently, but I've lived here my whole life. Maybe someone has been compiling grievances against me for years."

"Someone like Carrie Moore," Liam suggested.

"We've ruled her out. Unless your tests come back positive for cyanide, I don't think she's a suspect."

Hannah tapped to her notes app. "Here's the list so far."

Archer reached into a pocket of the jacket he'd laid on the seat beside him and pulled out the photos.

"We have the Stanton Building," Hannah said.

"No solid clues on that one." Archer wiped his hands on his napkin before sliding the Stanton window picture off the stack.

"The tree stump."

"The kid got a new bike, and he's off at college now. I don't think he's plotting revenge from the University of Kentucky."

"Jewelry store."

"That one is still a possibility. That guy was mad. Maybc I'll talk to the sheriff about that."

"Bakery. Aside from the Carrie angle, is there anyone else? Previous owner or employees?"

"Can't think of anyone."

"Then we've got two I didn't figure out." She pointed to the next picture, the one showing the peak of a roof with gingerbread trim they'd thought formed an *A*.

"That's the old supper club," Liam said.

"The Greensboro Club," Archer added. "Bryn and I went there a couple of times. No fires there. I don't know the owner or anyone who works there now, but it's been around forever." He took a sip of soda, then rubbed his temple. His eyes widened. "Stan Carlson was a busboy there when we were in high school."

Hannah tapped her screen. "That makes two things that point to him. Three, if we count the bakery, since he was sweet on Carrie while she was sweet on you." She smiled with the same kind of smirk he'd given her and Liam.

Archer groaned. "Leave my exes out of this."

"I think we need a spreadsheet to keep track of all of them."

Liam pointed to her phone. "Make a note of the lovers triangle—if you can even call it that—and let's move on to the next one."

The next picture showed two arched windows that looked like an *M*.

"That one was easy," Archer said. "St. Anthony's Catholic Church. Once again, no connection. I've been to a wedding and a couple of funerals there, but nothing personal."

Hannah added St. Anthony's to her list. "You said the lowercase *i* was a newel post. Anything else on that one?"

"Nothing." Archer slid it off the pile.

"And that photo you thought was of one of the new braces under the park bridge."

"Yep. I've run over that bridge a thousand times. No connection." Archer set it aside. "This one is clearly a downspout. Every building in town has them."

"That's going to be a tough one." She put a question mark next to it. "And that brings us to the flower shop."

Archer shrugged. "I've ordered flowers."

"For all the women falling at your feet?" Liam teased.

Archer rolled his eyes. "Yes. Hundreds of bouquets. But I've paid for all of them."

"Let's think outside the box," Liam said. "Forget about any connection to these pictures. Who have you aggravated recently?"

"Sounds like you have someone in mind."

"Actually, yes. Through no fault of your own. I think. Two names come to mind."

"Who?" Archer wasn't trying to hide the defensiveness in his voice.

"Emmett Shepherd for one."

An exasperated sigh ruffled the crumpled napkin Archer had set next to his plate. "That guy needs to get a life."

"Who is Emmett Shepherd, and what did you do to him?" Hannah asked.

"Nothing *to* him. He's a firefighter down in Scottsville. We went to the academy together. Two years ago we both competed in the Southeast Regional FCL Challenge in Nashville. I beat him fair and square. He's still mad."

"Sorry I'm so uninformed, but what's the FCL?"

"The Firefighter Challenge League. They host a championship series that pits firefighters from all over against one another on a challenge course that tests five functions. Things like forcible entry and victim rescue. It's timed, and there are winners in each division. I didn't win, but I beat Emmett's time, so he's mad. It's been like that since the academy. He can be my friend if he bests me, but if it's the other way around, he can't handle it." Archer flopped against the back of his seat. "I mean, I know I'm competitive, but I won't take it to that extreme. Anyway, add him to the list. He did spray-paint 'Loser' on my car. It was easy to wash off, but who knows what he might try next?"

Hannah gave that some thought. Maybe it was time for them to shift their focus. "Why are you so set on seeing these photo messages as something bad?" she asked. "Isn't it just as likely that someone is delivering the pictures just for fun, or to honor you for being a hero? Or what about the treasure hunt idea? Have you actually gone to each of the places? Maybe there are hidden clues."

"I don't have time for that." He looked at Liam. "Who's the other person?"

"Mike Durham."

"That was a crazy misunderstanding."

"Mike Durham." Hannah didn't know him personally, but she had encountered him. "My dad knows him. What did you do to aggravate him?"

"There was a fire in his barn a few months ago. I asked him all the usual questions, and he thought I was accusing him of arson. Which I wasn't."

Liam pointed to the stack of photographs. "He's also the former building inspector and a current member of the Kentucky Heritage Council. Let's just say he has a passion for preserving old buildings."

Hannah stared down at the stack of photos. "And most of the pictures are parts of old buildings. But what does that have to do with Archer?"

"Nothing I can think of," Liam answered.

Archer's brow furrowed. "Unless it has something to do with my girlfriend being vice president of the Revitalize the Valley committee."

Hannah cringed. "The committee some people are calling the 'Gentrify BV Disaster'?"

"That's the one. Gentrification has never been Bryn's vision. She has some great ideas for bringing in more business to build the local economy, but the last thing she wants is to change the small-town feel or make us a modern metropolis. Unfortunately, there are a couple of people on the committee who balk at change of any kind. She's fighting against them." Archer blew out another long sigh. "But the two opposing voices are loud. And Mike Durham is one of them."

Chapter Twenty-Five

Archer might have thought her treasure hunt idea was ridiculous, but Hannah meant to pursue it anyway. The thought had woken her up every few hours throughout the night. She opened one eye and looked at the clock. It was just before nine.

Judging by the sunlight glowing around the edges of her room-darkening blinds, it would be a decent day. She could handle the cold if it wasn't cloudy or windy. She reached for her phone and tapped Lacy's name.

"Good morning!" Lacy sounded breathless.

"Are you in the middle of something?"

"Mixing up my secret goat feed recipe. It takes longer than it should because Neil won't let me lift bags."

"Good man. They're, what, forty pounds each?"

"Yes, but I'm a farm girl. I come from pioneer stock. We're tough."

Hannah laughed. "No argument here. If I come out and lift bags for you, would you be free for a couple of hours to go on a treasure hunt?"

"Are you kidding? Of course. Are we going to hunt for what's buried on King Farm?"

"Not today. I have to wait for a time when Elaine and Liam are both free. We're going to every one of the places in Archer's pictures and look for clues."

"I'm in. I should be able to get everything else done by ten. Does that work?"

"That's perfect. That'll give me enough time to wake up."

Lacy laughed. "I've been up for four hours already. Of course, I went to bed about the time your dinner rush started. I'm dressed like a farm girl. Any chance lunch might be involved in this adventure, and I'll need decent clothes?"

"I'd say there's a good chance of that, but you don't have to be too spiffy. Just ditch the coveralls and stocking cap."

"You know me well. Okay, see you in an hour."

Hannah closed her eyes for a few more minutes, then eased out of bed. After showering and dressing in fleece-lined jeans and a cowl-neck sweater, she picked up her Bible and journal and headed to the kitchen. Coffee first.

She loved her little galley kitchen. It had everything she needed within arm's reach. Her apartment wasn't big enough for much entertaining, but that wasn't a problem. She owned her own restaurant. There were times, late at night or in the mornings before Jacob arrived, that she'd go downstairs and bake muffins or cookies or breakfast for herself, using all the space she wanted. Just because she could. She still couldn't believe she owned such a magnificent space.

As she waited for her coffee to percolate, she whispered a prayer of thanks.

Settled at her little table near the window, she stared out at Main Street and thought of the previous night's discussion about the committee for revitalizing Blackberry Valley. She'd been at some of the chamber of commerce meetings when the committee discussed some of their plans. She was in complete agreement with most of them.

In fact, soon after Hannah had opened the restaurant, Bryn hosted a "Spotlight on the Hot Spot" night that lauded Hannah's vision for retaining the original exterior and much of the old "feel" of the firehouse while creating a space that felt updated and contemporary. But there had been dissenters. The two loud voices Archer had mentioned. Not long before she'd put in an offer on the building, one of them had lobbied to turn it into a firefighter museum, lambasting all her plans to modernize the interior. Thankfully, he was in the minority.

She made a mental note to talk to her dad about Mike Durham, then began her devotional. The message focused on the eleventh verse of 1 Corinthians 13: "When I was a child, I talked like a child, I thought like a child, I reasoned like a child. When I became a man, I put the ways of childhood behind me." Unlike several she'd read in the past week and a half, this one wasn't as convicting.

Until she read the commentary.

The words stayed with her on her drive to Lacy's. Maybe talking it over with her best friend would help her put the message, and how it applied to her, in perspective.

She drove slowly up the lane to Bluegrass Hollow Farm. She loved seeing how the farm changed through the seasons, and the drive up to the big white farmhouse with its welcoming porch gave her the same kind of "coming home" feeling she got when she approached the house where she'd grown up. So many sleepovers, giggling talks about boys, and shared secrets had taken place in that house when she and Lacy were young.

She greeted three of the goats, Flower, Sprout, and Niblet, as she drew near their pen. These were the ones she felt a connection with, since she'd been there when they were born. She liked to think they felt the same about her. Their enthusiasm as they frolicked toward the fence the moment she got out of her car seemed to prove that. Of course, they also knew she hadn't come empty-handed. She pulled a bag of baby carrots from her pocket and laughed at the way they tickled her hand as they nibbled.

Next were the chickens. Though Lacy had names for all of her birds, there were only three that Hannah knew by name. Rocky, the rooster, acknowledged her with a loud crow. Eggatha and Hennifer came close, seeming to converse with each other as they scampered toward her. Hannah loved to imagine their conversation as they clucked and murmured. *There she is again. Wonder what she brought us this time. Hope it's blueberries. Grapes would be good. Not strawberries. Too sour.*

"You have Jacob to thank for these," Hannah said as she held out a handful of blueberries. They swarmed around her and gobbled the fruit from her hand. "He set them aside for you." Jacob hated wasting food and often said that saving produce that was past its prime for Lacy to give to her animals was another way to recycle. After all, much of it came back to them in the form of eggs from these very hens.

Lacy was in the tiny feed room in the barn. She waved a greeting from behind a low table with two five-gallon buckets perched on top. "Impeccable timing. I got everything else done. I'll do the measuring if you do the heavy lifting."

"Just tell me what you need."

They spent the next fifteen minutes mixing barley, oats, alfalfa pellets, broad beans, carob, and sunflower seeds in Lacy's precise "secret recipe." Hannah grabbed the mixing paddle from Lacy when she saw how much work it took to combine the ingredients.

"Between you and Neil, you're going to turn me into a sloth."

As Hannah laughed at the mental image of a very pregnant sloth, Lacy slipped out of her coveralls, pulled the stocking cap off her head, and washed her hands in the utility sink. She ran her fingers through mahogany-colored hair. "Presentable enough?"

Hannah appraised the trim jeans, copper-colored sweater, and wedge-heeled boots. "For a farm girl, you clean up right nice," she drawled.

"Then let's go find us some clues." Lacy snapped covers on the buckets, grabbed her jacket, and led the way out into a crisp but beautiful day. "Where to first?"

"Let's do them in order. Start with the Stanton Building, or rather, the BV Forum. Let's pay close attention to the window." Hannah handed her phone to Lacy as they walked to the car. "I made an album of all the pictures Archer's gotten so far."

"Are you giving up on the idea that the letters spell something?"

"Not giving up, but setting that theory aside to examine other possibilities. For one, what if there are clues hidden in the things pictured? We didn't look closely. Maybe there's a slip of paper tucked under the window frame." They got in the car. Hannah waved to Lacy's horses, grazing in the pasture, as they passed the picturesque sight on their way down the drive.

"Is Archer still thinking someone's out to get him?" Lacy asked.

"He has no idea, but for now that's where he's focusing. I really want this to be something fun to get his mind off missing Bryn. The poor guy is like a sad little puppy. He's got dark circles under his eyes, and that beard he's growing for her needs some trimming. I wish he could think of this as a fun guessing game, but every time I suggest the treasure hunt idea, he dismisses it."

"So our goal today is to prove him wrong."

"Yep."

As they headed into town, Hannah brought up her morning devotional. "I'd never heard anyone say that the 'thought like a child' verse was referring to love. But it makes sense since it's in the 'love chapter.' But when I first thought of reading it as 'When I was a child, I *loved* like a child,' it didn't make sense."

"That would be a good thing, right? Children love without reservation. I'm sure it was a kid who first said 'I love you to the moon and back.' Why do we put that away when we mature?"

"That was my thought, but then the devotional went on to talk about how children respond to the people they love when they're corrected or told 'no.'"

"Hmm. True. That's not always a pretty sight. I threw some award-worthy tantrums myself when I was a kid. Pretty sure there were times my parents wished I'd go to the moon and not come back."

Hannah laughed. "We expect that of children because, like it says in Proverbs, 'Foolishness is bound up in the heart of a child.' But as adults we're supposed to have grown beyond 'I want what I want when I want it or I'll make your life miserable.' That was the part that got to me."

"Hannah Marie Prentiss, you would never make anyone's life miserable." There was a hint of scolding in Lacy's voice.

"But it hit me that even though I can *act* mature, there are too many times when what I'm thinking amounts to a mental tantrum.

I've had a number of them in the past few weeks when Liam and I made plans and something interfered. I want my thoughts to match my actions."

"Ouch. I'm a card-carrying member of that club too, sister."

"Let's start holding each other accountable. Maybe we should memorize the Philippians 'think on these things' verse."

"Good idea. But let's not be too hard on ourselves for not having this mastered. Remember that plaque hanging in my hallway that my mom bought back in the seventies?"

She did remember. "'Please be patient with me. God's not finished with me yet.'"

There was that theme again. *Patience.* This time it took on a new meaning, reminding her that not only did she need to be patient with her circumstances and the people she dealt with every day, but also with herself.

Lord, change my heart and help me to extend myself grace as You work on me. When she found herself wanting to add "the sooner the better" to her silent prayer, she laughed out loud.

"What's so funny?"

"I just realized how impatient I am to become more patient."

Chapter Twenty-Six

Blackberry Valley
February 19, 1931

Evangeline yawned as she walked down the back stairs, carrying a tray of fresh-baked oatmeal cookies. For three weeks now, her restless mind, swirling with joy and possibilities, had awakened her long before the sun. Or maybe it was the soft click of a small metal door that had roused her from sleep.

She set the tray on the counter in the storeroom. Breath held in anticipation, she opened the milk box door and took out six cold bottles, then slid her hand along the inside top of the box, smiling when she found a tightly folded paper wedged in the corner.

Holding the page up to the thin light filtering through the small, high window, she tried to decipher it. Micah and his mysterious clues.

Like the growing stack of drawings she'd already received, it was a sketch of part of something. A building. The curved top of a window with many panes. Next to it was a mailbox. No. Not a mailbox. An alarm box. The fire station.

She swiveled to cast a bit more light on the page. In miniscule letters at the bottom it said, *We like cookies after supper.*

What was Micah thinking? She couldn't.

Pa knew everyone in town, and everyone knew about the Haley-Benton feud. If they met in public, Pa would know about it before nightfall. She tried to understand Micah's thrill at courting danger, but she didn't share it. Meeting outside in the alley like they'd done on Valentine's Day or at the gazebo Micah was building on his father's Pine Street property was risky enough. This was just plain foolish.

Then again, who could fault the manager of the mercantile for bringing cookies to the Blackberry Valley firefighters?

With a smile wider than she'd smiled in years, she packed the cookies into a cracker tin and set them aside. Her customers would have to live without them for a day. Today, she was going to show her appreciation to the fearless men of the fire department.

At six o'clock, Evangeline pulled down the shade, flipped the sign to Closed, stepped out the front door, and locked it. On legs that felt like they were made of jelly, she walked along Main Street, clutching the tin of cookies to her chest.

She wished she had more to bring to Micah. Her part of their plan to discover who had dug up the ring was to casually insert the names Linus Moss, Josephine Hamilton, and Paxton Cromwell into conversations with her customers. At first, she'd been worried about word getting back to her father. If he had any inkling she was dredging up the events of ten years ago, he'd be irate. "Let sleeping dogs lie," he'd said more than once. How she hated that phrase.

But after talking to a few of the older residents, she'd found ways to pepper those names into questions about the "good old days" before the economy collapsed. Yet despite all of her cautious inquiries, she hadn't spoken to anyone who knew anything that could help them.

She hesitated when she reached the firehouse, but as she took a deep breath and raised her hand to push the buzzer, the small door to the right of the massive arched doors flew open.

Micah, in his brand-new blue uniform, stuffed a rag in his pocket as he grinned at her. "You're a brave girl," he whispered as he took the can of cookies. "I've got some news." Then, in a way-too-loud voice, he said, "Thank you, Miss Haley. Would you like a tour while you're here?"

"I would love that, sir." She didn't quite match his volume, but anyone standing within a few feet would have heard her answer.

Micah led the way to the truck he'd apparently been working on. "Ain't she a beauty?" He took the rag from his pocket and wiped off a smear of dried wax.

"Yes, *she* is." Evangeline laughed. "Why do men call boats and automobiles 'she'?"

"I suppose because they're pretty, and if we're nice to them, they do what they're told and don't talk back."

She smacked his arm. "So that's the kind of woman that would interest you? A mousy little thing without opinions of her own?"

Micah's guffaw resounded in the brick-walled building. "Well, it would make life easier."

As she raised her hand again, he lifted his in mock defense. "But much, much more boring. I prefer a woman who speaks her mind and likes adventures." His gaze left no question he was talking about her.

She looked over her shoulder. "Standing here talking to you is about all the adventure I can handle today. My pa is good friends with the chief." She lowered her voice. "What did you find out?"

Micah straightened and pulled something out of his back pocket before tucking the cloth into it.

Evangeline looked down at the slip of paper. A name and an address—Fletcher Arnett, who lived on South Street. She looked up at Micah.

"He was Linus Moss's best friend. If anyone can tell us anything, it should be him."

Chapter Twenty-Seven

"I don't see anything." Hannah stood a foot away from the alley window outside the BV Forum. "No tiny scroll of paper or words scratched into the bricks. Nothing." She let out a disappointed sigh.

"Maybe there's a pattern," Lacy offered. "Maybe after we've examined each one, something will jump out at us."

"Hello again."

Both women yelped at the unexpected voice. Stan Carlson leaned against the alley wall beside them. Neither of them had noticed his approach.

"S-Stan," Hannah stuttered. "Nice to see you again."

"Our front door is usually open," he said. "No need to sneak peeks through the windows."

Hannah felt her cheeks warm. "Oh. No. We weren't looking inside."

Stan raised an eyebrow dubiously.

"We're on a treasure hunt. Sort of," Lacy said. "This window is a clue. Maybe."

"Interesting. Why don't you come in out of the cold? I'm sure Steph would like to hear about it too."

This wasn't part of the plan. They wanted to go to each spot, look for additional clues, and take pictures. Hannah didn't have all day. But since they'd been caught staring in the Carlsons' window, it seemed a wise idea to try explaining their actions. "All right."

They followed him into the building. Hannah admired their progress. "You've gotten a lot done in a week." The wallpaper was finished, the floors clean and gleaming.

Stephanie popped out from behind a box taller than she was. "Hello again. Yeah, we're almost done. Next job is assembling chairs. Hey, I need a break. Would you like a tour?"

Hannah hesitated, so Lacy answered for her. "We'd love that, if you're sure you can spare the time."

"I'm sure. If I didn't explain it when you were here before, all of this"—Stephanie gestured to the grand room they stood in—"was the bank lobby, added when the Stantons bought the building. From what we can tell from old photos and from things we uncovered while remodeling, the front of the original structure, the Haley Mercantile, was here." She put her hand on a doorway leading to the rest of the main floor.

"It's cool that you know that," Hannah said. "I love learning the history of old buildings."

"Me too. I'm making a slideshow of old pictures." She pulled out her phone and showed them a black-and-white photo of a young woman and a middle-aged man. They stood in front of a large window with *Haley Mercantile* lettered in an arch across the glass. "I love this one. The caption on the back said it was taken in 1929. That's Talbert and Evangeline Haley. I assume father and daughter."

Evangeline Haley. Until now, Hannah hadn't been sure the two names fit together. She leaned closer to get a better look at the woman with short, wavy blond hair. If Hannah had put the pieces together correctly, this was the Evangeline who'd received a valentine from Micah Benton—possibly a valentine that contained a secret message telling her to meet him in the alley Hannah and Lacy had been standing in mere minutes ago. She imagined that stolen moment. At least she and Liam didn't have to hide their time together.

"...way it was back then." Stephanie was leading them through the doorway. Hannah had missed a few words, but it didn't take long to catch up. Stephanie pointed to the shelves lining a room that was currently filled with ladders and paint cans. "This will be a private meeting space when we get it done." She tapped her toe on the floor, drawing their attention to the wide, worn planks. "Refinishing the floor is our next project. We want to keep as much of the original as we can and just give it a bit of twenty-first century vibe."

Hannah looked from the floor that showed signs of more than a century of use, to the crown molding surrounding the pressed tin ceiling. The molding and ceiling were painted white, the floor-to-ceiling shelves a glossy black that contrasted beautifully with the dove gray they'd painted the walls. The frame around the window she and Lacy had been inspecting sported a fresh coat of white paint. She tried to picture the space as it would have looked as the town's general store. Perhaps Stephanie had photos to help with that visualization.

They walked through another doorway into a smaller room. A back door led to the parking lot. A staircase on the left led to the second floor. "This will be used for caterers. It was probably a storeroom for the mercantile. We found some fun things here. Like this wall-mounted milk box." Stephanie opened a small silver cabinet with Brown's Dairy written in red, loopy cursive across the front.

"I haven't heard of a milk box," Hannah said.

Lacy the farmer chimed in. "Before refrigeration was a widespread thing, milkmen would deliver dairy products to homes—and apparently to this business, which probably sold them. Maybe artisan cheeses and such. Anyway, people would leave their empty milk bottles and payment in this box, and the milkman would pick them up and leave fresh ones."

Hannah had to admit that while the milk box was interesting, she couldn't see what was so special about it. Until she realized there was something inside it.

"It was evidently used for more than milk back in the day." Stephanie sent them a knowing smile then turned around and took something off a shelf. A paper in a plastic sleeve. "We found this all folded up tight inside it."

Hannah's pulse skipped a couple of beats as she looked at the familiar style of the sketch in the bottom right corner. A man, alone, standing with one arm reaching out as if beckoning. Or longing. Her gaze shifted to the words.

Angel, I'm so, so sorry. I shouldn't have put you—us—in that position. I should have known Fletcher might talk. I should have sent word, telling you not to go alone. I pray they will come to their senses and you won't lose your job or get kicked out. But please, let's stick to our original plan, just tomorrow instead. The ring will solve everything. I will wait for you. Tomorrow night. And always.

"Who is Angel?" Lacy asked.

"I'm guessing it was Evangeline Haley," Stephanie answered. "'Angel' could be a nickname for Evangeline, right?"

Angel. *A*. Short for Evangeline. Why hadn't Hannah thought of that?

"We found a ledger with receipts in it that were signed by Evangeline, so we assume she worked here, maybe even as the manager. We've been so busy I haven't had time to do any research. The story I've concocted in my head is that she was seeing someone secretly, but her father would have fired her if he found out. I think they were planning to elope, but got caught. I mean, that has to be what 'the ring' means, right?" Stephanie pressed the plastic sleeve against her chest. "Whatever was going on, it's incredibly romantic. What woman doesn't want to hear that a man will wait for her forever? I'm going to have this framed."

The ring will solve everything. Hannah's chest tightened. And why was the note in the milk box? Unless…was this their way of communicating? It would be the perfect way for Micah Benton to leave and retrieve messages. She had to agree with Stephanie. It was all incredibly romantic.

"Would you mind if I took a picture of it?"

"I guess not." Stephanie handed the paper to Hannah, a question on her face.

"I think I know who wrote it." She briefly explained about the other letters, but said nothing about Linus Moss's ring or any of the other questions spinning through her head.

"That's fascinating. I'll have to get over to the historical society soon. Maybe we should donate this and frame a copy."

"Or you could keep the original and donate a copy," Lacy said. "I'm sure the society would be thrilled either way."

Stephanie smiled at her. "Would you like to see the upstairs? We're living up there, but we haven't done any updating yet. I actually love it the way it is, but it needs a little TLC. We found some work orders from around the time the Stantons bought the building. They added some modern amenities, but we don't think much has been changed since then. The note mentions hoping the person it was written to didn't get evicted. Makes me think maybe Evangeline lived up here. It's fun to imagine what Blackberry Valley was like back then, isn't it?"

"And that picture was taken the year of the stock market crash," Hannah said. "I wonder how the Depression affected the store."

Lacy nodded. "I have pictures of my great-grandma from back then. Marcelled hair, sack dress, long pearls, leaning against a Pierce-Arrow car. I can almost hear the jazz music in the background. I know there was a lot of poverty and things were bad for a lot of people during the Great Depression, but the Roaring Twenties that preceded it were so romantic."

Hannah held back a smile as she thought of teasing Liam about his job being romantic. It was easy to idealize things from a distance. Probably something she needed to reflect on when she had time. She tended to look at Lacy's life as being idyllic. Husband, farm life, baby on the way. Yet she knew Lacy and Neil well enough to know life wasn't always sunshine and roses, and viewing anyone else through rose-colored glasses could only result in misplaced envy.

As they filed up the steep, narrow stairway, Hannah thought of something Stephanie had said. Evangeline may have been the store manager. Which meant she could have been the one to write the strange "Dear Sir" letter Hannah had found in the folder from the historical society. She wished she could remember it word for word. The gist of it was they were, or maybe *Evangeline was*, happy to have him as a returning customer and looked forward to working with him in the future. It had been signed "Haley Mercantile Manager," which Hannah had found strangely impersonal at the time. With what she now knew, or thought she knew, it may have been more of a love letter than a business transaction.

The apartment upstairs was quaint and cozy. Stephanie hadn't exaggerated when she'd said not much had been done to update it. Stepping into the kitchen was like entering a time machine set back almost a century. White upper cupboards reached all the way to the high ceiling. The mistress of the apartment would have needed a stepladder to reach anything kept in the glass-front cabinets four feet above Hannah's head. Hexagon tiles in white and pale green made up the countertops. The walls were painted the same minty color.

The appliances were new, but Hannah was delighted to see that whoever had chosen them had picked plain white to blend with the vintage style. It didn't take much to imagine the blond-haired Evangeline donning a flowery bib apron to cook at a massive cast iron stove. Nor was it hard to picture her sitting in the corner breakfast nook and reading her latest secret message from Micah.

Stephanie opened a drawer and pulled out a stack of old magazines with papers sticking out of them. "The markers are all on pages with sketches of people." She opened one and held it out.

Hannah's jaw dropped. Lacy let out a gasp that sounded more like a squeak.

In tiny letters, captioning a drawing of a Parisian woman in flapper attire with the Eiffel Tower far in the distance, was the name of the artist—Micah Benton.

Stephanie pointed toward the far end of the kitchen. "We had to remove a small section of cupboard to make room for a dishwasher, and we found this behind it." She opened a cabinet and held out a framed picture. A drawing, unmistakably Micah's work, of a tree with a winding creek in the background.

Hannah took in the details. A shovel leaned against the trunk and, above it, a heart was carved into the bark. A heart that encircled initials.

E. H.

\+

M. B.

Forever

"There was snow on the ground when the picture was taken," Lacy said, walking around the tree stump again. "Look at it closer. Was something written in the snow, maybe?"

Hannah brightened her screen and held it closer. "Nothing. Just melting snow with patches of grass poking through. Are we sure there aren't any carvings on the stump?"

As she asked, she crouched, examining the cut surface of what was left of the tree Archer had cut down because it had fallen on power lines. She was close enough to count the rings. The tree had been around fifty years old. But there were no markings that even an overactive imagination like hers could construe as clues. If the carving had ever been there, it must have been on the section Archer cut off.

She stared at the shed the tree limb had fallen on. The side facing them was a brighter yellow than the back of the building that faced the river. Other than that, there was nothing remarkable about it.

"Let's move on," she said, with a sigh that fluttered a curled brown leaf sitting on top of the stump. "If we don't find any clues at the jewelry store, let's call it a morning and head for lunch."

"The baby and I are in complete agreement." Lacy patted her middle.

They stopped at the top of the foot bridge, something they did whenever they walked in the park. It was where Neil had proposed to Lacy. Hannah watched her friend close her eyes for a moment and smile.

As Hannah watched, she couldn't help but wonder where her special place of remembering would be. Would Liam propose with some grand gesture, or, like Neil and Lacy, would it be a quiet, intimate moment, just the two of them? Would he even propose? What if things didn't work out between the two of them? A sense of calm washed over her. God already knew. If it was meant to be, He would make it happen in His time.

Just the way she hoped He had done for Evangeline and Micah.

Chapter Twenty-Eight

"I would want something simple but elegant." Hannah leaned over a glass case sparkling with engagement rings and wedding sets. "Like that one." She tapped the glass, pointing at a 4-carat radiant-cut pink diamond surrounded by a circle of small round diamonds and set in rose gold.

Lacy bent down and read the description, then sputtered as she read the price out loud. "I'll pass that on to Liam. He'll be happy to know you're the, uh, low-maintenance kind." She stepped to the next case and motioned toward a sapphire pendant the size of a dime. "And you can return the favor by letting Neil know this is what I want for our anniversary."

"Hate to disappoint you, but the traditional gift for the thirteenth anniversary is something made of lace."

"Aww. That's kinda dreamy. But I still want sapphires."

"Find something you like?" A stocky man with a shock of black hair Hannah guessed wasn't his real color approached them for the second time. They'd already told him they were merely browsing. His stance, arms akimbo, emanated impatience. Was this the man who'd blamed Archer for not risking life and limb to rescue his inventory?

"Thank you for your patience. We're just dreaming."

Hannah scanned the interior once again, continuing the search for clues that had begun even before they walked through the door.

Nothing jumped out at her, but she admired the sleek, minimalist decor that created the perfect backdrop for all that glittered.

She examined several framed engagement photos hanging on the wall behind the rings. One featured a couple standing on the store's second-floor balcony, gazing into each other's eyes. The woman's left hand, sporting a massive diamond, rested on the railing. Right above the wrought iron swag that looked like an *M*. Was it a clue?

"Such a beautiful store." Hannah extended her hand to the man. "I'm Hannah Prentiss, owner of the Hot Spot. I've seen you at chamber meetings, but we haven't actually met."

He took her hand, his demeanor seeming to soften a fraction. "Nicholas Adamo."

"I heard you had a fire a while back."

"We did." Unlike most salespeople, he seemed to be a man of few words.

"That must have been devastating. I'm so glad your building was saved."

He scoffed. "Lost half my inventory."

"I'm so sorry. It would be hard to bounce back after a loss like that. Thank goodness for insurance, right?"

He didn't make a sound, but the puckering of his face said it all. "Some of the pieces I lost were one of a kind. Irreplaceable." His hand tightened into a fist. "The fire department could have done more."

"They're usually so quick to respond. And thorough."

"They were. But—"

The door opened, and a young man walked in.

"Never mind." The jeweler strode away from them, calling a greeting to the young man. "Welcome in. What can I help you find today?"

Hannah and Lacy made a quick exit.

The moment the door closed behind them Lacy said, "You were baiting him."

"I wouldn't call that baiting. I was merely investigating."

"What will he think when he sees you walking down the street holding hands with the fire chief?"

"Maybe he'll think he shouldn't go implying to the public that the fire department isn't doing their job."

"Okay then." Lacy had apparently picked up on Hannah's irritation. "Moving on. Bakery?"

"I guess." Though she'd left things with Carrie on perfectly good terms on Saturday, she felt a little awkward at the idea of facing her again, considering all the speculation she'd been part of. What would Carrie think if she knew she'd been the topic of numerous conversations that involved her and poison? "But we're looking at the building itself, not the new employee."

"Right." Lacy, unhindered by the awkwardness Hannah felt, strode along the sidewalk.

Hannah stayed half a step behind her. Before they reached Sweet Caroline's, her phone buzzed. She slipped it out and glanced at the notification. A text from Liam. "Just a sec." She couldn't have asked for a better excuse to put off walking into the bakery. She slowed her steps, then stopped altogether as she read.

Two things: First, Colt's parents' Range Rover has been in the shop for a week. Second, got my test results back. I'm allergic to cardamom. I don't even know what that is.

"Lacy. Listen." Hannah read the message out loud.

Lacy laughed. "The poor guy. I've never even heard of a cardamom allergy."

"I know," Hannah agreed. "Here we were making Carrie out to be some crazy poisoner. I feel terrible." And yet she couldn't help but laugh. "Maybe someday, like decades from now, we'll all be good friends in a nursing home together, and I'll tell her about our wild suspicions."

"And she'll whack you with her cane, which you will fully deserve." The thought brought another wave of laughter for both of them.

"Get serious, Mrs. Minyard." Hannah wiped her eyes, then tried and failed to force her mouth into a stern line. "If we walk into the bakery laughing, she'll get paranoid."

"And think we were talking about her behind her back?" Lacy giggled. Exactly like she had twenty years ago when they'd stayed up all night sharing secrets and too much sugar. Finally, after a few deep breaths, she said, "I think I can do this."

Hannah stopped in front of the bakery window. "We need to study the outside first. We'll check for clues over by that corner." She pointed to the edge of the building where different-colored bricks overlapped. The spot her father had run into on his bike.

Lacy ran her fingertips along the mortar-filled spaces. "Nothing."

"Let's go in then."

"What are we looking for?" Lacy put her hand on the door handle.

"No clue, other than a clue."

"Funny."

"We do need dessert," Hannah pointed out. "The salads we had for lunch won't 'stick to our ribs,' as my grandma would have said. We need energy for the rest of the treasure hunt."

"Agreed."

The young woman behind the counter was not Carrie. She smiled. "Welcome to Sweet Caroline's. What can I get for you?"

"Thank you," Hannah said. "It might take us a moment to decide what we want."

"Take your time. I'll be right here when you're ready."

Lacy tapped Hannah's arm and pointed at a tray of cookies that resembled small elephant ear pastries. The cookies, which had been labeled simply *Caramel Palmiers* at the health fair, now had an additional descriptor. *Cardamom Caramel Palmiers.*

"Hannah!" The voice carried through the pass-through window, followed by Carrie's face. "Come back and see my latest creation."

The young women ushered Hannah and Lacy through an opening in the counter, and they walked through swinging double doors.

Carrie wore a bib apron and a hairnet. She gripped a piping bag with both hands. Hannah introduced her to Lacy, then gaped at the stunning four-tiered cake Carrie was working on. The elegant confection was frosted in ivory buttercream with green-stemmed pink roses covering the top tier. Carrie exchanged a few words of greeting with Lacy, then continued piping pink rosettes around the rim of the bottom layer. "I'm practicing. This is a trial run."

"This is a *practice* cake?" Hannah asked, not hiding her astonishment. "That's like Michelangelo saying the Sistine Chapel was a sketch."

Carrie laughed. "Thank you. I'm playing with ideas for my brother's wedding."

"That reminds me. Is your brother Derek Grayson?" Hannah asked.

Out of the corner of her eye, Hannah noticed Lacy's hand tightening on her purse strap until her knuckles whitened. What was that about?

Still piping, Carrie answered cheerfully, "Yes. I guess I should have mentioned that we have different last names."

Lacy cleared her throat. "He was in a calligraphy class I took a few years ago."

Carrie paused to meet Lacy's gaze. "I think I remember him talking about that." Her voice sounded strained. "He likes to try new things." She squeezed out another perfect rosette. "My future sister-in-law can't decide if she wants to go classic or non-traditional, so I'm showing her options. The next one will have square layers."

"What do you do with your practice cakes?" Lacy asked.

"I'm donating this one to an assisted living home. They're having a sweetheart dance tomorrow tonight. They're holding it before Valentine's Day so as not to interfere with the residents who have dates. Isn't that lovely?" She set down the piping bag and picked up one with a smaller hole in the tip. "This is their theme." She began to scroll flowing cursive words in mint green around the second layer.

Never stop dancing.

"That's beautiful."

"Thank you." Carrie straightened, rubbed her back, and stretched her neck from side to side. "I'm friends with one of the physical therapists who works there. She used to be a dance instructor, and she painted a mural on one of the walls in the therapy room that says, 'You don't stop dancing because you grow old. You grow old because you stop dancing.' I'm adopting it as a life philosophy."

"I like that."

Hannah was about to compliment Carrie's design one last time, but Lacy tugged her elbow and stepped toward the door, saying, "Thanks for your time, Carrie. We'll let you get back to it."

After they'd chosen their desserts and walked out of the bakery, Hannah took a final sweeping gaze of the pastel-painted room.

Not a single clue to Archer's mystery in sight. But a new mystery was five steps ahead of her on the way to the car.

"What was that about?" Hannah demanded when she caught up with Lacy.

"Derek Grayson. He was in the calligraphy class I took. It was only two nights, so I never even talked to him or paid attention to his work, but I remember the name because one lady said he should sign his name with a font from the Middle Ages because his name sounded like a hero in a Gothic novel."

Hannah hadn't told Lacy about Derek Grayson's interaction with Archer when he was working for her uncle. "That could be a coincidence. Lots of people know calligraphy." Though at the moment she couldn't think of anyone. "We're trying so hard to find clues that maybe we're seeing them where they don't exist. It's like they say—if you're a hammer, everything looks like a nail."

"'They' also say that when you're pregnant, you see pregnant women everywhere you go. It's true," Lacy admitted. "They were always there, but now I'm noticing them. Our antennae are up, so we'll see possible clues we wouldn't have noticed otherwise."

"I suppose." She should be excited at the possibility that this could point to Carrie's stepbrother being the one sending the photos, but she had put all suspicion of Carrie aside and didn't want to dig it up again. Besides, what could possibly be Derek's motive? Still, it seemed more than a coincidence. She pulled her sleeve back and looked at her watch. "I've got an hour. The Greensboro Club won't open until four, but we could drive out there and look around even though it's closed. What time do you need to be home?"

Lacy covered a yawn. "Nap time is between two and three, so that's perfect timing."

"If you're sure you're up for it. I don't want you getting overtired."

"Thank you, Mother," Lacy teased. "I'm fine. Let's do this."

As they drove out of town, Lacy looked up the club's website and read the history out loud. "'The Greensboro Club first opened its doors in May of 1929. After a successful summer that saw patrons driving all the way from Bowling Green to savor the Club's slow-roasted pork simmered in cherries and Kentucky Butter Cake, the market crash in September of that year forced the doors to close for another three years. Since reopening in 1933, the Greensboro has changed hands only twice.'"

Rather than focusing on Archer's mystery, Hannah let herself imagine Micah Benton and Evangeline Haley dressing up for dinner at the Greensboro. She could imagine Evangeline slipping into a mid-calf velvet dress, midnight blue, with rhinestone buttons all the way up the front. Strappy shoes, pearls, and a little hat that sat at a jaunty angle.

She wished she'd seen a picture of Micah so she could easily picture him as well. Perhaps he'd been tall and dark-haired, with a thin Clark Gable mustache, or maybe he'd descended from one of the Scotch-Irish families that had settled in the area in the 1800s. Broad-shouldered, muscular, with reddish-blond hair. Either way, he'd wear a tailored suit. Plaid or pinstriped.

The supper club would be lit by wall sconces and candlelight. White linen tablecloths, plush carpet on the floor. They'd be greeted at the door by a hostess in a sleek satin gown, her hair perfectly coiffed like Irene Dunne or Carole Lombard. Waiters would be dressed in black waistcoats with starched white shirts. And all of that would simply feed into the ambiance that made them gaze into each other's eyes late into the evening.

"...connection to the Greensboro?"

Hannah snapped back to the present. She'd watched way too many old black-and-white movies with her dad. All fodder for an overactive imagination. "Sorry. What?"

Lacy, who knew her well, grinned. "Does Archer have any connection to the Greensboro Club?"

"He and Bryn ate there. And Stan Carlson used to be a busboy at the club back in high school. Nothing that would lead to a...We need another word for suspect, something that allows for the possibility of this being all for fun. What do we call the person who's sending the pictures if he or she is not a suspect?"

Lacy was quiet for a moment. "Photographer?"

Hannah pressed the brake pedal, slowing the car as she turned to Lacy. "Why hasn't anyone ever thought of that angle? The photos are artistic. They could have been taken on a good phone, I suppose, but the lighting and the angles suggest to me that the person who took them knew something about photography." She put on her turn signal as they approached the sign for the Greensboro Club. "Once again, we might be looking in the wrong place."

Chapter Twenty-Nine

Blackberry Valley
February 23, 1931

She'd heard the clang of the fire bell. Seen the trucks rushing past the store. Smelled the smoke. It only took minutes for word to spread of the barn fire outside of town. Fortunately, the owners had gotten all their livestock out of the barn. Once she knew no one was hurt, Evangeline could turn her focus to how the emergency affected her. She'd have to meet with Mr. Fletcher Arnett by herself.

For the second time in a week, she left the store on shaky legs. Her fear came from the fact that she had no idea whether this man knew her father or Micah's. If she asked him to keep their meeting confidential, it could trigger more questions than she wanted to answer. So she'd pretend she was simply curious about the history of the land her family had lived on for ten years.

The six-block walk used up some of her nervous energy. She'd never paid attention to the small clapboard house nestled in a grove of pines. The sidewalk was swept free of the leaves that littered the tiny yard. Though she'd met a Mrs. Arnett, a once-a-month customer who had to be in her eighties if not older, she'd never heard of Fletcher Arnett. Was he Mrs. Arnett's husband? Son? Brother? Whoever he was, he kept to himself.

After a slow, deep breath, she knocked on the door, picturing a grizzly old character annoyed by her intrusion. And yet he had agreed to meet with them.

The door swung open, and the man who stood in front of her was anything but grizzly. Maybe mid-forties, and so tall he'd have to stoop to walk out his own front door. Red hair, broad shoulders. "Miss Haley, come in." A hint of brogue gave his words a lilt. "I heard the fire alarm and thought our meeting might be off."

"Micah is on the call, but since you set aside time for us, I thought I'd come alone."

"Wonderful. I'm so glad Micah found me. I only get back to the valley to see Nana every couple of months."

Nana. His grandmother. Fletcher no longer lived in town. That explained why she'd never heard of him.

As if on cue, the older woman stepped out from behind a curtain with a pot of tea. Mr. Arnett ushered Evangeline to a small, scarred table pushed against a wall in the miniscule kitchen.

"I bet you want to know about the ring that caused the feud," Mrs. Arnett said in a Scottish brogue thick as honey. Her lone sentence tossed all of Evangeline's lead-in statements out the window.

She decided to be honest. "Well, yes, I do."

"It came from Scotland," Mrs. Arnett said. "On the same boat that brought me and my late husband here back in '72. It was Linus Moss's grandmother's wedding ring. Such a beautiful piece."

"What did it look like?"

Mrs. Arnett squinted slightly, as if she were studying Evangeline. "You haven't seen it?"

"No!" Evangeline's spine straightened with defensiveness. She was so tired of everyone's opinions and speculations. "It was *stolen.*"

The thin line formed by the frail woman's lips conveyed doubt. Yet after a moment she gave a hint of a smile, as if willing to humor Evangeline's denial. "The stone was the clear blue-green of the fairy pools on the Isle of Skye, though I heard tell it likely came from Ceylon. It was set between two silver thistles." She brought her gnarled hands toward each other to demonstrate.

"It sounds stunning." Evangeline looked at Mr. Arnett. "Micah said you and Linus were childhood friends, and you used to pretend you were pirates hunting for buried treasure."

"Oh, aye. We did. Guess you could say we never grew out of it. I was the one who buried the ring for him beneath the chinkapin oak once the rains stopped that spring he left for the mine."

Evangeline's heart skipped a beat. She knew that tree, massive and old, its lowest branches far above her head, with leaves that looked more like chestnut than oak. It was not the tree Linus Moss had drawn on his map.

Mr. Arnett had made a mistake.

"Chinkapin? You buried it under the chinkapin?"

"Yes ma'am. Linus left in a rush after he got hired at the mine. He didn't have a chance to hide it when no one was looking. He said I was the only one he trusted with it. He wanted it put where none of his greedy kin could find it before he returned."

Evangeline nodded slowly, her thoughts in a daze. "Th-thank you. Both of you. I know it's rude of me, but I really must run. Thank you for the offer of tea. I hope to come back sometime for a longer visit. Thank you again." With that, she stood and darted toward the door with one thought on her mind.

She had to find Micah.

She had to tell him their fathers had dug beneath the wrong tree, and perhaps the rift between their families could be healed after all.

Chapter Thirty

Two days. Hannah sipped her second cup of coffee on Thursday morning as she watched the sun climb above the trees. She'd prayed over her to-do list, then added three more things. She made an attempt at numbering things in order of importance, but they were all important. Every single thing needed to be done by eleven o'clock on Saturday morning. Well, except for the things at the bottom of the page. *Ask Dad about Mike Durham. Ask Archer about St. Anthony's.*

Though not time-sensitive, she could cross one of those off right now. She tapped her father's number, and he answered before she heard it ring. "Good morning, darling daughter."

"Good morning, dearest dad. I have a question. What do you know about Mike Durham? Have you ever heard him say anything negative about Archer or Bryn?"

"Not about Bryn personally, but certainly about the Revitalize Committee."

"Do you have his phone number?"

"Sure do. I'll text it to you. Why do you want it?"

"He's on Archer's list of people who may have sent the photos. He and Archer had a bit of a confrontation, and it might not go too well if Archer talks to him directly. I thought I'd try."

"I see."

The contact information popped up on her screen. "Got it. Thanks."

"Anything for my girl."

Hannah stared at her phone. From what Archer had said, Mike Durham didn't respond well to anything that could sound like an accusation. She'd have to tread lightly. She held her breath as she tapped on the number.

"Greetings from sunny Green Valley. This is Mike. To whom do I have the pleasure of speaking?"

The cheerful voice did not sound at all like the man she'd heard raising complaints at the town meeting. And Green Valley?

"Mr. Durham, this is Hannah Prentiss."

"The Hot Spot lady. What can I do for you?"

"Well, first of all, how long have you been in Arizona?"

"Since the first of October."

Long before the first snow. And there was snow in at least two of the photographs.

"The wife didn't want to miss the fall colors in Blackberry Valley, but my arthritis doesn't like the cold. It's seventy-three and sunny here today. What's the weather like there?"

"In the thirties and cloudy."

Mike shuddered audibly. "That sounds miserable. Is there anything I can help you with?"

"Actually, no," Hannah said, realizing it was the truth. "I had a question, but since you're out of state, it really doesn't pertain to you. I'm sorry to have bothered you. I'll let you get back to that sunshine."

"All right. Let me know if that changes," Mike offered. They said goodbye and ended the call.

Hannah stared at the darkened screen of her phone. Another dead end. She and Lacy had struck out at the Greensboro Club and the Catholic church. They'd nosed around the supper club until one of the cooks walked out the back door and asked what they were doing. He'd only worked there two weeks, so he couldn't answer any of their questions.

A bored-looking secretary had given them a tour of St. Anthony's. They'd heard about the history of the cross-shaped building and admired the craftsmanship of the carved altar and intricate stained glass, but none of it had shed any light on Archer's mystery.

Hannah rubbed her eyes. She had a tendency toward all-or-nothing thinking. Being able to shut out distractions and concentrate on a single task or goal had served her well in college and in attaining her dream of owning her own restaurant. But in the past week and a half, she'd been a bit too "all" when it came to solving a mystery that had nothing to do with her. There was a reason she'd dubbed it Archer's mystery. Because it was *his*. He would eventually solve it, and then she'd have all the answers to all the questions that had preoccupied her mind. Today was the day to give it up and put her "all" into the list of details that still needed to be wrapped up before Raquel's birthday party and Saturday night's dinner.

Raquel. A jab of guilt wound through her thoughts. Though she'd asked her every day how she was doing, they hadn't had a real conversation since Monday. She printed *Raquel* at the top of the notebook page. She'd text and see if Raquel had time to meet at Jump Start for a few minutes before work.

She wouldn't give up on trying to uncover Evangeline and Micah's story, but nothing about that was time sensitive. She could put it on a shelf and pick it up after Saturday. It would give her something fun to do next week when Liam was gone.

Once again, the reminder that she'd be alone on Valentine's Day vied for her attention. *"Alone" with thirty-some birthday party guests and a constant flow of patrons for the dinner.* The irony almost made her smile.

In truth, she'd been without a date for many, many Valentine's Days—usually working, sometimes spending it with friends. And she'd never minded. But that was before she had Liam.

She had Liam. That was the thought she needed to focus on. She finished the last of her coffee, sent a text to Raquel, and marched toward the shower to wash away every trace of self-pity.

After spending a bit more time on her hair and makeup than usual, she headed downstairs. Sitting in her office, she crossed off the fourth thing on her list and powered on to the next. But the ring of her desk phone halted her momentum.

She scooped up the landline. "The Hot Spot. This is Hannah. How may I help you?"

"Hi, Hannah. This is Amethyst from the historical society. Do you have a minute?"

"I do. What's up?"

"I found something while I was filing stuff. It wasn't in the folder of love letters. I found a file for the Haley Mercantile. It was mostly old ledgers and order forms and things like that. But in the back of a book of inventory lists I found something I think you'll want to see."

Hannah could ask her to read it to her, but she gathered that Amethyst wanted to keep her in suspense. Whatever it was, she could spare a few minutes. "I'll be there in five."

When Hannah stepped into the library, she found Amethyst standing in the doorway of the historical society room, bouncing on her heels.

Phyllis stood behind her, hands folded and pressed against her chest. "I can't wait to see your face when you read this."

Amethyst stepped over to the counter and picked up a book with a black cover and dark red binding. She opened it and showed Hannah rows and columns of the products Haley Mercantile would have stocked. "I almost put this back in the file. I was flipping through the pages because I love looking at prices from a long time ago. So I was seeing things like how you could buy a loaf of bread for twelve cents, eggs for fifteen cents, and a whole chicken for thirty-five cents."

Phyllis, standing behind Amethyst, swept her gaze toward the ceiling. Hannah smiled. *Patience.*

"Then, way at the back, there's something that reads like a diary." Amethyst turned a chunk of pages at once and held the book out to Hannah. "Here."

Hannah read the words on the open page.

Tonight was the worst night of my life. No need for secrecy anymore. No more sneaking around giddily pretending we are Romeo and Juliet. The truth is out, and all of my worst fears have come to pass. I should have asked Fletcher Arnett and his grandmother not to say anything to anyone. In a town where gossip spreads like chickweed and takes root like crabgrass, I should have begged them to keep silent.

Minutes after we met at the gazebo, Micah's father showed up. With a gun. Right behind him was Pa. First time they've been that close together in a decade. Mr. Benton screamed at me. Pa screamed at Micah, then turned his anger on me, accusing me of stepping on his heart and crushing it. I started to tell them what I'd learned from Fletcher, but Micah squeezed my arm. Now I see. If we'd told them, one of them might have stolen it for real this time.

Isaiah is going to take over the store. Pa gave me two days to pack up and get out. My bag is already packed. I don't know where I'll go, but I'm leaving Blackberry Valley. I don't care about the ring. I don't care about ending the feud. Our fathers can take their mistrust and hatred to their graves.

But my heart is shattered at the thought of never seeing my mother again. How I longed to bring light back to her eyes. So many times since we started this quest, I have imagined her reunion with Thelma Benton. What joy it would have brought them to see their husbands reconciled.

The last thing Micah whispered in my ear was, "I'll come for you." Will he? Will he be strong enough to turn his back on his family? Was he just pretending to submit to his father tonight? Does he really love

The rest of the page was empty. "Wait. It ends there?" Hannah looked up at the women who were staring at her, both grinning.

"Turn the page," Phyllis said.

Hannah held her breath as she turned to the next page. Only two lines. And a picture.

Yesterday was the worst day of my life. Today was absolutely the very best. We found the ring! Tomorrow, we end the feud.

Beneath the words was a pencil sketch of the ring. Unlike the others, this one was drawn with colored pencils and not as artistically done. Perhaps Evangeline had drawn it. A round stone, shaded in blue and green, in a filagree setting. Or…

Hannah gasped then locked eyes with Phyllis and then Amethyst. “Is that what I think it is?”

Both women, even the one aged almost eighty, were now bouncing on their heels.

“It’s been torture, but we waited until you got here,” Phyllis whispered to Hannah as they stood in the doorway watching Amethyst practically run to the front of the library.

“Thank you. I wouldn’t have missed this for the world.” Her words came out as breathless as she felt as Amethyst pivoted and disappeared behind a shelf of books.

In moments, she popped out again, holding Evangeline’s hand and practically dragging her across the floor. Evangeline’s expression was a mixture of confusion and amusement. “What in the world is going on?” she asked as they both skidded to a stop.

“Come see.” Amethyst tugged on her hand, and Phyllis and Hannah parted to let them through.

“Let’s give her a little background first,” Hannah interjected as Amethyst picked up the book.

Amethyst groaned.

Talking as fast as she could while still making her words intelligible, Hannah caught Evangeline up to speed on all they'd learned about Evangeline and Micah. Then she nodded to Amethyst, who handed over the book, open to the worst day of the other Evangeline's life.

Evangeline's expression changed from confusion to empathy and back to confusion. "The poor girl. Why did she stop in the middle of a sentence?"

In unison, three voices said, "Turn the page!"

Evangeline gasped. Her right hand flew to her mouth, then she slowly lowered it and rested it next to the page. Next to the exact replica of the blue-green stone held by silver thistles on her ring finger.

"Where did you get your ring?" Amethyst asked.

"It was in my mother's jewelry box when she died. I don't remember ever seeing her wear it. I asked my father, and he called it an old piece of junk. I always thought he knew something about it, but wouldn't tell me."

"That's no piece of junk." Phyllis laid a hand on Evangeline's shoulder. "I'm going to call Kathryn Hobart again."

"Who's that?"

"She's the one who donated the letters in the Haley file, where we found the map and the other drawings. I left a message for her days ago, but she didn't return my call." Phyllis stepped behind the counter and paged through a book until she found what she was looking for, then tapped the number into the phone on the desk.

They waited in silence through three rings and then a click, followed by a recording.

"Hi, Kathryn, this is Phyllis Taft from the Blackberry Valley Historical Society. I have some questions I'd like to ask you about the old letters you donated before you moved. I'm wondering if you are related to either Evangeline Haley or Micah Benton. We're trying to unravel a mystery here, and you might be the very person who has all the answers. Please call me as soon as you can."

Chapter Thirty-One

TWO MORE. R YESTERDAY. U TODAY. SO IT'S "YOU OWE ME A MILL. WHY ARE YOU…?" ARCHER HAS NO CLUE.

Just when she'd cleared her brain to focus on everything she needed to accomplish and oversee in the next two days, a text from Liam reeled Hannah back in. He'd attached images of the photos to his message. She could have ignored it, shelved it until Sunday, if not for the location of the *R*.

It was a photograph of the curved iron side of a bench in front of the Hot Spot.

She'd found the bench in a pile of debris behind the building after she'd bought it. Her father had replaced the rotting wood then sanded and repainted the beautifully curved wrought iron. Was the location—the restaurant or the original firehouse—a clue? Was Liam right that the letters spelled out "You owe me a mill. Why are you…?" Or were they still, like she'd thought when she and Lacy had given up on the treasure hunt, completely off track?

She pulled out her desk chair, sat, and examined the second photo. This one was different than the others. Not as sharply focused. Or rather, it was a reflection. Part of a neon sign, taken at night, reflected in a window. She enlarged it and brought it closer to her face. Familiar. Someplace on Main Street. When it hit her, she laughed. "It's not a 'U'! It's a 'W'!" While the distorted image did make the second half of the letter appear like a double-image reflection, enlarging it showed the truth.

Just to be sure, she clicked to the website. There it was, right below a logo of a stylized vintage camera. It was the last letter in the top line of the sign on the window in front of ValleyView Photography.

Which completely wrecked the "You owe me a mill. Why are you..." hypothesis. But immediately brought Lacy's brilliant comment to mind.

What do we call the person who's sending the pictures? A photographer.

Her gaze landed on the list on her desk she'd abandoned hours before when Amethyst had called. *Raquel* jumped out at her. She'd be here in a few minutes, and Hannah needed to get her head back in the game. Not the Archer mystery game or the "How did one Evangeline get the other Evangeline's ring" game. And certainly not the mind-boggling "How do the two connect?" game.

Lord, help me to focus, to be fully present with Raquel. Help me be an attentive listener and an encourager or an empathizer, whichever she needs.

She sent a short text to Liam: IT'S NOT A U. IT'S A W. TALK TONIGHT. Then she set her phone on the desk, stood, and walked out of her office, closing the door and leaving behind all the questions.

For about ten seconds.

Raquel, still wearing her coat, was holding the front door open for Colt Walker.

What was he doing here? She couldn't think of another time he'd come to the restaurant alone when they weren't open. He was in uniform. Were they due for an inspection? Was he going to confess to sending the pictures?

Raquel motioned him toward a table. When she met Hannah in the middle of the room, she whispered, "He wants to talk to you. Alone."

"That's odd." It was also odd to see Colt without a smile on his face. "Hi, Colt. How can I help you?"

Colt set his hat on the table. "Liam said I should talk to you. My car alarm went off a little after three o'clock this morning. When I got to the window, there was an envelope under my windshield wiper, and a Range Rover almost identical to my parents' pulling away from the curb. It was right under the streetlight, so I got a good look at it. It definitely wasn't my parents,' and there was a bumper sticker on the back that said 'Jump-start your day at Jump Start Coffee.'"

"Really? Jack Delaney said there weren't any bumper stickers on the vehicle when he saw it. How many orange Range Rovers can there be in one town? But it must be the same one if you got an envelope," Hannah reasoned out loud. "Maybe we need to start casing the town. It shouldn't be that hard to track down."

Colt picked up his hat again, fiddling with it as if he were trying to decide what he wanted to say next. "I did. It was parked behind Jump Start. Where the employees park."

"Oh. That does narrow it down." She pulled out a chair and motioned for him to have a seat. "Who works there that would be delivering pictures to Archer? It must be someone who's close enough to him to know who his closest friends and family are."

"It was in Zane's parking space. The one with his name on it."

"Oh." *Oh.* "I've never seen him drive an orange SUV. Maybe he lets some of the other employees park there at times. But who else knows Archer that well?"

"Maybe they don't. Maybe someone has been stalking him."

"That is a possibility." Though she didn't want it to be the case.

"Archer stops at Jump Start almost every morning. I'm sure he's made connections with most of the employees." Colt shrugged his shoulders. "Liam said you should talk to Jacob."

"I will. Though I can't imagine Zane being behind this. Unless—maybe it's part of a promo for Jump Start. He and I sometimes send each other fun promotional ideas we see online." She pressed her lips together, thinking. "I'll talk to Jacob and see if the car belongs to Zane. And then I'll talk to Zane."

As Colt turned to leave, she said, "I don't think I saw your name on the reservation list for our Valentine's Day dinner. I'm sure there's some lucky girl just waiting to be asked."

"Nah. I'm taking a sabbatical from dating. Too much drama. But I do have a date."

"I'm not sure I follow."

"I'm taking my grandma out for dinner." His smile seemed to say there was more to the story, but she didn't ask.

"That's so sweet."

"Yeah. I guess." He waved, then walked out.

Hannah turned around, once again making an attempt to leave the questions behind. The next few minutes belonged to Raquel.

Hannah brought two mugs of coffee and a plate of heart-shaped cookies to the corner booth.

Raquel thanked her, adding, "It feels weird to have you waiting on me."

"You deserve to be pampered once in a while. And we're both helping Jacob by trying out his new sugar cookie recipe. I plan to wrap them in red netting and put one at each place."

"Love it." Raquel blew on her coffee, then leaned in. "Tell me everything. Do you know who's sending the pictures yet?"

"No. It gets more confusing by the day. But I didn't ask you here to talk about that. I want to know how you and Marshall are doing."

"We're...doing. He's still wavering, and I'm trying to enjoy every minute we're together. We've had some good talks. Indianapolis is a decent halfway point, so we've been looking at all the things we can do if we meet there on Sundays. He's been in communication with the guy who wants to hire him, and it looks like they'd want five restaurant reviews each week, so it's possible he could take Mondays off since lots of restaurants are closed anyway." Raquel took a sip of the coffee. "Perks of being in the same business, I guess. How are you and Liam?"

"We're good. Reading some of the notes between Evangeline and Micah has given me a different perspective. I don't know how long they had to keep their relationship a secret, but I get the impression they were focused on treasuring the time they could be together rather than whining about how little time that was. I, on the other hand, seem to lean toward whining."

"You and me both."

"It's the unknown that makes it hard, isn't it?"

"Definitely. But back to my original question. Tell me everything about Archer and Evangeline and Micah."

Grateful for the subject change, Hannah started with the good news, filling in her friend about the things Stan and Stephanie had found and the call from Amethyst that had led to Evangeline's ring.

"That's so cool! So our favorite librarian Evangeline has to be related to 'Evangeline my Valentine,' right?"

"Sure looks like it. Phyllis is trying to get in contact with the lady who donated the letters to the historical society. Hopefully she'll have some answers."

"Can't wait to hear how that turns out." Raquel eyed the antique firehouse clock. "Give me the summary on the Archer story."

Hannah did, then picked up her cup of coffee. "Do you happen to know if anyone who works at Jump Start drives an orange SUV?"

"Sure do. Zane just bought it. I love the color. It's called Madagascar Orange. Why?"

"Oh, Colt mentioned seeing it." Hannah stared at the door to the kitchen. She'd finally put one piece in the puzzle. Now to see if she could put the whole thing together.

Raquel stood. "Time to work."

Hannah nodded, but talking to Jacob was the next thing on her to-do list. Taking both empty cups, she walked toward the kitchen and through the swinging doors.

"Something smells scrumptious."

"Tortilla soup. Want a taste?" Jacob grabbed a soup cup without waiting for her answer. He filled the cup then garnished it with tortilla strips and sour cream. "Tell me if it needs anything."

She took a bite. And closed her eyes. With so many restaurants shorthanded, how was it that she had ended up with a five-star chef who could easily have his pick of positions at any big-city restaurant? "Perfect. This will be a hit."

"Thanks."

She ran her fingertip along the handle of the cup she'd just set down. "The coffee was especially good today. Are you picking up some secrets from your brother?"

Jacob snorted. "Where do you think my little bro learned everything he knows? I put myself through college working for one of the most acclaimed baristas in the world."

Hannah laughed. "Sorry. I should have known better. Hey, I heard he bought a new car."

"Yeah. It's a pretty sweet ride."

"How long has he had it?"

"About a week."

"Where'd he get it?"

Jacob tipped his head to one side. "Online. Why? Are you car shopping?"

"No. Just curious."

"Uh-huh." Jacob put both hands on the stainless-steel table and raised an eyebrow at her. "I'm more than a pretty face, you know. You were fishing. What aren't you saying?"

"Nothing. Just wondering where he bought it." She ate another spoonful of soup. "This is really, really good." She picked it up. "Think I'll savor it in my office. Thanks." She strode toward the door, once again leaving questions behind. Only this time, they were Jacob's.

Chapter Thirty-Two

Blackberry Valley
March 3, 1931

Evangeline scurried down the back steps, almost tripping in her hurry to open the door. The loud knock had made her jump and drop an earring before she realized she had no need to be afraid. She opened the door, letting in a blast of March air. And Micah.

"Come in, Micah James Benton!" she yelled, embracing the freedom that was soon to be theirs.

Micah's deep laugh echoed off the high ceiling in the storeroom. "Happy to, Evangeline Haley!" He closed the door behind him, picked her up, and swung her around in a tight circle. When he set her down, he stared at her for the longest time.

She could get lost in those sky-blue eyes. "Are you ready for this?"

"Couldn't be readier."

"How did you get your father to agree to it?"

"I told him it was finally time to settle the score. I said I had definitive evidence about what happened to the ring."

"Perfect. I told my pa I had some words to say to him face-to-face before I moved out."

"That's my brilliant girl." Micah shrugged out of his coat and hung it on the hook by the door. Resting his hands on her shoulders, he bent and pressed his lips to hers. "I've imagined this moment so many times in the past few months. In the past ten years, actually. Every time I've pictured this moment, it was in a beautiful setting with candlelight and music playing, but I just now realized that wherever we are together is beautiful."

To her shock, he lowered his hands, put one in his pocket, and dropped to one knee. When he opened his hand, his palm sparkled with a stone the color of the blue-green fairy pools on the Isle of Skye, nestled in its thistle setting. "I will make payments on this to our fathers for the rest of my life if need be, but this ring belongs to us. To you. Forever. Evangeline Adelaide Haley, will you marry me?"

Over a sob that tightened her throat and blurred her vision, Evangeline managed to squeeze out an emphatic "Yes!"

Another knock, this one at the front door, interrupted the magic.

Hand-in-hand, they walked to the door. To end a feud and begin a life. Together.

Chapter Thirty-Three

"Sorry. I had every intention of coming alone," Liam whispered into Hannah's hair on Thursday night. He squeezed her hand before sliding into a booth. Archer, appearing less scraggly than he had in days, took the bench across from him.

Hannah could have let it irritate her, but she chose to laugh it off. There were things she needed to tell both of them anyway.

Raquel brought their waters and asked if they were ready to order. "I highly recommend the tortilla soup. It's to die for."

"If I have to die, I'd rather it be in the line of duty, but I'll settle for soup." Archer winked at her.

Brow furrowing, Raquel studied him. "What's changed?"

"The guys made him trim the scruff." Liam smirked at Archer. "They chased him with a razor and threatened to tie him down and do it for him."

Until recently, Hannah had never seen Archer with a beard. Now that it was neatly trimmed, she thought it suited him. "But something else is different," Hannah said, sliding in next to Liam. "You just said something funny."

"I'm a funny guy."

"Not lately." Hannah and Raquel spoke in unison.

"Wow. Have you guys been rehearsing how to hurt my feelings?" He took off his jacket. "Okay. The truth?" He aimed the words at Raquel. "I'm in a good mood because it's almost your birthday."

Raquel didn't miss a beat. "While I'd love to believe you're ecstatic that I'm turning a quarter of a century old, I'm pretty sure it's actually because you're assuming a certain someone will show up."

His smile was what Hannah could only label hopeful. "I'm right, right?"

Raquel held up her hands. "I don't know. I haven't had any communication with her either."

"I might be the last person she wants to see on Valentine's Day, but she wouldn't miss your birthday. And when she shows up, I'm going to be ready. Flowers, chocolate, and lots and lots of groveling."

Hannah laughed. "And I'm capturing every second of it on video. But you can't seriously think that her being upset with you means she doesn't want to see you ever again."

"She hung up on me." That was all it took to bring back his gloom. Archer rested his elbow on the table and his chin in his hand. "And she could have called. She might not have phone service in the cabin, but she has a car and could get to her grandparents' place to call from there. She's not in the middle of Antarctica or anything."

No one answered. There was nothing to say. Hannah didn't voice the concerns she'd had since receiving a text from the Blessings & Bliss lady this morning. DON'T THINK I'LL BE ABLE TO DELIVER THE BASKET TODAY. SO SORRY. SALT TRUCKS ARE OUT, SO HOPEFULLY THE ICE WILL BE MELTED AND ROADS CLEAR BY MORNING. Would Bryn make it home by Saturday?

After a minute of silence, Liam said, "I'll have a cup of soup and the Five Alarm."

"Same," Archer said on a pitiful sigh.

Hannah exchanged a look of shared empathy with Raquel. "I'll take a bowl of the soup. Thanks, Raquel." She stared at Archer, wondering if the mention of Zane's new Range Rover would distract him from thoughts of Bryn—or send him down a dark path of wondering who was out to get him. When she couldn't think of anything else to say, she forged ahead. "I suppose Cole told you about Zane's SUV."

Archer nodded. "Did you talk to Zane?"

"No. We're playing phone tag. I'm sure he turns in early since he has to be up before the sun, so I'll try again tomorrow. Jacob said he just got the Range Rover a couple of days ago."

Archer ran a hand over his newly trimmed beard. "So Zane didn't own it when it showed up here, but he did own it when it showed up at Colt's place. That doesn't make sense."

"Nothing about this has made sense so far," Liam pointed out.

"I know Zane, but not that well," Archer said. "We've never hung out in the same circles or had anything to do with each other outside of the coffee shop. I can't think of any reason why he'd be pulling some kind of practical joke on me or sending me on a treasure hunt."

"What about anyone else working there?" Hannah asked. "Any girls who thought you were in love with them?" Somebody had to bring a bit of humor into the situation. "Anyone who bought a dress to wear for you?"

Archer fixed a baleful glare on her. "I'm sure there are many of them."

"Okay then. Let's table that for now. I have another theory. Actually, it's Lacy's. The photos are kind of artsy. Lacy suggested they might be the work of a professional. And then yesterday's photo was taken at ValleyView Photography."

"It was?" Archer's lips pressed into a hard line.

"You didn't know that?" As soon as the words were out of her mouth, she realized that of course he hadn't. She hadn't said that in her text to Liam. She'd only corrected their missed guess on the letter.

Archer picked up his jacket, pulled out the ever-present envelope that was fatter than the last time Hannah had seen it, and studied the latest photo. A muscle in his jaw tightened.

Liam took the picture out of Archer's hand. "What don't I know? I can't think of a thing that would connect you to this place. The city hired Wes Reid to take some candid shots at the department last summer. Did you complain that he got your bad side or something?"

He was trying to make light of it, Hannah knew, but Liam wasn't doing any better at it than she'd done. Months ago, she'd overheard Raquel and Bryn talking about the owner of the ValleyView studio. She hadn't heard much, but she got the impression Bryn wanted nothing to do with the man.

"I wasn't in any of those pictures. Intentionally."

"Your intention?" Hannah asked. "Or his?"

"Both. We have an unspoken mutual understanding to stay as far away from each other as possible, so I volunteered to speak at a junior high assembly that day. Pretty sure I wouldn't have ended up in any of those shots anyway." Archer crumpled his napkin in his hand. "He and Bryn were engaged once."

"What?" Liam dropped the photo onto the table. "How is it I never heard that?"

"Because I never wanted to hear the guy's name. I certainly didn't want to talk about it." He tossed the napkin in the air and caught it. "I confess, there might have been a little jealousy involved."

"But I heard Bryn talking about Wes once," Liam said. "It sure didn't sound like you had any reason to think he was a threat."

Except for the fact that he very well could be the one sending the pictures.

"I want to believe that. But *he* jilted *her.* Two weeks before their wedding. I met her about six months after the breakup. As far as a lot of people are concerned—him included—I'm probably the rebound guy." Archer dropped the napkin onto the table. "A few months after we started going out, he called her. Said he missed her. She hung up on him and told me all about it. I thought he'd give up after that. But what if these pictures are some kind of taunt? Maybe he heard we had a fight and he knows she's vulnerable. What if—"

"Stop that!"

The words came from the next booth. Raquel straightened, washcloth in hand, from where she'd been cleaning up after a family with two toddlers. "You are not going down that path, Archer Lestrade. Bryn loves you. Even if she didn't, she would never, ever go back to Wes, no matter what he said or did. So get that thought out of your head right now." She poked him hard in the shoulder. "There is no way she's ditching you over some dumb thing you did or didn't do. Think of the history you have. I know she wrote you mushy texts every single day. Go back and read them." She propped her fists on her hips and glared at him, waiting for a response.

Archer's shoulders sagged. "I hope you're right, but—"

"I am right. And that's that."

Elaine approached their table, menus in one hand, coffee carafe in the other. "Sorry to interrupt, but you've got a three-top, Raquel."

"Okay. Thanks. You stop talking nonsense, Mr. Lestrade." Raquel shook her finger at Archer, pivoted on her heel, and hurried away.

Elaine topped off Archer's and Liam's cups, then nudged Hannah. "I know you're crazy busy, but the guy I'm renting that pasture to is going to be moving one of his bulls out there, so tomorrow's our only safe window if you want to poke around."

Now that they knew Evangeline and Micah had found the ring, going out to the tree didn't seem as important. Yet she was curious about the headstone. It could be Evangeline's or Micah's. She eyed Liam. He still hadn't told her what time he was leaving on Saturday, but she knew their time together was limited. Especially since he probably had to work the following day.

Liam smiled back with that look in his eyes she wanted to think he reserved just for her. "If we go early enough, that should work. Is nine too early?" He addressed the question to Elaine.

"That works. I can be done with chores by then."

Liam slid his arm around Hannah's shoulders. "It's a date then."

Hannah suppressed a laugh. She might not have a date for Valentine's Day, but she would for Valentine's Eve. Just her and Liam. And Elaine.

"Who's up for a date in a cow pasture?" Liam picked up Hannah's jacket from the arm of her couch.

"You sure know how to treat a girl."

"It comes natural with a girl like you."

Hannah groaned at his sappy answer, but it only made her smile wider. He held out her jacket for her to slip into.

As they walked to his Jeep, she said, "I love how you spoil me."

"My pleasure, ma'am."

They'd planned enough time to stop for coffee—and maybe a few questions—before heading out to King Farm. Instead of parking in front of Jump Start, Liam drove behind the building. The orange car with the bumper sticker was parked near the back door. In the space with Zane's name on it.

Once inside, Hannah looked around for any signs of a new marketing plan. Maybe there was an ongoing contest they hadn't heard about yet. But there were no black-and-white photographs or posters or anything that would hint at a link to Archer's mystery.

When they reached the head of the line, Zane greeted them with a smile as always. "Any breakthroughs on the photo mystery yet?"

"Funny you should ask," Liam said. "Can we talk in private for a minute?"

Zane's expression morphed into one of concern. "Sure."

"We'd also like two coffees to go." Liam took out his wallet. "One black, and a caramel macchiato."

Zane rang up the order, then called to the young woman bagging doughnuts at the other end of the counter and asked her to watch the register for a bit. He motioned Liam and Hannah to an unoccupied corner table. "I'll join you in a sec."

Hannah and Liam sat next to each other.

Zane brought their drinks and sat across from them. "How can I help?"

"At least two of the envelopes containing photographs were delivered in your new car. We understand you've only had it for a few days, so it seems likely the previous owner was driving it the first time."

Zane nodded. "Interesting. I had no idea she was the one who—"

"She?" Hannah jumped in. "She who?"

"Carrie Moore."

Chapter Thirty-Four

"*Carrie Moore*?" Liam and Hannah echoed in unison.

"Yes. I've known her for years. She recently started working at the bakery." Zane stared at Hannah. "Haven't you met her yet?"

Hannah simply nodded, too surprised to utter a word.

"So she's been out to get Archer this whole time," Liam muttered.

Zane gave an almost imperceptible jerk backward. "Out to get him? I doubt it was personal. Pretty sure she was just doing her job."

"Her job? What does delivering photographs have to do with baking?" Liam waved a hand as if trying to swipe away the confusion. "Start from the beginning. Tell us what you know."

"Carrie's brother Derek started a courier service a few weeks ago. Unfortunately, right after he got his first few clients, his dad—they're stepsiblings—was in a car accident, so Derek had to fly to Phoenix to help him. Carrie has been making deliveries for him before work, but she started having car trouble. She bought a new car but hadn't gotten it yet, so I let her use mine."

Hannah nudged Liam. "We need to go talk to her."

"No time." He held out his hand to Zane. "Sorry if I acted like I was conducting an interrogation."

"No worries. I'm as intrigued about this as anyone. Let me know what you find out, but I guarantee Carrie was only doing her job. Or, I should say, Derek's job."

"Thanks, Zane." He'd given them another crucial puzzle piece. And more questions.

Was Carrie really delivering for a client? Or for herself? Had Derek written Archer's name on the envelope as a service to a client—or for himself?

As soon as they got back in Liam's Jeep, Hannah looked up Sweet Caroline's number on her phone, then placed a call on speaker.

"Sweet Caroline's. How can I sweeten your day?"

Hannah had spoken to Carrie enough times to recognize that this wasn't her. "May I speak to Carrie, please?"

"She's delivering a wedding cake. Can I help you?"

"Do you know when she'll be back?"

"Not for a couple of hours. Can I take a message?"

"No, thank you. I'll call again later." She swiveled in the seat to gaze at Liam. "Now what?"

"I had a thought while you were on the call. I know Carrie hasn't worked at the bakery very long, but from what you've told me, she's been baking the whole time she's been back here. Since she makes wedding cakes, it's very possible she's crossed paths with Wes Reid at weddings."

That connection hadn't crossed her mind. "You're thinking they might have joined forces?" Her imagination spun with possible scenarios. "There was a bridal show in Bowling Green last week. What if they were both there and Carrie saw that Wes had displayed one of the Stanton Building windows and that reminded her of Archer and—"

"Whoa. You're losing me."

But the idea was coming together so quickly in Hannah's mind that her mouth could barely keep up. "Stan Carlson was interested in Carrie at the same time she had her eye on Archer. So what if she told Wes about that and how Archer humiliated her? And as soon as Wes heard Archer's name, he claimed to Carrie that Archer stole Bryn from him, even though he's the one who left her, and the two of them—"

"Slow down, Hannah." Liam reached out and clasped her hand. "I was only thinking that maybe Wes hired Carrie's brother to deliver the photos. Maybe we should stick to the facts for now."

She gave him a sheepish smile. "But adding a bit of melodrama makes this all so much more fun. All right, let's talk facts. We know Wes wanted to get back together with Bryn. And we know Carrie delivered the envelopes. And it's not too much of a stretch to assume Derek wrote Archer's name on each one."

Liam's quizzical look reminded her she hadn't explained about the calligraphy class.

When she finished, he said, "Lots of people use calligraphy."

"True." Hadn't she said those same words? But to be fair, she didn't know of any others with a possible connection to this case. Yet.

"And we know Archer got photos of a bunch of other places that don't seem to have anything to do with him or Carrie or Wes." Liam flicked on the turn signal and slowed around a corner.

"You're right. I keep jumping at possibilities. I think I just want this mystery to be solved once and for all. How long is Archer going to keep receiving mysterious pictures? Whoever is sending them hasn't given a single clue about what he or she wants. Unless we're all too dense to figure it out."

"We might be a little dense, but we're not *too* dense."

Hannah laughed. "Hey, the sky is blue, the sun is shining, and we're together. Let's make a pact. No talk about Archer or Carrie or photos for the next hour. Deal?"

"Deal. Let's just talk about a different mystery from a hundred years ago."

"Oh, yes, let's," Hannah agreed at once. She chuckled. "We're hopeless."

"Hopeless romantics the day before Valentine's Day? There are worse things to be."

"I agree." Liam still hadn't mentioned any specific plans for a Valentine's Day rain check. Maybe it was time to set that thought aside and move on. From this point on, she was not going to revisit it. She *wasn't.* "What time do you have to get on the road tomorrow?"

"I need to leave the house before eleven, but I'll plan on enough time to come and see my Valentine."

The smile that accompanied his words might just be enough to let her float through the next week.

On one end of King Farm, tangled skeletons of blackberry bushes covered the ground. In a matter of weeks, they'd start turning lush and green. Liam turned into the drive leading to Elaine's farmhouse. Like Lacy's property, Elaine's farm was bare and almost desolate this time of year. The plastic-covered hoop house appeared empty, but she imagined there were already seedlings sprouting in trays of potting soil as the dormant farm geared up for spring. Off to one side, beneath a red maple tree that had blazed with color in October, stood the original cabin built by the first settlers on the farm.

Elaine was waiting for them on the front porch and came striding toward the Jeep with Banjo, her rescue dog, at her heels. The pup's floppy ears bounced as he trotted behind her. Elaine held up one hand when Liam opened the door. "Let's drive," she called out. She held what appeared to be a clutch purse and a foldable camp shovel. Liam rolled down his window, and she explained, "It's a bit of a hike. Are you up to some off-roading?"

Liam patted the dashboard. "It's why I bought her."

Elaine got in the back seat and buckled her seat belt. Then she gave Liam instructions to follow a tractor path that ran between a blackberry field and one covered in cornstalk stubble. As he started along the bumpy trail, Elaine handed Hannah what had appeared to be a clutch. "I found this in the attic." It was made of leather, folded in thirds, and tied with a strip of darker-colored leather.

Hannah untied and unfolded it. Inside was a two-page yellowed document with a single handwritten letter tucked inside. She skimmed the first page of the document, reading portions out loud. "'State of Kentucky, County of Barren… I, William McLeash, Clerk of Courts for the city and county aforesaid, certify that the foregoing deed was this day lodged with me…'" She flipped to the next page. "'This deed of conveyance, given under my hand this 25th day of October, 1947, between Talbert and Viviene Haley and Lemuel and Olive King…'" Her breath hitched when she read the name *Haley*, but she kept reading. "'A ten-acre tract of land situated to the east of Sugar Creek and to the north of…'"

She picked up the letter. It was written on Haley Mercantile Letterhead.

Dear Lemuel and Olive,

Having lived next to this property once owned by Linus Moss for all these years, I know you are familiar with much of the story of how this parcel ended up in my hands. I have rarely talked about it, but thought that now, as I prepare to sell a portion of my land to you, it is time to put the facts in writing. It may well be that this piece of history will be passed down to my descendants and yours, along with our land, for many generations.

On March 9 of 1921, I was working in the Pond Creek Coal Mine next to Linus Moss and Oren Benton when an explosion collapsed the roof, trapping us and fatally wounding Linus. Before he took his last breath, he gave us a map of his property in Blackberry Valley and a letter willing it to Miss Josephine Hamilton, the woman who had broken his heart. He also said he wanted her to have the ring he had buried on the land.

After Oren and I were rescued, we contacted Miss Hamilton, who was by then Mrs. Paxton Cromwell III. She said she wanted nothing to do with Linus's land or the ring and said we could have it all. Though we had no legal proof the land was ours, we moved our families to Barren County with dreams of going into farming together. That dream did not last even a full day after our arrival.

The morning after we arrived, my daughter's puppy ran into the pasture. Fearing it would be trampled by the bull we had acquired in the transaction, I ran after it. Oren assumed

I was trying to get a jump on digging up the buried ring, and he attacked me. Later, he and his son dug up a box that should have contained the heirloom ring we had hoped would support our new venture. Oren claimed the ring was not in the box. I didn't believe him, and he didn't believe I hadn't taken it. That ended our partnership and friendship.

We divided the property down the middle of Sugar Creek, and didn't speak to each other for ten years, until my daughter Evangeline and Oren's son Micah began secretly meeting and falling in love. They began investigating, talking to people who had known Linus, and discovered that Linus had given the ring to a friend to bury under the red oak tree near the river. That friend, Fletcher Arnett, misunderstood Linus's instructions and buried it under the chinkapin oak, causing Oren to dig under the wrong tree.

To bring this story to a beautiful conclusion, Evangeline and Micah found the ring and brought an end to a decade of their fathers' foolishness. They also united our two families in the most wonderful way. Ten years after the mine collapse that turned our lives upside down, Micah and Evangeline were married under the chinkapin tree with the ring that had come from Scotland with Linus Moss's grandmother.

Blessings,

Talbert Haley

Hannah swiped at the dampness on her lashes as Elaine said, "Stop here," in a hushed tone that mirrored the wonder Hannah felt.

Without talking, they got out of the Jeep. Elaine pointed at the chinkapin tree, and they approached it in silence. Hannah had hoped to see a remnant of initials carved in a heart, but after almost a century, there were no signs.

"If I'm remembering right, the headstone is on the other side of this tree. I talked to my brother this morning, and he said he didn't think it was actually a headstone, but he said there are words on it."

Liam led the way to the other side of a tree so massive the three of them could have stood around it with their arms outstretched, and their hands would not have touched.

If they hadn't been looking, they would have missed the patch of gray, about the size of Liam's hand. It looked like an ordinary smooth rock buried in the dirt. Liam knelt and brushed it off, then accepted the shovel Elaine held out. After a few minutes, he had uncovered the edges of a rectangle about a foot wide and two feet square. A bit more digging, and he was able to pry it up and flip it over.

Hannah crouched beside Liam for a closer look at the weather-worn words. It wasn't a headstone, but rather a fitting closure to the century-old mystery as they knelt beneath the branches that had stood guard over the ring that now graced Evangeline Cooke's hand. The same branches that had arched over Micah and the first Evangeline as they pledged their lives to each other, joining two families forever.

DELIGHT THYSELF ALSO IN THE LORD;

AND HE SHALL GIVE THEE

THE DESIRES OF THINE HEART.

PSALM 37:4

As they drove back into town, Liam suddenly slowed the Jeep and pointed to a man crossing the street. "That's Wes Reid. How about we break our rule about ignoring Archer's mystery and go talk to him?"

"Why not?"

Liam parked in front of ValleyView Photography. They waited in the Jeep while Wes unlocked the front door. "You have the photos on your phone, right?"

"Most of them. What's your plan?"

"I'm the straightforward guy, remember? If it were up to me, I'd walk in and ask him if he was the one sending the pictures. I'm guessing you may have a softer, more roundabout approach."

"I have an idea. Trust me?" She put her hand on the door handle.

"Always." He grinned at her. "Well, usually, anyway."

Wes sat behind a desk when they walked in. He raised his head and gestured to two chairs on the other side of the desk. "Welcome to ValleyView Photography. Have a seat and let me know what I can do for you."

"This will only take a moment." Hannah took out her phone. "A friend of ours has received some interesting photographs, and he's trying to find out who the photographer is. We thought this was a good place to start." She handed her phone to him with the photo of the Stanton Building window on the screen. "Swipe left to see more."

Wes's bushy brows rose and fell as he swiped through the collection. "Definitely interesting. Whoever took these has a good eye for perspective, but they aren't high enough resolution to be professional shots. I'm confident they were taken with a smartphone rather than a camera. Architectural lettering photographs were very popular a decade ago, but I'm guessing these were taken more recently. Wish I could help you with a name."

"Thank you," Liam said. "That helps."

As they walked toward the car, Liam asked if she believed Wes.

"I do. I watched for any tells, but he didn't seem the least bit uncomfortable." She sighed. "Another one crossed off the list."

"That's a good thing, isn't it? We're narrowing it down."

"To what?"

"Good point."

When they reached her building, Liam put his arm around her and walked her up the stairs to her door. "A lot to process and it's only ten a.m."

"It was the perfect way to spend the morning before Valentine's Day. It helps me not mind so much that I don't get to spend tomorrow with you."

Smile lines fanned out around those deep brown eyes she could get lost in. He leaned down and brushed his lips across her forehead. "I need to get to work. And I'm covering for Cole tonight, so I'll see you tomorrow."

"Until tomorrow then." *When I have to say goodbye to you on Valentine's Day.* As Liam headed down the steps, Hannah stuck her hand in her pocket for her keys and felt her phone vibrate. She pulled it out to see she was getting a call from the historical society. "Liam. Wait a second."

He stopped halfway, and she answered the call, putting it on speaker. She wanted Liam to hear this with her, whatever it was. She told herself it wasn't simply an excuse to delay saying goodbye to him.

"Hannah, this is Phyllis. I finally heard back from Kathryn Hobart. I've got you on speaker, and Evangeline is here. We're going to try not talking over each other."

"Okay." Hannah motioned for Liam to come closer. "Go ahead."

"We spent the last hour drawing up a family tree," Evangeline said. "My family tree, which turns out to be someone else's too."

"Whose?" Hannah sat down on the top step and Liam perched next to her.

"Well," Phyllis said, "I've only met Kathryn a couple of times, so I had no idea she is Heather Reynolds's mother."

Hannah stared at Liam. His eyes reflected her surprise. "She's Bryn Reynolds's grandmother?"

"Yes." This time it was Evangeline who answered. "And get this—Kathryn's grandmother was Evangeline Benton!"

Hannah squinted and rubbed her temple. "So Bryn is Evangeline Benton's...great-great-granddaughter?"

"You got it."

"But how is it your family tree too?"

"It's on my mother's side. You know, the one I never knew much about because of how early I lost my mother. I never had enough curiosity about it until this whole thing came up with the ring. Then Phyllis was kind enough to help me track my family tree through official records. Apparently, my mother was Kathryn's aunt. Which means—"

"Evangeline Haley Benton was your maternal grandmother!" Hannah finished for her in excitement. "You were named for your grandma. And that makes you and Bryn...what?"

"First cousins twice removed."

"That's incredible. I'm so happy you figured that out." But as the women started talking over each other in excitement, more questions bubbled to the surface.

The first photo Archer had received was an exact replica of the drawing that hung in the library display. The drawing that had been donated by Bryn's grandmother. That couldn't be coincidence. But how did it connect to Archer?

Chapter Thirty-Five

Hannah looked at her watch as she hung up her desk phone. Half an hour until Raquel's party.

She'd finally gotten ahold of Carrie, and the answers she'd obtained were evasive. When Hannah had asked for the name of the client who was sending the letters to Archer, Carrie had answered, "I'm sorry, Hannah, but Derek handles all of that. Even if I knew, I wouldn't be able to tell you." So Hannah had taken it a step further and asked, in her best non-accusatory voice, if they were from either her or her brother.

There'd been a moment of silence, and then Carrie replied, "No. Of course not. Why would either of us be sending photos to Archer?" Once again, she'd sounded completely genuine. And even slightly offended.

But now was not the time to think on that. Every ounce of Hannah's energy and all her focus had to be on the celebration for Raquel and tonight's dinner.

Hannah looked at her watch again. Twenty-eight minutes until the birthday party and Liam still hadn't shown up. She'd hoped he might text her last night and invite her out for breakfast. Or join in the decorating fun before he had to get on the road.

She stood, taking in the tiny room crowded with valentine decorations that would transform the dining room from birthday party fun to romantic elegance. Nothing would deter her from enjoying every minute of this day. Once again, she closed her office door behind her and imagined leaving all her frustration behind in a pile on her desk.

As the door clicked, her phone buzzed. She pulled it out and looked at the name on the screen. *Liam "My Valentine" Berthold.* When had he done that? Any lingering frustration fled as she answered. "Good morning, Valentine."

"Happy Valentine's Day. I'm on my way. Anything you need while I'm out?"

"Just you."

"Coming right up. See you in a few minutes."

She stepped into the dining room with a smile that probably advertised who she'd been talking to.

Elaine and Dylan had spent the morning decorating with her. Bouquets of silver and teal helium balloons sprouted from the corners like spring flowers. More balloons hung from streamers that looped across the dining room. The tomatoey-garlic smell emanating from the kitchen made her stomach growl in anticipation. "It's perfect in here, guys."

Elaine and Dylan stepped away from the food table and beamed at Hannah as the kitchen doors swung open. Jacob backed out, carrying the four-layer tiramisu creation that would be the centerpiece on the food table. Hannah joined Elaine and Dylan to chorus their admiration. Another voice joined them.

Raquel stood just inside the front door, Marshall at her side. "This is so beautiful! You guys are the best." Her face crumpled, and she leaned against Marshall, who engulfed her in a hug.

Hannah's own eyes smarted as she strode toward Raquel. She knew these were happy tears, but there was a tinge of bittersweet. Marshall had made his decision yesterday. He was leaving for Chicago on Monday.

Marshall stepped back, and it was Hannah's turn to hold out her arms to her friend. "Happy twenty-five." At that moment, Raquel's phone rang. "Better get that. Somebody probably wants to wish you a happy birthday."

Swiping at tears, Raquel stepped away. Hannah turned to Marshall, only then noticing that he held something in his right hand. An envelope that was becoming all too familiar.

Before she had a chance to ask about it, the door opened behind Marshall. Liam and Archer stepped inside. Liam walked over to Hannah and put one arm around her. "Happy Valentine's Day."

"Happy Valentine's Day to you." She leaned into him, savoring the moment, no matter how fleeting. At least he would only be gone for a few days. Raquel would have to miss Marshall for a much longer time.

"I have something for you. Not exactly a valentine, but I thought you might be able to find a place for it." From behind his back he brought a framed black-and-white picture of a group of firefighters. Above each man was a name written in white ink. "I knew I'd seen this somewhere." He pointed to one of the men. Dark hair. Tall and handsome.

"Micah Benton. He was a firefighter." Another connection to him and Evangeline. She whispered the word she'd just said about the decor. "Liam, it's perfect."

"Raquel asked me to get here early and bring all the photographs," Archer said. "How come?"

"Sit over here." Raquel's tears were replaced by a grin as she motioned to a table in the center of the room. "I have something for you."

"Huh? It's your birthday. I have something for *you*." He patted his pocket.

"Me first. Humor me." She pulled out a chair for him.

Archer sat, looking as confused as everyone else.

Raquel held out her hand to Marshall, took the envelope from him, and set it on the table in front of Archer.

"Another one?" Archer raised his eyes to Hannah. "Did Liam tell you what I got yesterday?"

With everything going on yesterday, she hadn't even thought about it. "No. What was it?"

"Another *R*. Liam identified it. It's part of the carving on the altar at church."

The old altar at the front of the Faith Community sanctuary was the only thing salvaged from the original church, built in the 1800s, which had burned down in the forties. How was that connected to Archer?

Raquel tapped his shoulder. "Open it."

Archer tore open the envelope. A photo fluttered out. Everyone drew close. The picture showed a faded *Y* painted on brick. Hannah knew she'd seen it before. On the side of one of the old buildings on Main Street. But which one?

"That's the dress place," Liam said.

"The dress place? Oh! You mean the bridal shop," Hannah said.

"That's right."

"Did you bring the other pictures?" Raquel asked.

Archer pulled out both his phone and the envelope, which was starting to get a bit tattered at the edges.

"Spread them out."

He set his phone on the table, then did as Raquel had ordered, saying each letter out loud as he laid them on the table in the order he'd received them. "U-O-M-E-A-M-I-L-L-Y-R-W-R-Y. Makes no sense at all."

Archer's phone vibrated. He glanced at it and his face lit with a grin wider than Hannah had seen in weeks. "It's Bryn." Hope shone in his eyes as he tapped the screen, but his expression soon turned to confusion and then disappointment. "It's just about the game. She finally gets a phone signal, and the first thing she does is remind me to play a stupid game?"

Hannah stepped closer and read the single word on the screen. SHUFFLE. The name of the online word game Archer and Bryn played. "But it must mean she's on her way home."

She turned her attention back to the pictures spread across the table. Did the places mean something? Or the letters? Or neither?

Mentally, she catalogued the locations. *Stanton Building, now the Forum. Tree stump at the park. Jewelry store. Bakery. Supper Club. St. Anthony's. Newel post…somewhere. Park bridge. Downspout somewhere. Flower shop. The Hot Spot. Photography studio. Church altar. Bridal shop.*

As she listed off the locations, she noticed Raquel staring at the pictures and typing on her phone. Was she doing the same thing?

Oh. Hannah let out a tiny squeak. "Shuffle!" The word popped out of her mouth as the letters rearranged in her mind, followed by a giggle. "Shuffle the letters." She turned to Raquel, who was now beaming and nodding.

Archer, however, gaped at the photos, seeming completely bewildered.

Raquel and Hannah flanked him and began rearranging the pictures until they'd spelled out two words: *WILL YOU*

Archer looked from Raquel to Hannah. "Will I what?"

"No wonder Bryn always beats you at this game." Raquel reached over his shoulder and rearranged three more letters until they spelled out, *WILL YOU MARRY ME*

A light suddenly went on in Archer's eyes as they widened in astonishment—just as the front door opened.

Bryn Reynolds walked in, her parents and Archer's right behind her, followed by Archer's parents. Bryn carried an 8x10 photograph in front of her.

A photograph of a question mark.

"Well," she said, "will you?"

Archer shot to his feet and ran to her, crushing the picture as he picked her up and swung her around in a tight circle. "Yes. Absolutely yes!"

"A threat? You thought I was threatening you?" Bryn stood with hands on hips, gaping at Archer.

The moment he'd stopped spinning her and had kissed her soundly, and the cheers and clapping and congratulations died down, Archer started peppering her with questions.

"Not you. I had no idea who was sending these. I thought someone was out to get me. Or you. Or, I don't know what. Didn't you stop to think what I might think?"

"What I thought was that you'd think it was fun. I thought it would give you something exciting to do and connect you with people. It never occurred to me that you'd consider it anything sinister."

Bryn took a step toward him. Her hand rose to his beard. "You haven't shaved since I left."

"You wanted to see how I'd look with a beard."

"And for the record, it was awful," Liam interjected. "At least until the crew made him trim that thing."

"The crew." Bryn tipped her head to one side. "At the station?"

"Yeah, but don't change the subject." Archer stepped back, and Bryn's hand dropped to her side. "Why did you—" His question went unfinished when Bryn started to laugh.

"When I stopped in to say goodbye, I put a note in your bathroom drawer. Under your razor. A note telling you to expect a clue every day until Valentine's Day."

Archer took another step back and grabbed a chair, then dropped onto it.

Liam walked over to him and rested his fist on top of Archer's head. "Seriously? You put us through all this just because you were too lazy to shave?"

"I wasn't lazy. I was doing it for her."

Bryn pressed a hand to her chest. "I do love it." She was clearly struggling to keep a serious face.

Archer pointed at Raquel. "Did she know all along?"

"Nobody knew anything until today. When I called her and found out you hadn't figured out the theme of what was supposed to be a fun diversion while I was gone, I asked her to get you here early with all of the pictures."

"When you hung up on me, I thought you—"

"Hung up on you? I've never hung up on you. Ever."

"When you were on your way. I asked if you were sure the drive was worth it, and you hung up on me. I thought you thought I was questioning your commitment to your dissertation, and after the other boneheaded things I'd said and done recently, you were deciding whether you even wanted to be with me anymore."

Bryn's hand flew to her mouth. "I lost the signal. I just assumed you'd guess that." She stepped toward him, then kneeled in front of him, putting her hands on his arms. "Archer Lestrade, I promise I will never, ever hang up on you. And the last thing in the world I want to do is leave you."

Archer bent to press his forehead against hers. "I can't tell you how glad I am to hear that."

Liam slipped his arm around Hannah. "What a ride, huh?"

"It was an adventure. All this time we were hoping the pictures would get his mind off Bryn, when the whole thing was designed to make him think about her."

Behind them, the door opened. Though she would have loved nothing more than to stay right there, nestled against Liam, it was time to start the party. She turned to greet the first guests and was delighted to see Ted and Evangeline Cooke. Hannah held out a hand to Evangeline.

"Are we interrupting something?" Evangeline asked.

"Not at all. In fact, your timing couldn't be better." Hannah leaned in and whispered, "Bryn just proposed to Archer." She led Evangeline over to Bryn and Archer. "Bryn, I'd like you to meet your first cousin twice removed."

Bryn stood. Mascara smudged her face, but she'd never looked happier. "I already know Evangeline. Wait—what did you call her?"

"I'll explain everything in detail," Evangeline said, "but for now, all you need to know is that I've found out that my grandmother was your great-great-grandmother."

"Really?"

"Really. Now, I understand congratulations are in order."

Bryn beamed at her. "Thank you."

Evangeline reached out and took Bryn's hands in hers. "I'm so happy for you, Cousin. But it seems something is missing." She turned to Archer. "Do you have a ring for this woman?"

"Not yet."

Evangeline let go of Bryn's hands. "I think I can help with that." She removed a ring and handed it to Archer. "This ring crossed the ocean from Scotland in the 1800s. It was buried under a tree for over a decade, and then it was passed to my grandmother, Bryn's great-great-grandmother, and then to my mother. I found it in her jewelry box after she died. Nothing would please me more than to pass it on to you to give to your bride-to-be. That is, if the two of you would like that."

The sparkle in Bryn's eyes was all the answer anyone needed.

Archer admired the aquamarine stone surrounded by thistles. Then he stood, motioning for Bryn to take the chair. Kneeling before her, he said, "Bryn Reynolds, I'm sorry for being so clueless so often and for thinking I had to build us a house and have everything perfect before I asked you to spend the rest of your life with me. I *will* marry you. And for the record, I was on the verge of buying a ring until I thought you were going to dump me." A murmur of laughter swept the room. He lifted her hand and slid the ring on her finger. "But this means so much more. I love you with all my heart. Will you be my valentine forever?"

Tears streaming down her face, Bryn nodded and whispered, "Yes."

Wrapping paper littered the floor. Only crumbs were left on the cake stand. As guests headed for the door, many of them promising to be back in a couple of hours, Hannah walked over to Liam. She hadn't expected him to stay until the end of the party. "When do you have to leave?"

"Not for a while."

"I don't want you driving after dark. You could hit a deer or—"

His kiss on her temple stopped her. "Let's start cleaning up. You've got another shindig to get ready for." He started to gather serving dishes, but laughter caused them both to turn around.

Archer sat at a table with all the photographs spread out in front of him. His hand covered his face. "What about that one?" Through splayed fingers, he looked up at Bryn, who stood beside him.

Liam and Hannah stepped closer. "Don't mind us," Liam said. "We're not really eavesdropping."

"I don't believe that for a second." Bryn grinned at them. "Please join us. I've just started pointing out how clueless my new fiancé really is. And by the way, before I forget, thank you for the beautiful basket. And the note. I didn't get it until last night, or I might have tried to get home to my poor man sooner."

"What basket?" Archer asked.

"It's a girl thing." Bryn grinned at Hannah, then pointed to the photo of the roof peak. "I took this at the Greensboro Club where we had our first date. I got the idea from a bunch of sketches my great-great-grandfather did. My grandma has them—close-ups on parts of buildings like the bakery and the jewelry store." She picked up another photo. "This one is the newel post on the railing in front of the altar at church."

Archer groaned. "Okay, I admit I was dense for not catching on to the whole wedding theme."

"We all were," Hannah said.

"But some of these don't fit. I think you stuck some in just to throw me off." Archer tapped the picture of the tree stump. "Like this one."

"That tree, before you cut it down, was where we had our first kiss."

"Oh." Archer closed his eyes as his face reddened. "Suppose I should have remembered that."

"I suppose it wasn't all that memorable for you." Bryn's feigned expression of rejection was priceless.

Archer rolled his eyes. "You know better than that." He pointed at the photo of the bench outside the Hot Spot. "What about this? I mean, we come here all the time. Is that it?"

"Right there, on that bench, is where you told me you loved me for the first time. And then you almost had to do the Heimlich maneuver on me, because I wasn't expecting you to say that and I choked."

"Oh. Yeah. I remember." He gave her a sheepish smile. "I do."

"Say that again. You need to practice."

"I do. I do. I do. Happy?" Archer winked at her, then turned back to the photographs and pointed to the downspout photo. "I hunted all over town for this one."

"It's not in town. You tripped over it, dislodged it, and had to put it back together. Remember? You got scratched by the rosebushes?" She pointed at the bushes behind the L-shaped spout. "I thought you would remember almost breaking your neck."

Archer's confusion slowly faded as comprehension dawned. "The courthouse in Glasgow, the county seat. When we went with those friends of yours to get their marriage license, and I tripped over the downspout." He grimaced. "Courthouse. Marriage license. Church. Bridal shop. Jewelry store. How could I have missed it all?" He held out his hand and grasped hers, kissing her fingertips. "But in my defense, I was so distraught at the thought of possibly losing you—the beautiful, intelligent, kind, amazing love of my life—that my brain wasn't functioning right."

It was Liam and Hannah's turn to groan. He took her hand and whispered, "Let's let these two talk in private. Besides, I need your full attention for a moment."

Hannah took a deep breath, knowing he was going to say goodbye. But it didn't have the sting she'd thought it would. "I have something to give you before you leave." She let go of his hand and strode to her office, where she picked up an envelope she'd stuffed the previous day.

When she walked out, he was standing by one of the two-tops Elaine had finished decorating. She took a moment to admire the white tablecloth, red cloth napkins, and shimmering crystal glasses.

The menus she'd labored over rested on bread plates, and the heart-shaped fairy lights gave the space a rose-colored glow.

Liam stepped aside, and she noticed the reservation card in the center of the table. The card read *Berthold*. Her lips parted as she stared up at him.

"I do have to leave, but only to go home and change." He smiled at her confused expression. "Colt is covering for me at the conference tomorrow. His grandmother lives in Owensboro, so he's up there taking her out for dinner tonight. Tomorrow he's going to help with setup for the conference. I don't have to be there until Monday morning."

Her eyes stung. No words came to mind, so she simply hugged him, then held out the envelope. He beamed at the sappy vintage-inspired card she'd made herself, then took out the envelope she'd slipped inside. She'd written *For stolen moments* on the outside and filled it with gift cards for the movie theater, restaurants, bowling, and even the firefighter museum she wanted to take him to.

"This is perfect. And it appears we were on the same page." Liam picked up a flat red package with a white bow from the bench beside him. "Happy Valentine's Day."

The package was flexible and only about a quarter of an inch thick. Hannah tore off the paper. Inside was a calendar that started with February and went on through December of the following year. There were large spaces for writing. She gave him a quizzical look.

"This is going to become our new best friend. I'm going to arrange the schedule so I'm off on Mondays, like you are, whenever possible, and we're going to fill this up with plans of fun things to do together. We might end up crossing some stuff out, but we're going to start being intentional about time together. Proactive rather than reactive. How does that sound?"

"It sounds like the best Valentine's gift ever."

Cupping her face in his hands, he brushed his lips over hers. "I was hoping you'd say that."

From the Author

Dear Reader,

I hope you enjoyed following Hannah around Blackberry Valley as she tried to solve Archer's mystery and uncover the truth about a century-old Romeo-and-Juliet romance. Are you as impatient as I am to see what's next for Hannah and Liam and Raquel and Marshall? Speaking of impatience, could you identify with Hannah's frustration? We all, at times, "want what we want, and we want it now." Are you in a place like that today?

Writing about a character learning to be patient offered lessons for me too. It gave me the opportunity to ponder the real meaning of patience in God's definition. I've come to the conclusion that we can't have true patience without trust. Sure, we can bridle our tongues and control our whining, but what's going on inside? If our emotions are still in turmoil, we've only put a bandage on the problem. True patience, the kind that allows us to rest as we wait, requires believing that God is in control of the timing and the outcome, and His ways are far better than ours.

Hannah surprised me by her realization that she also needed to be patient with herself. I know readers often assume writers are in control of their characters, but that's not always the case! I love the thought that God not only wants us to be patient with our circumstances and with the people in our lives, but also with ourselves. We are all works in progress and should, maybe daily, look in the mirror and say, "Please be patient with me. God's not finished with me yet."

My prayer for you is that the Lord will help you to trust Him more and learn to rest in His perfect timing.

Blessings,
Becky

About the Author

Becky Melby lives in the southeastern corner of Wisconsin with Bill, her hubby of fifty-plus years, and a few backyard chickens. Together (without the chickens), they enjoy hiking and seeing the country in their motorhome.

Becky is the annoyingly proud mom of four sons and grandma to fifteen grandkids who mess up her house and light up her life. She has authored more than twenty-five contemporary fiction books, including ten other cozy mysteries for Guideposts. She loves encouraging women to live out the truth that God's mercies are new every morning.

The Hot Spotlight

Kentucky Family Feuds

If you say the name "Hatfield" to almost any American, they will immediately connect "McCoy." But that infamous feud wasn't the only one. A map displayed in the Kentucky History Center in Frankfort shows eight major feuds that ripped apart families in the 1800s. If you're looking for some entertaining reading on a rainy day, research the Tolliver-Martin Vendetta, the French-Eversole Feud, or the Strong-Amis, Hill-Evans, Howard-Turner, Baker-White, and Hargis-Marcum-Cockrill-Callahan feuds. But for now, let's take a look at some interesting facts about those infamous Hatfields and McCoys.

Like our fictional Haley-Benton feud, the dispute between the Kentucky McCoys and the West Virgina Hatfields began with a misunderstanding. During the Civil War, most of the Hatfields and the McCoys fought for the Confederacy—with the exception of Asa Harmon McCoy, who fought for the Union. The first record of violence was Asa's death, purported to be at the hands of William Anderson "Devil Anse" Hatfield in 1865. It was later discovered that Anse was home sick at the time of the murder, but the fuse had already been lit.

The next recorded confrontation took place in 1878 over an argument about who owned a hog. Randolph McCoy claimed the notches in the pig's ears were McCoy marks. In reality, the hog belonged to Floyd Hatfield. And they were at it again. The feud escalated with a Romeo-and-Juliet relationship between Roseanna McCoy and Anse's son Johnse Hatfield. As you can imagine, that romance did not end well. Things became so intense that, in 1888, the United States Supreme Court got involved.

Why so many disputes in this area? According to a group of doctors who studied the families in 2007, genetics might have played a part. They found an unusually high rate of Von Hippel-Lindau disease, a condition that can increase "fight or flight" stress hormones. Anecdotal stories of the combative nature of many members of both families seem to confirm the possibility.

It's a sad story, but the legends surrounding these two fighting families have given Americans an endless source of entertainment:

- In 1979, descendants of the original family were contestants on the game show *Family Feud*. The McCoys won the cash prize—and a pig.
- In Pike County, you can take a self-guided driving tour of the famous feud sites.
- The feud is the theme for a musical comedy dinner theater show in Pigeon Forge.
- Peace was finally declared, gaining national attention. On June 14, 2003, a truce was signed by more than sixty descendants, along with the governors of Kentucky and West Virginia.
- More than a dozen movies have been based on the dispute, starting with a 1923 Buster Keaton comedy, and including cartoon versions, like one starring Betty Boop.

- The "us against them" theme inspired by the feuding families has shown up in TV shows like *The Andy Griffith Show, Bonanza, The West Wing, NCIS,* and *Bones.* Elmer Fudd, Rocky and Bullwinkle, and the Flintstones have all portrayed feuding characters. Even *My Little Pony* joined in with an episode called "The Hooffields and McColts."

These two feuding families were also the inspiration for the much less violent happy-ending story you just finished reading.

From the Hot Spot Kitchen

JACOB'S TIRAMISU CAKE

Three layers of coffee-soaked vanilla sponge cake frosted with a fluffy mascarpone cream and dusted with cocoa powder are sure to turn any event into a special occasion.

Ingredients:

Cake:

1 cup cake flour*

Pinch salt

1¼ teaspoons baking powder

4 large eggs, room temperature and separated

½ cup granulated sugar

½ teaspoon vanilla extract

2 tablespoons hot water

Mascarpone Frosting:

1½ cups whipping cream

1 egg**

2 tablespoons sugar

1½ cups mascarpone

1 cup espresso or strong coffee

Topping:

¼ cup cocoa powder

Directions:

1. Preheat oven to 340°F. Lightly grease and flour, or spray, one 8-inch round cake pan. Springform pan works best.
2. In a medium bowl, sift flour, salt, and baking powder together.
3. Beat egg whites until stiff. Set aside.
4. In a separate large bowl, beat egg yolks and sugar. Add vanilla, then add flour mixture a little at a time, alternating with the hot water, and beat until combined. Gently fold in the egg whites.
5. Transfer batter to prepared pan and bake 30 to 40 minutes or until a toothpick comes out clean. Cool in pan 15 to 20 minutes, then move to a wire rack to cool completely. When cool, cut into three layers.
6. While the cake cools, beat together sugar and eggs until frothy, then add mascarpone and cream, beat until thick.
7. Place 1 layer of cake (sliced side up) on a large plate, spoon 1/3 coffee over the top, and cover with 1/3 of cream mixture. Repeat with the remaining layers. Frost the cake with the remaining cream mixture. Chill for 3 to 4 hours or even overnight. Bring to room temperature for 30 minutes. Sprinkle with unsweetened cocoa and serve.

Notes:

- *If you don't have cake flour, take one cup all-purpose flour, remove two tablespoons and replace with two tablespoons cornstarch or arrowroot. This adds to the cake's fluffiness.
- **If you don't wish to use raw eggs, substitute pasteurized eggs or egg replacer. You can also leave out the eggs but substitute powdered for granulated sugar.

Read on for a sneak peek of another exciting book in the *Mysteries of Blackberry Valley* series!

The Cookbook Clue

BY ELIZABETH PENNEY

The parish hall at Grace Community Church was filled with chatter, laughter, and the aroma of fresh coffee. Letting the door swing shut behind her, Hannah Prentiss stood for a moment to get her bearings. She had grown up in Blackberry Valley, Kentucky, so this was her home church even after years in California working as a chef. Now she was back in town, the proud owner of a thriving farm-to-table restaurant called the Hot Spot, located in a beautiful former firehouse.

Hannah's gaze fastened on the reason they were there on this chilly March evening: Julia Miller, nationally acclaimed cookbook author and Appalachian foodways professor. Julia was working on a new cookbook featuring Kentucky cuisine, and her family connection to Blackberry Valley had led her here in search of classic, time-tested recipes.

The battered, stained notebook Hannah held under one arm might well contain a recipe Julia would choose for her book. This honor was the aim of all the women attending tonight with their recipe boxes, community cookbooks, and notebooks like Hannah's, which had belonged to her great-great-aunt, Mabel Prentiss Byrne.

Hannah also hoped to discover historic local recipes for the Hot Spot's menu during the multiweek project, which the ladies had dubbed the Cooking Club. If so, she would feature the creator's name and biography, maybe even a photograph. Hannah also thought that the Cooking Club would be the perfect antidote for the late winter doldrums. Spring was coming as it always did, but there was still plenty of wet, chilly weather to get through first.

"There you are." Lacy Minyard, Hannah's best friend, strode across the polished tiles, one hand smoothing the barely visible baby bump under her loose top. Lacy and her husband, Neil, were expecting their first child, and both were over the moon about it. "I was afraid you weren't coming."

"Got sidetracked at the restaurant," Hannah explained as they moved to the table where Lacy was sitting. "Made the mistake of checking my email." The Hot Spot wasn't open on Mondays, and Hannah used the time to get caught up on endless management tasks.

Lacy rolled her eyes. "Yeah. That happens to Neil all the time." Neil owned Legend & Key Bookstore, a new and used bookstore in town. The couple lived on Lacy's family farm, where she kept a flock of chickens and other animals. Lacy was one of Hannah's restaurant suppliers.

"A hazard of working for yourself," Hannah said. "The buck stops with you." Despite the long hours and occasional uncertainty, Hannah wouldn't trade owning her own eatery for anything.

At the table, Hannah set down her notebook and bag, then unzipped her jacket and draped it over the back of the chair she'd chosen.

Elaine Wilby, Hot Spot hostess and another good friend, bustled up to the table. "Decaf tea for you," she said to Lacy as she placed two disposable cups on the table. "Coffee for me. Sorry, Hannah. I didn't see you come in."

"Just got here. I'll go grab my own. Maybe some cookies too." Hannah was confident the ladies had brought a tempting array of baked goods, as they did to every gathering.

"Cookies!" Lacy's cry followed Hannah as she made her way to the buffet. Hannah grinned at her friend's enthusiasm. Exuberant, outgoing Lacy made everything more fun.

Hannah filled a cup with steaming coffee and then wandered down to the treats. A plate of cookies with frosting seemed to call her name.

Miriam Spencer, a women's group fixture in her eighties, appeared at Hannah's elbow, leaning on her cane. "Those are my butter cookies. My mama's recipe."

"Like the cake?" Butter cake was a Kentucky classic. Hannah selected a cookie and, unable to resist, took a bite. The texture was soft, the taste creamy and subtly sweet with a hint of vanilla. "Wow. These are great."

Miriam hid her pleasure behind a quick adjustment of her eyeglasses. "That means a lot, coming from a professional chef."

Hannah shook her head. "I still have plenty to learn from experienced home cooks, believe me."

Being in this room reminded Hannah of potlucks through the years. Many women had their specialties or creative twists on basic recipes. Food was nourishment and comfort, but also a reflection of skill and personal expression. Those early experiences had shaped Hannah's approach to her profession. Joining the church women's group had helped her realize how much.

As Hannah loaded a plate with treats for herself and Lacy, Miriam refilled her own coffee cup. Then the pair returned to the same table, Miriam taking a seat beside Connie Sanchez, the church secretary, and Lorelai Dawson, the pastor's wife.

"Did you hear about the storms coming later this week?" Miriam asked anxiously. "We could get several inches of rain, they said."

Julia Miller, who had been passing out stapled packets to the attendees, said, "Oh, dear. My poor husband." Thirtysomething Julia wore a white bibbed apron over a crisp blue cotton dress, her brown hair neatly pinned up in a bun.

"What do you mean?" Hannah asked.

Julia smiled. "I'll explain in a minute, when we get started." She hurried to take her place at a podium, set up with a table, laptop, and projector screen.

Someone dimmed the lights slightly, and Julia switched on the laptop, making the large screen behind her come to life. The title slide read: *Kentucky Food Traditions.*

"Good evening," Julia said into the microphone. "Can you all hear me?" They all confirmed that they could. "I'm a professor of Appalachian studies at Tennessee State." She quickly put up a hand. "But before you kick me out"—the women laughed—"my great-grandparents were from Blackberry Valley."

"We'll let you stay then," one woman called, to more laughter. "Who were they?"

"Glad you asked," Julia said. "Their names were Bud and Velma Hicks. Their son moved to Lexington, so we lost the connection to the valley after they passed in the sixties."

Frowning, Miriam mouthed the names *Bud and Velma Hicks*, then gnawed at her bottom lip. Hannah guessed the names rang a bell for the longtime resident.

"We're glad you're back," Connie said. "This place calls people home."

"That it does." Julia held up a book titled *The Humble Biscuit*. "In addition to teaching, I'm a chef and a cookbook author. This was my first book, a compilation of the many ways people make biscuits, as well as their importance and history in Southern cuisine."

Hannah smiled, thinking of calorie-conscious Los Angeles, where she'd worked for years. Biscuits were on the forbidden list for many, although she'd seen them becoming more popular.

"Tonight, though, we're not going to talk about biscuits. Or rather, not only biscuits. My new cookbook will feature a range of dishes from Kentucky. I'm hoping that you'll share your treasured family recipes with me, with credit, of course. We'll make some of them and enjoy them together. We'll also plan a church supper featuring our dishes and invite the rest of the congregation." She smiled. "My husband, Erik, will be joining us."

"Where is he?" someone asked. "Back in Tennessee?"

"Right now, he's on a leisurely multiday bicycle trip through Kentucky. His position as head pastor is pretty intense, and this is how he likes to unwind. Me, I cook."

Her audience chuckled.

No wonder Julia was concerned about the weather, with her husband out and exposed to the elements.

"I hope he doesn't run into those storms they're predicting this week," a woman said. "We might even get a tornado." Others echoed her concern, and Miriam looked even more troubled.

"How will you know where he is?" another asked. "I'd worry too much to let my husband do something like that. All alone, on a bicycle. Anything could happen."

Julia touched a key on her laptop. "I have a way to track him, believe it or not." She brought up a program. "This cycling app monitors his progress." She enlarged a map. "See that dot? That's Erik. He's stopped for the night at a campground. I spoke to him before our meeting, and he's doing well."

"What a great use of technology," Lacy said, and Hannah murmured agreement.

"With those storms in the forecast, we'd better pray we don't have a repeat of March 1965," Miriam said. Her grim tone caused a chill to settle over the room.

"What do you mean?" Julia asked.

"Unexpected tornadoes came through Blackberry Valley," Miriam said. "They caused a lot of damage, including to the church. We had weather forecasting at the time, but it wasn't as accurate or detailed as it is now. We didn't have a chance to truly prepare."

Several older members chimed in, confirming Miriam's memory of the storms.

"We'll definitely be praying," Julia said before bringing the meeting back on track. "I'd like to talk about a certain dish that we can experiment with. A dish that every cook puts his or her own spin on. Something that's well-known—famous, even. Can anyone guess?"

Hannah racked her brain. What could Julia be referring to? Kentucky was known for quite a few delicious recipes.

Lacy bounced up and down in her chair, waving her hand.

Julia smiled at her. "Go ahead."

"Burgoo," Lacy declared. "It's got to be our most famous dish. They serve it every year at the Kentucky Derby."

"Great guess," Julia said. "Give Lacy a round of applause, everyone." After that died down, she changed the display to a photograph of a bowl full of stew. "No one is exactly sure when burgoo was first made. It is thought that it's based on Irish mulligan stew. The first known mention was before the Civil War. Called a survival dish, it was originally made with whatever was handy from wild game, vegetables, and beans."

Julia went on to display other slides showcasing the progression of the dish. The stew was now made most commonly with a combination of pork, beef, and chicken, and all the ingredients were the cook's choice. At the derby, the stew was made in huge kettles over open flames, a tradition many looked forward to each year.

As Julia talked, Hannah realized that burgoo would be a great addition to the Hot Spot's menu. Since the farm-to-table concept meant that different ingredients were available to her at different times of the year, a flexible dish like burgoo would help to highlight the variety.

"The first step," Julia said, "is to start with our own recipes. We'll try various combinations together and come up with an amazing Blackberry Valley Burgoo. Does anyone have a recipe to share?"

Chatter broke out as women leafed through their recipe boxes or checked the indexes of community cookbooks their relatives had contributed to.

"There's no right or wrong way to make burgoo," Julia said as she strolled among the tables. "So don't be shy. We won't judge anyone here. It's not like a cake, where a mistake can make it sink. Or refuse to rise at all."

Hannah had briefly glanced through Aunt Mabel's notebook after she'd found it among her late mother's books. She'd been surprised, because Aunt Mabel's diaries were donated to the library. In fact, the 1965 diary included the tornadoes Miriam mentioned earlier. Somehow this compilation of recipes and hand-scrawled notes had been missed.

Hannah located a burgoo recipe near the end of the book, marked by a folded piece of lined paper. Hannah unfolded the page, which held handwritten notes on the back.

Ladies' Group Meeting. March 23, 1965. Fundraising—church supper.

Miriam had said the church was damaged. It was no surprise to Hannah that the ladies had immediately ramped up efforts to help repair the building.

Near the bottom of the page, a note set off by itself caught her eye.

Bud Hicks—cross?

"Miriam," Hannah said. "Do you have any idea what this means?" She slid the paper across the table and pointed to the note about Bud.

"What's going on?" Lacy asked.

"Aunt Mabel wrote something about Bud Hicks and a cross," Hannah explained.

Lacy glanced toward Julia, who was leaning over a table while an attendee showed her a recipe card. "The Bud Hicks Julia is related to?"

"He was the only Bud Hicks in town." Miriam tapped the page with her finger. "And yes, I do know what this means. When the tornado hit the church, our gorgeous gold altar cross went missing. It seems to me that Mabel suspected Bud had something to do with that."

Loved *Mysteries of Blackberry Valley?*
Check out some other Guideposts mystery series!

Whistle Stop Café Mysteries

Join best friends Debbie Albright and Janet Shaw as they step out in faith to open the Whistle Stop Café inside the historic train depot in Dennison, Ohio. During WWII, the depot's canteen workers offered doughnuts, sandwiches, and a heap of gratitude to thousands of soldiers on their way to war via troop-transport trains. Our sleuths soon find themselves on track to solve baffling mysteries—both past and present. Come along for the ride for stories of honor, duty to God and country, and of course fun, family, and friends!

Under the Apple Tree
As Time Goes By
We'll Meet Again
Till Then
I'll Be Seeing You
Fools Rush In
Let It Snow
Accentuate the Positive
For Sentimental Reasons

That's My Baby
A String of Pearls
Somewhere Over the Rainbow
Down Forget-Me-Not Lane
Set the World on Fire
When You Wish Upon a Star
Rumors Are Flying
Here We Go Again
Stairway to the Stars
Winter Weather
Wait Till the Sun Shines
Now You're in My Arms
Sooner or Later
Apple Blossom Time
My Dreams Are Getting Better

Secrets from Grandma's Attic

Life is recorded not only in decades or years, but in events and memories that form the fabric of our being. Follow Tracy Doyle, Amy Allen, and Robin Davisson, the granddaughters of the recently deceased centenarian, Pearl Allen, as they explore the treasures found in the attic of Grandma Pearl's Victorian home, nestled near the banks of the Mississippi in Canton, Missouri. Not only do Pearl's descendants uncover a long-buried mystery at every attic exploration, they also discover their grandmother's legacy of deep, abiding faith, which has shaped and guided their family through the years. These uncovered Secrets from Grandma's Attic reveal stories of faith, redemption, and second chances that capture your heart long after you turn the last page.

History Lost and Found
The Art of Deception
Testament to a Patriot
Buttoned Up
Pearl of Great Price
Hidden Riches
Movers and Shakers
The Eye of the Cat
Refined by Fire

The Prince and the Popper
Something Shady
Duel Threat
A Royal Tea
The Heart of a Hero
Fractured Beauty
A Shadowy Past
In Its Time
Nothing Gold Can Stay
The Cameo Clue
Veiled Intentions
Turn Back the Dial
A Marathon of Kindness
A Thief in the Night
Coming Home

Savannah Secrets

Welcome to Savannah, Georgia, a picture-perfect Southern city known for its manicured parks, moss-covered oaks, and antebellum architecture. Walk down one of the cobblestone streets, and you'll come upon Magnolia Investigations. It is here where two friends have joined forces to unravel some of Savannah's deepest secrets. Tag along as clues are exposed, red herrings discarded, and thrilling surprises revealed. Find inspiration in the special bond between Meredith Bellefontaine and Julia Foley. Cheer the friends on as they listen to their hearts and rely on their faith to solve each new case that comes their way.

The Hidden Gate
A Fallen Petal
Double Trouble
Whispering Bells
Where Time Stood Still
The Weight of Years
Willful Transgressions
Season's Meetings
Southern Fried Secrets
The Greatest of These
Patterns of Deception

MYSTERIES OF BLACKBERRY VALLEY

The Waving Girl

Beneath a Dragon Moon

Garden Variety Crimes

Meant for Good

A Bone to Pick

Honeybees & Legacies

True Grits

Sapphire Secret

Jingle Bell Heist

Buried Secrets

A Puzzle of Pearls

Facing the Facts

Resurrecting Trouble

Forever and a Day

Mysteries of Martha's Vineyard

Priscilla Latham Grant has inherited a lighthouse! So with not much more than a strong will and a sore heart, the recent widow says goodbye to her lifelong Kansas home and heads to the quaint and historic island of Martha's Vineyard, Massachusetts. There, she comes face-to-face with adventures, which include her trusty canine friend, Jake, three delightful cousins she didn't know she had, and Gerald O'Bannon, a handsome Coast Guard captain—plus head-scratching mysteries that crop up with surprising regularity.

A Light in the Darkness
Like a Fish Out of Water
Adrift
Maiden of the Mist
Making Waves
Don't Rock the Boat
A Port in the Storm
Thicker Than Water
Swept Away
Bridge Over Troubled Waters
Smoke on the Water
Shifting Sands
Shark Bait

Seascape in Shadows
Storm Tide
Water Flows Uphill
Catch of the Day
Beyond the Sea
Wider Than an Ocean
Sheeps Passing in the Night
Sail Away Home
Waves of Doubt
Lifeline
Flotsam & Jetsam
Just Over the Horizon

A Note from the Editors

We hope you enjoyed another exciting volume in the Mysteries of Blackberry Valley series, published by Guideposts. For over seventy-five years, Guideposts, a nonprofit organization, has been driven by a vision of a world filled with hope. We aspire to be the voice of a trusted friend, a friend who makes you feel more hopeful and connected.

By making a purchase from Guideposts, you join our community in touching millions of lives, inspiring them to believe that all things are possible through faith, hope, and prayer. Your continued support allows us to provide uplifting resources to those in need. Whether through our communities, websites, apps, or publications, we inspire our audiences, bring them together, and comfort, uplift, entertain, and guide them. Visit us at guideposts.org to learn more.

We would love to hear from you. Write us at Guideposts, P.O. Box 5815, Harlan, Iowa 51593 or call us at (800) 932-2145. Did you love *No Love Lost*? Leave a review for this product on guideposts.org/shop. Your feedback helps others in our community find relevant products.

More Great Mysteries Are Waiting For Readers Like *You*!

Whistle Stop Café Mysteries

"Memories of a lifetime...I loved reading this story. Could not put the book down...." —ROSE H.

Mystery and WWII historical fiction fans will love these intriguing novels where two close friends piece together clues to solve mysteries past and present. Set in the real town of Dennison, Ohio, at a historic train depot where many soldiers once set off for war, these stories are filled with faithful, relatable characters you'll love spending time with.

Mysteries & Wonders of the Bible

"I so enjoyed this book.... What a great insight into the life of the women who wove the veil for the Temple." —SHIRLEYN J.

Have you ever wondered what it might have been like to live back in Bible times to experience miraculous Bible events firsthand? Then you'll LOVE the fascinating **Mysteries & Wonders of the Bible** novels! Each Scripture-inspired story whisks you back to the ancient Holy Land, where you'll accompany ordinary men and women in their search for the hidden truths behind some of the most pivotal moments in the Bible. Each volume includes insights from a respected biblical scholar to help you ponder the significance of each story to your own life.

Mysteries of Cobble Hill Farm

"Wonderful series. Great story. Spellbinding. Could not put it down once I started reading." —BONNIE C.

Escape to the charming English countryside with **Mysteries of Cobble Hill Farm**, a heartwarming series of faith-filled mysteries. Harriet Bailey relocates to Yorkshire, England, to take over her late grandfather's veterinary practice, hoping it's the fresh start she needs. As she builds a new life, Harriet uncovers modern mysteries and long-buried secrets in the village and among the rolling hills and castle ruins. Each book is an inspiring puzzle where God's gentlest messengers—the animals in her care—help Harriet save the day.

Learn More & Shop These Exciting Mysteries, Biblical Stories, & Other Uplifting Fiction at **guideposts.org/fiction**

Printed in the United States
by Baker & Taylor Publisher Services